I0764632

ALEX DETAIL'S REBELLION

ALEX DETAIL'S REBELLION

THE SEQUEL TO *ALEX DETAIL'S REVOLUTION*

DARREN CAMPO

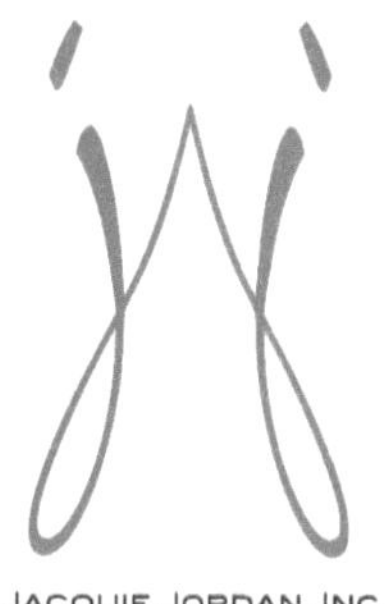

JACQUIE JORDAN, INC.

Alex Detail's Rebellion

Published by Jacquie Jordan Inc.

Interior book design by Barbara Aronica-Buck
Book cover art and sketches by Daniel Rhone
Author photo by Suki Zoe

ISBN-13 9780981931159

www.TVGuestpert.com
www.JacquieJordanIncPublishing.com

First Printing October 2010
Printed in the United States of America
10 9 8 7 6 5 4 3 2 1

For my sister,
Nicole Campo

ACKNOWLEDGMENTS

They say you can't pick your family, but in my case I think someone gave me an exception to the rule because they're all who I would have chosen. As a writer with a vivid array of family experiences I suspect the adventures we have been on secretly move my stories and characters in ways I could never fully be aware. The great adventure started on day one with my parents and my sister Nicole. It continued on with my grandmother Jacqueline, aunts Elizabeth and Lisa, Andrea and uncle Bob, cousins Allen and Sarah, and my grandparents of blessed memory, Judith and Romano Campo, and Robert Brunelle.

Special thanks to Jacquie Jordan, my champion who knew the story must continue and published the sequel you are holding, Stephanie Cobian, who gave me insights and a touching ode to George Spell, editor Victoria Hanley who continued her amazing work from the first book, and Ryan Finley for taking the treacherous trip to find the Axiom.

Sometimes, indeed, there is such a discrepancy
between the genius and his human qualities
that one has to ask oneself
whether a little less talent might not have been better.

– C.G. Jung

CONTENTS

CHAPTER 1 • The Assassination of Alex Detail **1**

CHAPTER 2 • The Perilous Planetarium **16**

CHAPTER 3 • The Kidnapping of George Spell **28**

CHAPTER 4 • Madeline Spell's Last Resort **35**

CHAPTER 5 • Flagship Space Race **39**

CHAPTER 6 • Search for the Axiom **45**

CHAPTER 7 • But Not Quite Human **49**

CHAPTER 8 • Return of the Reaper **54**

CHAPTER 9 • The Tricky Trap **65**

CHAPTER 10 • Madeline Spell and the Generationists **70**

CHAPTER 11 • JuneMary's World **75**

CHAPTER 12 • The House of June **85**

CHAPTER 13 • George Spell and the Sorceress **91**

CHAPTER 14 • The Captain's Concisely Convincing Cadence **96**

CHAPTER 15 • The Magic and Danger of First Sleep **105**

CHAPTER 16 • Ancient Conspiracies in New Africa **111**

CHAPTER 17 • The Dark Things on Venus **125**

CHAPTER 18 • The Power of Details **132**

CHAPTER 19 • Approaching the Terminator **139**

CHAPTER 20 • Madeline Spell's Shock and Awe **144**

CHAPTER 21 • The Adventures of George Spell and the Cat **150**

CHAPTER 22 • Living in the Shadow of Alex Detail **153**

CHAPTER 23 • Getting to the Other Side of the Board **158**

CHAPTER 24 • Fulfilling a Short Destiny **167**

CHAPTER 25 • Revenge of the Harvesters **172**

CHAPTER 26 • Extinction Level Event Horizon **184**

CHAPTER 27 • How to Save the World at the Speed of Light **197**

CHAPTER 28 • In the Interests of the Greater Good **206**

CHAPTER 29 • Until Next Time **211**

EPILOGUE **217**

CHAPTER 1

•

THE ASSASSINATION OF ALEX DETAIL

The most upsetting thing to Alex Detail about attending his promotion ceremony was that it took place inside a giant sphere, which meant this was the day George Spell would kill him.

What an inconsiderate promotion, not like before.

The first time Alex had been promoted after winning the Harvester War, he was just fourteen years old and given the lofty rank of Admiral. Now, *that* had been a first-class affair, held in the proper venue of Carnegie Hall, without the threat of a genius clone intent on assassinating him.

But now, it seemed his clone knew what Alex had been up to since the end of the Second Harvester War. It was clear that George Spell knew the only place Alex was vulnerable was inside a sphere. George must have covertly planted a subconscious thought in the mind of his mother, House of Nations Speaker Madeline Spell: *The New York City Planetarium is the best location to publicly announce Admiral Alexander Detail's promotion to Chief Admiral.*

For security reasons, the location of the event was not made public until Alex was in the official motorcade to-car that would only stop and unlock its doors once the procession had arrived at the planetarium entrance. By the time Alex arrived, a crowd of nearly five thousand people had packed the street outside the planetarium, hoping to catch a glimpse of the 18-year-old who was about to become the second most powerful person in the world.

Well, so be it, Alex thought as he checked his dark brown hair in the mirror, pushing his long bangs to the sides of his temple. He had gotten out of tighter spots, and it wouldn't do to turn tail and go home. *What if I said I left my oven on?* No, Alex had just as much access to the mind of George Spell as George had access to his. *So let him try to kill me.*

There were only seventy-two ways George could kill him, and Alex had just run through them all in those few moments between exiting the car and approaching the planetarium entrance. Still, Alex had been distracted these last several months, while George had clearly been planning this for some time.

It had been six months since the destruction of the Harvesters, and Alex had grown angrier every day that passed. Why had the Harvesters thought the best way to save humanity would be a mass abduction? Clearly, they had the ability to bring some of their universe to this one. There could have been a way to keep the powers Pluto had brought, if only Alex had had time to figure it out before George Spell destroyed the Harvester ships. If only anyone had even had the sense to attempt it or even consider it, through the cloud of euphoria in those days that Pluto orbited Earth. But no, once again, Alex had held the one thing he had longed to hold his entire life—an escape from the omnipresent trap of time—only to see it slip out of his grasp. Thwarted by the only one who was not at all affected by the Harvesters: George Spell. Thwarted by his very own clone that he'd had a hand in creating, tricked by the lure of the Generationists, planted right at his feet by Madeline Spell.

But not this time. This time Alex Detail was going to get what he wanted. And for the past six months, the remains of Pluto orbiting Earth had been providing him with everything he needed. While Alex knew the link he had with the Harvesters was similar to the one they had established with the late Peevchi Derringkite, Alex was no Derringkite. And he had other plans for the Harvesters this time. But there was an ironic fear that the only person able to kill Derringkite was George Spell. Alex recalled the grisly sight of Derringkite's gashed torso lying on the bridge floor and the blank look on George's face. The horror was magnified by George's nonchalance—the barely three-feet-tall boy tapping instructions into a panel, a panel level with his bright platinum hair—as if committing the gruesome murder had been a minor inconvenience.

At least the creation of his clone had accomplished the one intended effect of reversing Alex's mental decline.

The only problem was having George's pesky mind always poking through Alex's thoughts. And that little mind must have known that the only time Alex Detail's link to the Harvesters got severed was inside a sphere.

The New York Planetarium was the largest sphere in the world.

Alex entered the planetarium for the pre-show, "Flight of the *Cronus,*" a specially programmed holo to entertain the guests before his official promotion was announced. The first person he saw standing at the entrance, looking tall, magnanimous and somewhat tired in her blue and white suit, was Madeline Spell, the one who would make the announcement. Next to her stood her impossibly small son, wringing his hands and staring at Alex with narrow green eyes.

"Congratulations, Admiral Detail," Madeline said, shaking his hand in that awkward side-by-side handshake that had to be endured with smiles for the official photographer. Alex was keenly aware that even in boots that added an extra inch to his five-foot-nine height, he was still a bit shorter than Madeline Spell. The camera captured their images and Detail was able to extract himself from the handshake and take a half step forward.

But suddenly, George Spell stepped in front of Alex and extended his hand.

The sight of George Spell always had an unnerving effect on Alex. His clone was only three years old but the Generationist age-acceleration allowed Madeline Spell to claim that George was seven. The boy looked much smaller than Alex imagined a normal seven-year-old would be. And George's piercing green eyes and intense focus suggested the presence of something far more menacing than a young boy.

The maneuver forced Alex to stop short and then bend down to shake George's hand, placing his head close enough to hear George sharply whisper directly into Alex's ear, "Enjoy looking up at the show in the dark, Alex Detail. I hope there are no throat slashers in the audience."

A small jolt ran through Alex, but he quickly smiled and whispered back, "I see you still haven't found those files that show how you were made." If George was susceptible to self-doubt, Alex hoped his comment would strike at the heart of it.

Alex moved on, looking over his shoulder at George. His young clone smiled at him, then reached out with his right hand and held his mother's left hand. It was an unusual show of affection by George. Alex had never seen George hold Madeline Spell's hand in the numerous encounters they'd had since the destruction of the Harvesters. And it appeared to take Spell by surprise; she glanced down at George with a curious expression. He turned away from Alex and looked up at his mother with the same beaming smile. She appeared touched by her son's display of affection, smiling back and holding his hand more firmly.

Not looking where he was walking, Alex bumped into something very solid.

Captain Odessa.

With her pursed lips and red hair pulled tightly back, the five-foot-tall Odessa at once seemed to fill the planetarium with her vigilant stance. Having forgone a dress uniform for her standard ARRAY blue service officer uniform, Odessa appeared ready to captain the planetarium if need be.

"Congratulations, Admiral," Odessa said, not at all phased by having Alex barrel right into her. She stopped a waiter carrying a tray of foods to the reception area. Quickly grabbing three cashew-encrusted chicken skewers, she ate all of them in one raptor-like swipe. "What is wrong with you?" Odessa asked Alex before she had swallowed her treats. "You are distraught and frightened. Doctor take away your laudanum?"

Alex had no idea what that was, but he assumed Odessa's remark was some sort of barb, as she seemed rather pleased with herself. Having grown accustomed to Odessa's penchant for peppering her speech with archaic expressions, Alex reflexively asked, "What?"

"You are emitting a strong metaxemone scent that makes these inedible biolegume skewers they pretend are chicken taste more putrid than I thought possible." Odessa stopped another waiter and swiped three skewers of coconut shrimp, eating them in the same manner. "Inedible," she said.

"Walk with me, Captain," Alex said, moving toward the seating area.

The New York Planetarium sat on the corner of 81st Street and Central Park West, built over the location of the old Hayden Planetarium adjacent to the Museum of Natural History. The new planetarium was a gigantic sphere constructed entirely of clear carbon fibers with microscopic iron filaments that made it appear to be a glimmering crystal orb. The base was held in place by four exterior legs, while the top of the planetarium was connected to a mooring attached to an arm that extended from one of the adjacent museum walls. Transparency of the entire sphere could be controlled to make the planetarium appear crystal clear or completely opaque. The floor and seats were made of a similar transparent material, allowing a 360-degree view of the sphere's interior and exterior. At the moment, it was opaque to those outside but clear inside: No one outside could see in, but those on the inside had the feeling of standing within a colossal sun-filled globe. Alex and Odessa walked toward the center of the seating, a gentle concave area two hundred feet across—the exact radius of the planetarium.

Alex stopped as they reached the center of the sphere and stood on the thirty-foot-wide circle of transparent floor that served as a holographic projector augmenting the optics in the sphere walls.

"Captain, I really need your help with something," Alex whispered to Odessa. "George Spell is going to try to kill me in here."

"Oh, please," Odessa scoffed.

"Just look at him!" Alex whispered.

Captain Odessa looked back over her shoulder at Speaker Spell and her son. George had his sights fixed on Alex, but was still holding his mother's left hand as she greeted people. "Well, he certainly has a lethal look in his eye," Odessa agreed. "But why do you imagine he will be attempting to put an end your life on this day? You have been in his company numerous times and you seem perfectly alive. Perhaps if you would quit meddling with what's left of the Harvesters then he would not feel compelled to murder." Odessa stuck her nose in the air and said haughtily, "Why, *the only person* that I know of who George Spell has *ever* killed was the Harvesters' precious little pet, Peevchi Derringkite." Odessa thought for a moment, then added, "And I must say he did a fine job of it. So if you do not wish to end up a slaughtered carcass like Derringkite, I recommend you not do anything George Spell might find similarly provocative."

So, Odessa knew Alex had attempted to establish some link to the Harvesters. But if she really knew the extent, she wouldn't be so vague. Alex self-consciously looked at his right thumb, and then quickly back up at Odessa. No, she didn't know. She probably just had some primitive command program spying device made by her ever-present lap dog, Vice Captain Horace Witaker.

"My studies of Pluto's remains have been completely sanctioned by ARRAY, Captain," Alex said. "It is inappropriate of you to suggest I have had any intent to communicate with the Harvesters."

Captain Odessa waved a hand at Alex. "You may cease and desist with that high and mighty business immediately. You would not be in mortal fear of young little George Spell if your studies were purely scientific. So why, Admiral, do you believe he is going to attempt fratricide?"

"Huh?" Alex looked over her shoulder at George. The boy wasn't making any attempt to pretend his full attention was trained on anyone but Alex. "Fratricide?" Alex asked.

"The murder of one's sibling," Odessa said with a gleam in her eye.

Alex huffed. "You mean clonicide? But please, listen, Odessa. He just said something to me that makes it seem like he knows something no one should know."

"What was that?" Odessa asked. "That you conspired to mutiny aboard the *Virgin Mother*?" Her voice grew more sarcastic, "That you convinced my first officer to build a sham bomb when we were ordered to destroy Pluto? That perhaps if you had not taunted Witaker with that 'being a tiger' nonsense Derringkite put into your head, we might have destroyed Pluto and prevented all of this?"

"Keep your voice down!" Alex whispered harshly. "I see your fling with Witaker has gotten you the information you wanted. How hurt he'll be to find out he was used."

Odessa snorted. "Oh, do have fun with your fruitless speculation. As if anyone would think Alex Detail knows anything about interpersonal romantic congress." Odessa raised an eyebrow and smirked. "You may know how to penetrate a command program, but no one who knows better would question my prowess."

Alex held his hands in front of his face with disgust. "Okay, can we stick to my problem? It doesn't matter what George said, just know he is a great threat, and not just to me. His programming would justify killing every person in this building if it meant my death."

The thing troubling Alex was indeed what George had said. It wasn't that Alex seriously thought George would produce a knife and slit his throat during the show (though George *had* killed Derringkite with a knife). But what George said indicated there was something far more sinister in play.

When Alex Detail was six years old, his mother had brought him to this very planetarium. It was the first time he had ever been to a planetarium and he was delighted that the seats leaned far back to allow one a clear view of the sky above. However, from what little Alex remembered of his mother, she was often wildly manic and prone to moments of paranoia which she delighted in sharing loudly in public settings. During their visit to this planetarium, just as the lights went out before the show began, as they lay with their necks exposed to the planetarium dome in the pitch black, Alex's mother leaned toward him and said, "I hope there are no throat slashers in the audience."

Was it just a coincidence, or did George have access to far more of Alex's consciousness than Alex realized?

Odder still, Alex had not thought about his mother in years. He was aware ARRAY had attempted to remove his natural bond with her shortly after he was taken from home, but Alex doubted if that attempt or any of their other earlier attempts to alter him had been very successful. After all, he'd still lost his mega-IQ, still was prone to gloominess and resignation. And as far as he could recall, his parents were more than eager to hand him over to ARRAY. He remembered experiencing an emotionless curiosity years ago at his parent's lack of contact, but then, he was equally relieved. What could those simple people who were his parents want from him? Money? To bask in his fame? No, they had let Alex go; handed him over to the state, as he imagined they thought was properly their duty in a time of war. And Alex had also let go of them.

Alex was startled out of his reverie by a woman's voice. "Well, if Mary didn't have a baby named Jesus! I haven't seen you two together in a space age!"

Alex and Odessa turned to find JuneMary standing before them, accompanied by her father, RK June, Madeline Spell's Secretary of Intelligence.

Captain Odessa held out her hand and greeted the two. "Ambassador JuneMary. Secretary June."

Alex hugged JuneMary. "You came all the way from Venus just for this?" The vivacious 91-year-old New African woman nodded and beamed with joy.

"The Lord didn't send me on a trip to Pluto and back with a stop in-between to heaven knows where, to keep a little trip from getting in the way! What I really came for was this."

JuneMary pulled Odessa toward her and gave her a big hug. Odessa appeared to try to smile but it was more of a grimace. After a few moments of not knowing what to do with her hands, likely because she was still clutching the chicken and shrimp skewers, she was relieved by Alex, who reached behind JuneMary and took the skewers. Her hands now freed up, Captain Odessa patted JuneMary on the back, but in an oddly practical manner that looked more to Alex like Odessa was wiping food off her fingertips.

"All right now, that's enough of that," Odessa said, taking a step back.

"Oh, same old mother," JuneMary said. "Now we're just missing handsome Horace. Where's that boyfriend of yours?"

Captain Odessa pursed her lips and said to JuneMary, "I see your appointment to Ambassador from New Africa has done little to quell your penchant for sophomoric gossip."

The colonized area of Venus that had been named New Africa was the only member of the House of Nations still using an official ambassador. The House of Nations had abolished those positions early in its existence, under the philosophy that a united world did not need ambassadors, as the very nature of an ambassador implicitly symbolized cultural differences that could not be addressed through normal bureaucratic relations.

However, Venus had always been given special treatment.

Venus was never seriously considered to be a planet that could be terraformed like Mars because it presented too many extraordinary difficulties. Its atmosphere was so thick that it would crush anyone on the ground. Its temperature of 450 degrees C would boil just about anything living. And worst, its slow spin, a sluggish one rotation for every one hundred seventeen Earth days, prevented it from having a magnetic field capable of shielding it from cosmic radiation that would instantly kill any organic life. Making Venus habitable was just too big a job.

But, while the greatest scientific minds were busy building an atmosphere on Mars, the CEO of a rather old-fashioned rocket propulsion factory that was manufacturing guided missiles to take materials to Mars came up with an ingenious idea—and just before any laws could be passed to prevent her from enacting it. Kade Kabede, chief executive of Somolian Industries, had her eyes on the giant asteroid, Radius-9, that passed through the solar system every two hundred seventy years. Radius-9 was about a year away from passing Venus's orbit when Kade realized a slight alteration of its vector might just produce a miracle. The asteroid, composed of a mantle that surrounded water ice and a rocky core, was just the right size for the job she had in mind. It was not too difficult to disguise Operation Aphrodite within the corporation's large-scale test rocket programs. Once she had attached a few of Somolian Industries more powerful rockets to the asteroid, she double-checked some calculations and fired them up.

Naturally, this was soon discovered by observation satellites, and the House of Nations immediately arrested Kabede and seized control of her company.

But in doing so, the House of Nations violated several of their Articles of Powers that could only be enacted during a global crisis. The courts barred the House from Somalia Industries. However, that didn't stop the House of Nations from sending ARRAY forces, placing the facility under military control.

Didn't matter. Kabede had made allowances for that, and ARRAY was unable to take control of the propulsion system she had fashioned for Radius-9. By the time the courts allowed the House of Nations to issue the executive order that ARRAY needed to destroy the facility, it was too late.

Operation Aphrodite was completed and Radius-9 slammed into Venus at just the right angle to eject most of the planet's dense carbon dioxide atmosphere and increase its spin by a factor of forty. A large chunk of the asteroid vaporized, releasing enough water vapor to create an oxygen rich atmosphere.

It took several decades for the atmospheric maelstrom that resulted from the asteroid's impact to settle enough for a manned exploration of Venus. But Kabede got her miracle. The outcome was a planet with a rotation of 72.1 hours, a magnetosphere that could protect organic life from solar radiation, and a mean surface temperature of 250 degrees F.

Still too hot for humans to live on, but Kabede had her sights set on the highlands of Venus's northern hemisphere, a landmass approximately the size of Australia, named Ishtar Terra, home to the planet's highest plateau, Maxwell Montes. Rising eleven kilometers above Venus's average surface elevation, Maxwell Montes had an average temperature of 110 degrees F, and became home to the first shelters built by the Federation of African Nations. In 2195, the House of Nations formally recognized the Maxwell Montes settlement as an autonomous member of the African Federation. Five years later, the African Federation granted complete autonomy to the Maxwell Montes settlement, officially bestowing the name New Africa.

Considered home to some of the most advanced scientists in the solar system—perhaps due to technological necessities forced by the harsh environment, and perhaps due to the audacity of its origins and first settlers—the planet and its inhabitants were held in high regard by the House of Nations. Its population of twenty million people was governed by a simple council of five volunteers who met once a week and officially interacted with the House of Nations through two appointed ambassadors.

JuneMary had served for nearly a decade on the council after her early career with ARRAY. She left to serve as the lieutenant governor of the University of New Africa before being drafted back into service aboard the *Cronus* during the second war with the Harvesters.

Now, Ambassador JuneMary stood before Alex and Odessa, teasing Captain Odessa with her "sophomoric gossip."

"Yes, it was my turn to do some more work," JuneMary said. "The House is still pestering me about that black hole we came up with. Being short of ships was a good excuse to keep putting that off, but President Innsbrook was kind enough to send *UC One* for me. Lord, us June's just keep on going, don't we, Dad?"

Secretary RK June was looking across the room, distracted. "What's that now, sweetheart? Oh, yes." It was rumored that the exceptionally long lifespans of New Africans was directly connected to living on the planet Venus. But JuneMary's father had spent most of the past fifteen years on Earth as a member of the speaker's cabinet. It was unusual to see RK June unfocused.

"What's got you so absent-minded, Father?" JuneMary asked.

"You've heard of Speaker Spell's special advisor during the war?" RK asked.

"Brother Lonadoon?"

Nodding, RK June indicated a man across the room. "That's him. I had better let the Speaker know he's here." In a troubled voice, he added, "I'm darn certain he was not invited by Secretary Hiramoto. Must be something Spell cooked up on her own."

RK left to attend to the matter, and JuneMary was about to resume her interrogation of Captain Odessa when the tall and muscular Vice Captain Horace Witaker joined the group, wearing his usual air of mild depression.

"So, it's a reunion," Alex said, as he, Odessa, JuneMary and Witaker stood together for the first time in six months.

Suddenly, the light-hearted camaraderie they had outwardly displayed was wiped away, and a wave of loss and sadness was shared between the four people who had faced life and death together and the weight of saving humanity. It was an awesome and heavy feeling, and the next thing Alex knew, JuneMary started crying.

"Here now," Vice Captain Witaker said, handing JuneMary a napkin.

"It's just a mighty thing seeing us all here all of a sudden." JuneMary blew her nose.

Alex didn't entirely feel the full rush of emotions. His anxiety was rising. What would happen if he just left, right now? Or was that what George Spell was planning on? Of the seventy-two ways George could kill him, there were several that could make a door deadly.

Captain Odessa nodded and blinked rapidly. Was that a tear in her eye?

Horace tentatively raised his hand as if to offer a comforting touch to Captain Odessa's arm, but Odessa stiffened and said in commanding voice, "Let us not be swept away unawares by a foreign discontent."

It wasn't clear to Alex whether Odessa had intended the remark to pertain to the entire group, or a subtle warning to Vice Captain Witaker to keep his affections to himself, but it appeared to strike a nerve with him. He withdrew his hand and looked up at the sky. A little too quickly, as he accidentally looked directly at the sun above them, then squinted and looked away, rubbing his eyes.

Alex suddenly had a dreadful thought. There was a seventy-third way George could kill him. "Why the hell is it so bright in here?" he asked.

"No doubt for your privacy," Witaker said, wiping tears from his eyes. "The walls allow light in but none out. And just in case any of the media outside have photo static polarization equipment, the EM filter is probably at maximum. Not even the smallest photon particle could escape these walls."

That's when Alex Detail realized the brilliance of George Spell's assassination plan. George had good reason to jump in front of Alex and shake his hand as he entered. Of course, he knew about the glass shard in Alex's thumb, and as George pressed his palm into Alex's, it would have been a simple matter of imagining a certain geometric shape that would cause the Harvester shard to emit a certain particle.

That meant that as Alex stood there in the center of the planetarium sphere, a sub-atomic particle was bouncing around the interior of the convex-opaque sphere at the speed of light. And in seconds, it would collide with the only thing dense enough in the room to stop it—the shard of Harvester glass in his thumb.

The resulting explosion would vaporize Alex and anyone within ten feet of him.

As she greeted the last of the attendees, Madeline Spell, still holding George's hand, said, "Come on now, George. Let's go take our seats and watch the show."

"Okay, Mom," George replied.

But before they could take a step Madeline saw secretaries Guy Hiramoto and RK June walking toward her with another man in tow.

Brother Israel Lonadoon.

What the hell is he doing here?

Not only was Spell certain Lonadoon had not been invited, Madeline had personally greeted every one of the nearly five hundred guests. But she had no recollection of greeting Lonadoon.

He stopped before her and gave a slight bow.

"Bother Lonadoon," Madeline said, returning his greeting with a slight tilt of her head. "I was not aware you were invited."

"Neither were we," Hiramoto said, exchanging worried glances with RK June.

"I apologize for surprising you like this," Lonadoon said. "But I had a rather urgent issue I needed to speak to you about. May we have a moment?"

Spell glanced at Hiramoto and RK June, and then nodded. "If you wouldn't mind, gentlemen?"

Hiramoto and RK June reluctantly moved off toward the edge of the seating area a short distance away.

But George stayed put, still holding Spell's hand, staring maliciously at Lonadoon.

Madeline knew the only subjects so urgent as to cause Brother Lonadoon's sudden appearance after leaving six months ago had to be either the Harvesters, Alex Detail, or George. Most likely all three.

"George, please go stand with your father and Secretary June," Spell said.

George didn't reply, but slowly let go of Spell's hand, shot Lonadoon one last searing glance, then left them.

"Of all the places in the world, what is so urgent?" Spell asked Lonadoon in a sharp but hushed tone.

Lonadoon glanced sideways at George, and then said, "Your repairs are not working."

Spell frowned. "Could you please be more specific?"

"Speaker, I do not believe you understand the extraordinary extent of … why, indeed, did you bring George with you, today?"

"He wanted to come," Spell said matter-of-factly.

"Why would he want to come here at this time? Today? Surely you could arrange for him to see a show at the planetarium anytime."

Spell nodded and smiled over Lonadoon's shoulder at Hiramoto and RK. George was standing next to them, wringing his hands. "Brother, we have already been speaking too long. Please get to the point."

Lonadoon whispered. "George came here today because there is something particular about these circumstances and it certainly involves Alex Detail's presence. I warned you against putting them in this type of situation. You underestimate both of them."

"Oh, this again," Spell said. "I've been at this for many years and I have never underestimated either of them."

"You would unleash their powers here?" Lonadoon asked. "Have you forgotten the purpose for which George was created?"

"Oh, I see. You, of course, know Alex Detail has been dallying with things he ought not. So, you think George is going to kill Detail?" Spell decided to speak as sarcastically as possible to show Lonadoon how ridiculous he sounded.

"Well, who am I to intervene? Alex has forced me into this situation, giving me no choice but to put him in command of ARRAY. And believe me, he does not want the job, he just wants to use that position to scheme up his Harvester immortality quest. So, which is more dangerous, Brother Lonadoon? Alex, with the world's greatest military at his command, or George, a young boy with his only weapon being a young Detail's mind?" Spell sighed.

"I see," Lonadoon said. "You think it's all very simple. Perhaps George does indeed attempt something, an improbable accident suddenly befalls Alex Detail. How convenient for you. But make no mistake, Speaker. They both have ambitions that go beyond what you can imagine, and if they are put into a position of adversaries, their powers could destroy all of us." Lonadoon peered around at George, then spoke sharply under his breath to Spell, "Would you be responsible for the extinction of humanity?"

Spell was already turning to leave this conversation. "I have heard enough, Brother. I would thank you to make your way out now."

Lonadoon nodded. "Very well, Speaker. Consider yourself warned for the last time."

A tremendous explosion blasted them off their feet.

As Spell was falling to the floor, a strange sensation flooded her, and it was certainly accompanied by a horrific flood of guilt and grief, but most prominently, the feeling she experienced was one of relief.

The explosion could mean only one thing: Lonadoon was right.

Alex Detail was dead.

It takes approximately 300 milliseconds for information to travel along a neuron in the brain. Then it takes another 300 milliseconds for the information to be processed by the brain as a thought.

This was fortunate for Alex Detail, who needed to process a lot of thoughts in the last few seconds of his life.

Of course, despite his every effort to shield his Harvester work by distracting George with thoughts of the Generationist Research he so desperately sought to extract from Alex's mind, he obviously had not been able to prevent George from learning about the chip.

Alex had gone to great lengths to obtain the chip they removed from Peevchi Derringkite's thumb and replace it with a useless replica. While on the *Virgin Mother*, the crew had not analyzed the Harvester chip to learn enough of its true nature to be able to recognize a decent counterfeit. And before they disembarked from the ship, Alex had taken the true chip and replaced it with a decent counterfeit.

Derringkite's Harvester chip, when in contact with an exposed nerve, worked by responding to the carrier's thoughts of particular geometric shapes. A properly conceived shape, such as an isosceles triangle, golden rectangle, dodecahedron, etc. would cause the chip to emit any number of sub-atomic particles that could convey messages to the Harvesters, so long as there was an "antenna" to their universe. And one still existed: The remains of Pluto orbiting Earth still contained a link.

It was clear now that George knew all of this. And when he shook Alex's hand, he had directed a shape thought right into Alex's mind. That thought released a particle that would not be able to escape the sphere, and it would bounce around at the speed of light until it struck the only material that could stop it: the shard embedded under the skin in Alex's thumb.

So, there were a few things Alex could do. He could find the planetarium controls and adjust the sphere walls to allow light out. But that would take at least a minute. He could run for an exit, but he suspected that would not be so easy: Doors could mysteriously lock; perhaps someone would shout, "Stop him!"; it could all take even longer than a minute. And the further danger was that he would be close to people when the particle struck his thumb, killing ten, perhaps twenty in the area around him.

Alex had run the math. In his first minute after shaking George's hand there was a ten percent probability the particle would collide with the Harvester shard. The risk increased exponentially after that, meaning that by the time he understood what was happening, he had only seconds left.

So, the third option occurred to him concurrently with the first two. It was the simplest, fastest, and could be done in seconds without anyone noticing.

Alex was still holding the food skewers he had taken from Odessa. While pretending to continue his conversation, he put his hands behind his back, dug a skewer into his thumb, pushed out the chip, and pretended to pluck a piece of lint off his uniform, which he flicked a good thirty feet away into an area of unoccupied seats.

Then it was only a matter of seconds.

Alex saw George Spell standing with RK June and Secretary Hiramoto. He caught George's attention and smiled at him, giving him a slight head shake. *Not this time, George.*

Turning his attention back to the group, *whose lives I have just saved, once again*, he saw that Odessa had apparently fully recovered from her brush with emotion and was addressing JuneMary in full lecture mode , "...truly it is important to consider ARRAY's concerns with the renegade practices of your radical scientists on New Africa. House citizens must be able to live their lives built on the trust that they are safe from the ill-conceived hazards of—"

Odessa was interrupted by one of the few things that could actually cut off her thundering voice—a thunderous explosion.

CHAPTER 2

•

THE PERILOUS PLANETARIUM

Captain Odessa had conducted numerous training exercises with new ARRAY cadets on the subject of explosions. She would pace before the officers-to-be lined in front of her and say, "Close proximity to an explosion is an unnerving experience. The shock wave slams into you while you are simultaneously traumatized by a deafening noise. Your pitiable minds will be flooded with all manner of phantom terrors. Am I severely injured? Will I die? Is another explosion about to hit me? Unprepared, you will find yourself in a state of absolute petrifaction, stunned and unable to instantly respond to the adrenaline flooding your body while a painful ringing in your ears drowns out all other sound."

Odessa would then make her point by suddenly setting off a loud explosion behind the cadets, then issuing them an order they were incapable of hearing or paying attention to. Once their hearing returned, they would be subjected to a lengthy lecture on how their inadequacies would cost them their lives and those of their crew, leading to battle losses and the end of the world simply because they were weak and unprepared for a loud noise.

Shameful.

Experiencing an explosive shockwave inside a perfectly-shaped sphere is more painful than any other enclosure. As the waves hit the concave walls they reverberate back in upon themselves with energy crossing and destroying itself in a series of explosive echoes.

The explosion in the planetarium rendered everyone paralyzed in those moments when action must be taken.

Everyone except Captain Odessa.

During her service in the First Harvester War, Odessa had experienced firsthand the disorientation and confusion of explosive shock waves. It irritated her that something as innocuous as sound could put one at a sudden disadvantage, a needless disadvantage. Odessa subsequently incorporated all manner of explosive and disorienting sounds into her personal battle training. In time, she began to enjoy the thrill of a big bang knocking into her. As much as Odessa detested bland food that failed to ignite her sense of taste, so too did she prefer sounds to be much louder than most people would find comfortable.

As Odessa saw the first sparks of an explosion across the planetarium, she had already pre-processed what was coming. And before the sound wave had even reached her, she was braced against it, feet firmly planted as she launched herself at Alex, JuneMary and Horace, taking them down in an efficient tackle.

By the time the blast wave and tiny fragments of translucent carbon fibers that had once been seats blasted over them, Odessa and her group were already falling toward the floor.

And that's why I win so many battles, Odessa thought.

The moment the blast had passed, Odessa was back on her feet. But a sudden quake nearly toppled her.

The explosion had taken place right on top of one of the legs holding the giant sphere in place, dislodging it from the base and jolting the planetarium. Odessa shouted, "Evacuate!" Her cry was not necessary, as everyone was shouting and running toward the nearest exit, following the swarm of security that had already surrounded Madeline Spell.

Witaker had helped JuneMary to her feet and they were moving with Odessa toward the exit.

That's when Captain Odessa noticed two very strange things.

The first was that George Spell was looking toward the area of the explosion with dismay. Not fear, not surprise. Not normal. He clearly expected the explosion but was not pleased with the results. Security officers swarmed George and swept him away.

So, Alex Detail had been right.

The second strange thing Odessa noticed was that Alex was not with them. As she helped herd people to the exit, she spotted Alex frantically searching the floor near the perimeter of the explosion. This was certainly not the behavior of an ARRAY officer. Training dictated immediate evacuation of civilians away from the site of the explosion, as it was the most likely location of a secondary attack.

But Alex appeared to be following a small spatter pattern on the seats nearest the explosion. He knelt down, patted his hand on an area of the floor, then jumped back up and ran toward the exit. He caught up with Captain Odessa as she hustled the last of the people out of the exit.

"Did you find what you where looking for?" Odessa asked Alex.

"What?" Alex yelled.

Odessa rolled her eyes. Of course fancy-pants Admiral Detail had not undergone typical ARRAY training. He obviously did not know that with his hearing temporarily compromised, he should be focusing on reading lips in those critical moments following an explosion.

As they exited into the sunny park surrounding the planetarium, Odessa noticed that the thumb of Alex's right hand was dripping with blood. But rather than holding it in his left hand, as would be the natural reaction, his left hand was clenched shut.

Odessa was close enough to Alex to notice he was no longer emitting the strong metaxemone scent. Since that indicated he was no longer in his state of panic, Odessa deduced that Alex had figured out how George had caused the explosion and was no longer in fear of another attempt on his life. And rather than appearing shaken by the incident, Alex seemed to be rather pleased with himself.

What are those boys up to?

Odessa did not have time to ponder this question further. As the senior officer (after Admiral Detail) in attendance, it was her duty to take command of the crisis. She grabbed the nearest security officer.

"Were you in the planetarium?" she asked.

"No sir," the officer said.

Good. Someone who could hear her. "Immediately set up a perimeter," Odessa ordered, pulling out her hand window. "No one is to leave the grounds until they have been searched and questioned. Where is the Speaker?"

The officer was listening to his earpiece and reported, "The Speaker has been secured in her car. She is waiting for her son before leaving."

Odessa could see Madeline Spell's car nearby, surrounded by her personal House security detail. Other officers were escorting Secretary Hiramoto and George to the car.

"Hand me your sidearm," Odessa commanded, and the officer gave her his gun.

As the officer left to execute Odessa's orders, she turned and grabbed Alex Detail. Pointing to her mouth, she shouted, "Can you hear me?"

Alex nodded. "Yes, barely." But he wasn't paying attention to her. He was looking over at the officers escorting Hiramoto and George Spell past them.

"Listen to me now," Odessa said. "There is no ARRAY officer here who would question the great Alex Detail, let alone search your person. I, however, intend to get some answers."

"I told you he was trying to kill me," Alex said. "Why don't you go detain George? You waste time with me. Are you afraid to take George Spell into custody?"

"Don't be ridiculous," Odessa snapped. "You have a self-inflicted wound on your thumb and I watched you remove something from the explosion site which you are now holding in your left hand."

Alex raised his clenched left hand, held it in front of Odessa's face, and opened it.

It was empty.

Odessa gave a disgusted grunt. "Your sleight of hand does not amuse me, Admiral. But perhaps a full cavity search would amuse you?"

"Oh please, Odessa," Alex said. "Yes, you got me! I was able to unbutton this uniform and shove a piece of stolen evidence into it, then button it back up all while running out of there with all these people."

Undeterred, Odessa continued, "Well, since you recently had all admiral uniforms re-designed, quite ridiculously while we were attending to more important matters like rebuilding half the planet, who knows what secret pockets and pokey-holes you may have devised!"

A sudden ruckus caused Odessa to turn around.

George Spell had slipped away from his security detail and was pushing his way through the crowd. Odessa stepped between George and Alex just as he approached.

"Admiral Detail," George yelled. Then in a whining, plaintive voice, George said, "Alex, come to the car with us. I don't think it's safe out here!"

Secretary Hiramoto and his guards caught up to George, but he jumped forward as they tried to grab him. Odessa caught George Spell by the shoulder and held him firmly in place as he tried to squirm past her. "Young man, you will go with Secretary Hiramoto! You are to be in a secure location!"

Then the ground shook.

Everyone turned to the planetarium as the second of the support legs collapsed. The huge sphere had hit the ground, shaking the earth as it began to roll forward. Above, the support that attached the top of the planetarium to the giant arm was beginning to detach. If it failed, the 400-foot sphere, constructed of 97,000 tons of extremely dense carbon fibers, was on enough of an incline that it would roll over everyone, crushing a deadly path through the thousands of people mobbing the street, and leveling several blocks of city buildings before it stopped.

Horace Witaker was at Odessa's side within moments. "A flier with a repair crew has been dispatched," he reported to Odessa. "But it has an ETA of almost three minutes."

The street was now a logjam of thousands of people trampling each other to get out of the way. The people who had evacuated the planetarium were running past the perimeter established by ARRAY security and rushing out of the park into the mobbed street.

How convenient for whomever was responsible for this, Odessa thought. Simultaneously, she said to Witaker, "Three minutes! All the barricaded routes have been overrun with people. None of the cars are getting out of here that soon even if they try running over people, including the Speaker's! We need someone up there now!"

Odessa had never been one to appreciate the beauty of impractical architecture, and this was a perfectly good example of why not. What would the degenerate designers of this modern marvel think of their creation after it had crushed a thousand people, killed the Speaker of the House of Nations and half of the government leaders? All because of whatever battle had been provoked between Alex Detail and George Spell.

Win two wars against the Harvesters only to be crushed to death by a giant ball.

Ridiculous!

George Spell had not moved from his spot near Odessa, but his body language had changed. Upon hearing that his mother and House leaders were in danger of being killed, his body went rigid and his attention turned from Alex Detail to the planetarium. His eyes were squinting, and he stared at the gigantic orb as it strained against the damaged mooring at its top.

Suddenly George turned to Odessa and said, "The explosion created a fracture in the attachment's forth quadrant that was weakened two minutes after the first leg collapsed. The fracture is expanding at twenty picometers per second. Total collapse will occur within one hundred and five seconds."

George grabbed a light knife from a junior ARRAY officer's uniform. He began to run toward the planetarium. As he ran, he shouted over his shoulder, "Shoot your gun ahead of me!"

Looking ahead of George, Odessa thought perhaps there might be someone he needed shot out of the way, something Odessa would have been happy to do for George since it appeared he was going to attempt to climb to the top of the planetarium. But there was no one in his way as he arrived at one of the remaining legs and began running up the steep 45-degree angle.

"Excellent initiative," Odessa said to Alex and Horace. "He will make a fine ARRAY officer one day."

Alex rolled his eyes at Odessa. "Well, what are you waiting for?"

"I've seen no obstacles," Odessa replied. Then it occurred to her that George needed something to help him scale the nearly 157-foot portion of the globe's lower convex exterior between where the leg attached and the "equator."

As George reached the top of the leg, Odessa, the best shot in all of ARRAY, set her gun on auto, aimed, and fired.

The gun's standard ammunition, a T-boride bullet, shattered against the planetarium's carbon filaments, spraying the area with shrapnel.

"Try these," Horace Witaker said, handing Odessa a magazine of "solid mercury" rounds—a non-shatter artificial compound with the hardness of diamond nonorod.

Odessa quickly made the switch and fired again.

This time, the blasts from her gun struck the globe just above George's head, creating an indentation. George leaped up and grabbed the handhold. Odessa continued firing, creating a series of gouges in the globe approximately one foot away from each other, and George scaled the side of the globe as fast as she could fire. She just hoped he didn't get too far ahead of himself and end up getting shot.

"Why the hell are you firing at my son?" Madeline Spell, trailed by Hiramoto, the Junes, and a retinue of security was reaching for Odessa's arm. Odessa ignored the Speaker. Concentration was paramount.

Alex explained. "She's creating handholds for him. Look at him go, like a little spider."

Spell waved her security detail over. "Go over there beneath him! If he falls ..."

"Then it ain't gonna matter worth a darn!" JuneMary said. "Cause we'll all be squashed—so let's let mother concentrate here."

It was a strange scene. Thousands of screaming people continued to flee as the 400-foot-tall planetarium threatened to roll over them at any moment. And standing directly in its path was the Speaker of the House of Nations, JuneMary with her father, and Alex Detail, all surrounding Captain Odessa as she fired her gun repeatedly, the bullets striking just ahead of the small boy scrambling up the side of the giant orb.

Alex Detail was irritated.

Once again George Spell was about to publicly upstage Alex Detail.

Not that Alex was totally convinced George would make it to the top of the planetarium in time. It was more likely he would fall, or the planetarium would come loose. And, Alex thought, it would be a shame if someone bumped into Captain Odessa, causing her to accidentally shoot Alex's would-be assassin.

If Alex had thought it was a completely hopeless situation, he would have been SO out of there with the screaming mob. He'd be the first to agree that "run for your life" was really good advice.

But whether or not George made it, the attempt would be viewed as heroic. Whatever the outcome, Alex was irritated that he was outdone once again by his little clone. Surviving the assassination attempt was one thing, but to then have this little copy of him publicly attempt to save the day was just too much for him to bear.

There had to be another way to stop this massive globe from crushing half the city.

So, while he listened to Madeline Spell's backseat driving as Odessa tried to concentrate on shooting grooves for George's superhero scramble to the top of the planetarium, and while some more courageous members of the media recorded this great heroic attempt, Alex pulled out his hand window and started making some calculations.

Thankfully, to his relief, another solution occurred to him.

Alex accessed the city government's operational systems and within seconds assembled the modules of a program. Now all he needed was an executive order.

All he needed was George to fail.

Or fall.

Alex lowered his window and looked up.

George had made it past the underside curve of the globe and was now at a full-on sprint to the top. Good lord, it appeared he was going to make it. As he watched his best and brightest genes at work, Alex decided to put a stop to it right then.

Alex put one foot in front of another, leaned forward, and directed his thoughts at George.

That's when George tripped.

Madeline Spell gasped.

George fell forward and rolled onto his side.

Alex tried to will a wall of force to knock his clone right off the planetarium. It's not like falling would kill him, what with Madeline Spell's goons there to catch him. And if somehow the fall was lethal, they'd have him at the House healing center and stitched back together in no time. *Let him fall,* Alex thought. *I have the situation under control.*

But then imagine how the public would respond to that. The child who risked his life and almost died saving the city.

No, that was much worse.

George caught himself before rolling off the globe and reached the top of the planetarium just seconds after almost falling off.

Just as he was approaching the creaking mooring, the sound of a flier filled the air.

"Now they get here!" Spell said.

So much for Horace's estimate of three minutes. Alex would have blamed the mistake on Horace's obviously distracted mind, his infatuation with Captain Odessa, but even that wouldn't have caused Witaker to be wrong by such a large margin. It hadn't even been two minutes.

Witaker checked his hand window. "That's not the flier that was sent," he said.

"Well whatever it is, thank God it's here," Spell said. "Contact them and get George off of there."

Odessa was looking at Witaker's window. "Speaker," she said, "that's not a house flier, and its channels are closed."

"What?" Spell asked. "Then who sent it?"

"Its beacon is disabled, which is highly suspicious. The specifications match the *UC One* flier," Witaker said.

President Innsbrook's spaceship transport?

Witaker continued, "Telemetry reports confirm it descended from *UC One*'s orbit over five minutes ago, landed behind the museum on Columbus Avenue and just took off from there."

This was very perplexing. Why would Innsbrook put his flier down in Manhattan where they were prohibited? He would have had to send it on its way before the explosion.

How would he know there would be an emergency? How would he know there would be an explosion and a flier would be needed to fix the top of the planetarium?

Alex looked around as he realized Innsbrook would not have known.

But Brother Lonadoon was another story. And neither man was anywhere in sight.

As they watched, the flier was close enough for George to climb in. But George was intent on finishing his mission. He had his light knife in hand and was about to fuse the broken mooring when a hand reached out of the flier and yanked him inside.

As soon as George had boarded, it should have been a simple matter for someone to hop out and fuse the failing planetarium mooring.

That didn't happen. The flier instantly took off into the clouds.

"That did not look like a rescue," Alex Detail said. "It looked more like a kidnapping."

"They just kidnapped George!" Spell shouted.

Unfortunately, there was nothing they could do about that for the moment.

The force of the flier's engines accelerated the crack in the failing mooring.

The planetarium broke loose and nearly one hundred thousand tons of dense carbon began to roll over them.

Alex Detail immediately swung around and grabbed Spell just as everyone turned in a futile attempt to run.

"I can stop it," Detail said.

Spell froze and stared at him.

As she looked into Alex's eyes, he realized she didn't trust him, didn't like him, and wasn't sure if she believed him.

But what choice did she have?

"Authorize this," Detail said, pointing to his window.

Spell had no time to read whatever was on his screen. She held up her hand. Alex grabbed it and shoved her index fingertip onto a box on his window.

The giant globe was gaining momentum, rolling toward them, casting a giant reflective light shadow as its massive weight made the ground rumble. There was nowhere to run. It was like having a small planet about to bulldoze over them.

Then a sound began emanating from the very ground they were standing on. It was low-pitched with high screeching overtones muffled by the earth, and it vibrated through everyone like the low bass of a giant speaker.

As the planetarium rolled toward them, close to crushing them, it suddenly shook violently. The sound from the ground increased and the planetarium abruptly ground to a halt, then rolled back fifty feet toward its original spot by the museum, where it gradually shuddered to a stop against the museum wall. As it stood still, the globe began sinking into the earth.

Alex smiled at Madeline Spell, who still appeared to be in a state of shock at having watched her son be abducted.

Odessa grabbed the window from Alex's hand and said, "What did you do?"

Alex snatched back his window. "I created a massive surge of electricity through the subway tracks beneath us. It's acting like a giant magnet." He turned to Speaker Spell, "Thank you, Speaker, for authorizing emergency control over city infrastructure."

"Now," Alex continued, in a voice loud enough to be heard by the approaching crowd, and perhaps clearly recorded by some nearby reporter. "Captain Odessa, see to it that this entire area is evacuated. The amount of electricity running through those tracks is going to melt them in a matter of minutes. Also, dispatch a fire team to the subway."

There were a few cheers and some applause from the crowd.

Odessa raised her voice and issued the orders through her window, handing them to Vice Captain Witaker to ensure their proper execution.

Defense Secretary Guy Hiramoto was listening to an implant in his ear while simultaneously exchanging windows with RK June.

"Guy?" Spell asked. "Tell me we have some answers."

Guy nodded. "Yes. The flier that took George has docked on *UC One* and the spaceship has broken orbit."

"Have you contacted Innsbrook?" Spell asked.

"Yes," Hiramoto said. "The White House said they were not authorized to open communications or give the president's present location."

JuneMary grumbled, "Well, what is that old boy up to?"

"I think it is a reasonable assumption that President Innsbrook has kidnapped your son to gain some strategic leverage," Captain Odessa said to Madeline Spell.

Hiramoto nodded. "I agree with Captain Odessa, Speaker."

"But that's absurd!" Spell said. "Jonathan cannot leverage a criminal act against me. It would be political suicide."

Alex shook his head. "As usual, Speaker, Innsbrook has a bigger plan than you can wrap your head around."

Spell stared coldly at Detail. "Enlighten me, Alex. How could Innsbrook possibly be serious about kidnapping George?"

"Never mind. It doesn't really matter," Alex said sarcastically. "How silly of me! I mean, why not let President Innsbrook keep George? You can always just make another copy of me."

"That's enough!" Hiramoto shouted.

The grounds were sufficiently clear by now. The speaker's car pulled up beside them and she motioned everyone to get in.

Once inside, Hiramoto continued. "Alex, you keep your mouth shut about that when we are in public."

Alex felt like punching Hiramoto in the face. Parading around as if he were truly George's father. These people, so ungrateful! "How many times do I have to save your lives before I get a little respect?" He turned to Madeline Spell. "And for your information, it doesn't take a cloned genius to realize President Innsbrook has obviously hitched his wagon to someone more powerful than you."

"There is no one more powerful than the Speaker of the House of Nations," Hiramoto said.

"Oh, really? I guess I must be mistaken, Secretary Hiramoto, father of George Spell," Alex replied. "By the way, has anyone seen Brother Israel Lonadoon?"

Madeline Spell's eyes widened in shock as the possibility dawned on her.

"That's right," Alex said. "Another one of your mistakes that I will most likely end up having to clean up."

Just then there was a loud screech followed by a rumble.

"Uh oh," Alex said, looking at his window.

He had forgotten about that.

The rail on the northbound subway track was undergoing repairs. The electrical current he had sent through it had burned out the temporary repair rail, causing an emergency breaker to cut the current.

Without the extra magnetism of the north track, the planetarium was pulled in the direction of the southbound track.

But that track was not strong enough to hold it alone.

On the afternoon of Alex Detail's promotion, (which had been wrecked when his clone made an assassination attempt that almost caused a planetarium to squash thousands of people, but who was then kidnapped by the UC President and some mystic) the 400-foot planetarium popped free of the magnetic bonds Alex had created to salvage the situation. The huge sphere then rolled across Central Park West, crushed the stone wall, barreled down the steep slope into the park, and flattened a path of 500-year-old trees. Next, it wiped out half of Belvedere Castle, sending large chunks of granite and brick flying before coming to a giant splashy rest in Turtle Pond.

CHAPTER 3

•

THE KIDNAPPING OF GEORGE SPELL

Madeline Spell had to figure things out pretty quickly. The best way to do that was get her top people into ARRAY's war room at the House of Nations and initiate a total lockdown.

As soon as Spell's car arrived at the House of Nations, she gathered Alex Detail, Captain Odessa, Secretary of Defense Guy Hiramoto, Secretary of Intelligence RK June, and Ambassador JuneMary in the central command chamber. Vice Captain Witaker did not have the seniority required to attend the meeting, so he was left outside but placed under heavy guard.

As soon as the door was shut, Spell said, "House computer, initiate communications shielding and secure all entrances. Discontinue auto record."

The computer engaged the chamber's shielding and locks, but auto record was another matter. In order to prevent the creation of any intelligence that could not be classified and shared with the appropriate members of the House of Nations, all military matters were automatically recorded. The recordings could be classified and held up for security reasons as long as possible; they could be completely declassified and shared at a later time—or any combination in-between. But it was illegal for the Speaker of the House of Nations to make decisions of a military nature without the house auto record on her own.

The computer answered her request, "Authorization to discontinue house auto record must be provided by one house member executive civilian and one active military officer with alpha level clearance."

That meant the speaker required a member of the house cabinet and an ARRAY admiral to authorize her request.

Fortunately, she had both in the room.

Secretary Hiramoto said, "Computer, discontinue auto record, Secretary's authorization *****." The audio mute stopped the sound waves coming from Hiramoto's mouth from traveling farther than it needed to read them.

Spell looked at Alex Detail. "Admiral, will you please?"

Alex appeared to be thinking it over. Spell was not surprised. Alex was not inclined to offer help to her of all people, and if he did, he would be certain to get something in return.

Alex did not speak, but held up his window and sent a message to Spell's window.

She read his message: *I will comply. But in return, you must agree to allow me to fully participate in any attempt to retrieve the clone, George Spell.*

Spell had anticipated that, and had already made arrangements to keep Alex under her full control if she were forced to allow him to go after George. But she was disturbed Alex felt he could be so reckless as to put the words "the clone" in writing.

Spell sent a message back: *Agreed.*

Alex read his message, nodded, then said, "Computer, discontinue auto record, admiral's authorization *****."

"Auto record discontinuation authorized," the house computer replied. "An advisory of the auto record shut-off will be sent to the House Judiciary Committee. All authorizing personnel present during auto record suspension may be subpoenaed to testify on the matter. Do you wish to continue?"

"Yes," Spell said.

"Auto record discontinued," the computer confirmed.

Where to begin?

The past six months had been hard on Madeline Spell. Harder perhaps than the two wars she led against the Harvesters. It wasn't enough that planet Earth had been ravaged and citizens traumatized, but there were all the other loose ends everywhere she turned.

Foremost was Alex Detail. He had changed after the war. The Alex Detail she had known since he was seven years old was a vain, self-obsessed introvert who liked the trappings of fame and power but shielded himself from any true responsibility. Detail held the rank of admiral but did not command any fleets or serve on any official committees. When Alex was fourteen years old he just wanted the title, but remained the official head of ARRAY Science.

He was happy to go throw his title and name around but then disappear into his own world for weeks.

Not now. Today was the day he was to assume responsibility for all of ARRAY, a job he was not qualified for and would not be good at, but a job no one could refuse him. He hadn't even asked her for it. Alex had simply visited the House of Nations during a general assembly and announced that he would finally take on the role of chief executive of ARRAY since Fleet Admiral Sevo had committed suicide. He acted as if being the Chief Admiral of ARRAY was a position that had been offered to him repeatedly but that he had reluctantly declined his whole life.

Well, the house members might be glamorized by Alex Detail, but Madeline Spell knew him better than that. *A petulant genius might be good in a pinch, but that doesn't make him a qualified military administrator.* Still, how could she go before the House of Nations and refuse Alex Detail as the head of ARRAY? The house delegates and the countries they represented perceived Detail as the mastermind who had brought about victories in both wars. Not only that, but there was also the matter of George Spell.

Hiramoto had stated it clearly to Speaker Spell: Alex would tell the world about George, and that would be the end of her. And he meant it. She had no choice. Spell would be compelled to direct other senior ARRAY officers and department heads to do the real work while Alex pretended to run ARRAY. Meanwhile, what did he really want?

Hiramoto had approached Captain Odessa to help find the answer. She was the one person they both trusted to take a direct order from her civilian bosses to spy on Alex Detail. Odessa had never respected Alex as a true ARRAY officer so she understood her task without explanation.

Unfortunately, Odessa had turned up very little. All she had found was that Alex was openly studying the remains of Pluto orbiting Earth. Madeline Spell believed the only explanation for his interest would be if he hoped to somehow resurrect the power he'd experienced while on Pluto. Even *she* remembered the blissful consciousness the entire world had experienced once Pluto had arrived at Earth. To return the world to a state of mass "enlightenment" might seem a noble cause, but the Harvesters had provoked two wars, killed many, and Alex Detail was no saint. Sadly, however, he had enough people in his corner now. So, Spell was left to turn the full global military over to Alex Detail, knowing all the while that he was likely to use it to further his own ends.

Then there were the Harvester cults that they could not really call cults anymore. Very well-organized groups had formed to study the experience of no-time. And they wanted to know more. It was the sort of thing a zealot idolizer of Alex Detail could suddenly turn into a vast movement. Was that what Alex wanted? An army of devoted followers? Doubtful. But the fact Alex could snap his fingers and raise an army with the power to stage some manner of rebellion was a very real threat.

The matter of George was another terrible burden. While it looked like his genetic engineering could not be significantly undone, Spell firmly believed nurture could overcome nature. Just so long as she could keep the rumors at bay.

Spell had no real reason to think George was a threat to anyone now that the Harvesters were gone. She had arranged dinners that included George for Alex to attend, had made sure they were exposed to each other at a handful of carefully attended gatherings. George had never said or done anything to make her think he was dangerous or plotting an attempt on Alex Detail's life.

Today had proved she was wrong.

Lonadoon had been warning her, and that irritated Madeline Spell to no end. She began to regret ever befriending the man and worse, giving him the direct knowledge of George's origins. She had finally cut him off; she had made certain he had no access to either George or herself.

Then he shows up on the day this actually happens?

These were the sorts of things that had forced Spell to censor information, threaten groups with instant retribution, and issue a litany of executive orders that made her more a dictator than elected head of state. She despised what she had become, and her rationalizations about how her actions had saved the world twice were not helping. All those clever acts that had been so brilliantly masterminded by herself and Hiramoto were now known by certain people, thus giving them leverage, damn it all.

Now this.

Spell looked at the group of people she had assembled, and naturally turned to Hiramoto first. "Have we been able to locate Innsbrook's ship?"

"No," Hiramoto replied. "It does not register on any tracking sensors. The Pentagon has not been forthcoming with any information, which leads me to conclude they know about as much as we do."

"Alex," Spell said. "Admiral. What happened? What caused the explosion?"

"The clone tried to kill me," Alex said, again flaunting the forbidden syntax.

"Yes, yes," Spell said, sick of Alex's constant victim act. "Do you know how, or more importantly, why?"

"How?" Alex asked, incredulously. "How the hell would I know how? As for why, I suggest you ask the people you directed to create George."

Spell sighed. "So, you don't know how or why, but you purport to know that George is responsible? It seems you cannot answer the question without self-incrimination."

"Oh, come off it, Madeline," Alex said. "Everyone here knows George thinks I'm bringing the Harvesters back to get us."

"Are you?" Spell asked. She held up the report that had already been submitted by Captain Odessa. "What did you retrieve from the site of the explosion?"

Alex said, "Oh for god's sake. Why am I suddenly on trial? I'm not the one who kidnapped your son."

The purpose of Madeline Spell's intense interrogation of Alex Detail was to keep him occupied while the command center's highly powerful internal sensors performed a thorough magnographic scan of his body. Odessa's report suggested he may have acquired some foreign material from the Harvesters similar to the glass shard they had found on Peevchi Derringkite. But as he was arguing, the scan was taking place and the results were negative. There was a wound on the thumb of his right hand but the cause was indeterminable. It could have been self-inflicted to remove something or he may have accidentally cut himself on something during the planetarium explosion. If Odessa's hunch was correct, then whatever Alex Detail might have retrieved was no longer on his person. And, Madeline Spell realized, she was spending far too much time questioning Alex Detail: It was beginning to appear to be the result of some irrational paranoia.

Madeline Spell rubbed her forehead. "My apologies, Alex. I find myself jumping at shadows, and where the kidnapping of my son is concerned, you will understand my need to be thorough in any possible line of thought."

Alex wasn't paying attention to her anymore. He was tapping away at a console. Looking up, he waved JuneMary over to him. "JuneMary, is there someone we can contact on New Africa to send us a report on eddy currents?"

JuneMary thought a bit, then said, "The Kade Institute would give you the best data, but that would be a big old report. Lots of things cause eddy currents."

Alex nodded. "Yes, but there is a way to cross-reference eddy currents with an active ship q-field." Alex looked up and motioned to Hiramoto. "Have Mars Century Systems create a similar report. We can triangulate from a ship outside Earth's magnetosphere. Even a vague telemetry report will point us in the right direction."

Hiramoto looked at Spell. She nodded and he sent the message.

There was nothing more they could do from here, Spell thought. She had no choice but to send a ship to try to find the *UC One* vessel.

"Captain," Spell said to Odessa. "Assemble a minimal crew. You are hereby ordered to take command of the *Virgin Mother* and locate and retrieve George Spell."

After retrieving the chip from the explosion site, Alex attached it to the admiral's insignia on his uniform's left arm. But he knew he had to get rid of the chip before entering the war room at the House of Nations. Odessa had seen enough in the planetarium to know he had retrieved something after the explosion. It would have to be something so valuable it was worth the risk of going near the explosion site. And since his search was quick, Odessa had correctly assumed he had found what he was looking for. Whether they suspected it was the chip from Derringkite was something Detail doubted. The facsimile he had created from Dr. Kaykez's files on the *Virgin Mother* was perfect. And since the shard was microscopic, they wouldn't think it could be easily retrieved. But Alex had grafted the real chip onto a larger piece of glass; the glass was only the size of a pinhead, but large enough for Alex to handle more easily. Plus, he'd designed it to be photosensitive to the retina in his left eye. It wasn't hard for Alex to find by sight, appearing to him as a glittering green gem visible in even the dimmest light.

Only one other person would be able to see it the way Alex could. And George had been removed before Alex retrieved the chip.

Nevertheless, it was reasonable to assume Odessa had already shared her suspicions with Madeline Spell. Once sealed inside the command center, Alex would be at the mercy of its highly sensitive scanners.

He would be scanned, and they would find it.

It was also reasonable to assume that if he could hide the chip, he would be part of the group Spell sent off to retrieve George. So, where to put the chip during the meeting?

Horace. He would not be allowed to attend an alpha clearance meeting. He would be left outside. So, as Alex walked into the House of Nations central command, he brushed his arm against the door frame, pulling the admiral's insignia from his uniform. It fell to the floor. Behind him, he could hear Horace Witaker pick it up.

"Admiral," Horace called.

That was when Alex Detail used a trick he'd learned from the teachings of the 21st century doctor, Gerald Epstein. A nice trick intended to take the mind off of temporal matters and stop the anxiety and terror that accompanied states of emergency. Epstein had taught that all human aging and illness was the result of being in constant states of false emergency. A true emergency triggers the fight-or-flight response, flooding, the body, totally juicing it up with all sorts of chemicals intended to help with either fighting or fleeing. The problem? True emergencies rarely occur in a person's life, but people spend their lives flooding their bodies with the chemicals of fight-or-flight anyway—in response to being late for something, having to meet someone, and worrying about things that don't ever happen. Then the body has to spend a lot of time cleaning out all that junk, which causes worry over health, which leads to more false emergency states . . .

So, what to do? Well, the good doctor suggested that being honest in evaluating whether a given situation warranted a true emergency state might be a good start. He then suggested if you find yourself in one, use a paradoxal response. For example, if a guy puts a gun to your head and says, "Your money or your life," you say, "But it's 4:30." That puts your robber totally off, and maybe you get to just keep walking.

Alex needed to just keep walking into that room without calling attention to his dropped rank pin.

Here goes.

"Admiral Detail," Horace repeated.

Alex turned, just as they were entering the war room, and held up his window to Witaker. "Did you see this picture of JuneMary's niece?"

Horace was too polite not to look, and by the time he had, Alex was nearly through the door.

The moment he stepped through, the guards shut the door.

CHAPTER 4

MADELINE SPELL'S LAST RESORT

After sending Captain Odessa and her crew as well as Alex Detail on the rescue mission, Speaker Spell met with secretaries Guy Hiramoto and RK June in her office.

"RK," Spell said, "Have you drafted an announcement to the press regarding this afternoon's events?"

RK nodded, and Spell called up the report on her desk window. The statement explained that an overheated element in some catering equipment caused a small explosion in the planetarium, which resulted in structural damage that exacerbated a newly-discovered design flaw in the planetarium mooring. It further went on to say that George Spell had attempted to scale the planetarium to fix the problem, when, fearing for his safety, Spell dispatched the nearest flier to rescue him. The flier happened to be Jonathan's Innsbrook's *UC One* transport. Innsbrook had successfully rescued George from the top of the planetarium, but not before the situation went critical, threatening thousands of lives. Alex Detail was able to quickly fashion a magnetic field using the electricity in the subway tracks that directed the planetarium away from the crowd and into Central Park. There had been no injuries, and she thanked the President of the United Countries of America for saving her son.

"That should keep things quiet for a while," Spell said after reading the report. "RK, please deliver this to the press."

RK nodded and was about to leave when Spell's intercom beeped.

"What is it?" Spell asked her assistant.

"Chief Justice Schleiff is requesting to speak to you," her assistant responded.

"That was fast," Hiramoto said.

Justice Schleiff was put on the line. "Speaker, I have just received a notification of the house auto-record shut-off. As you know, I must invoke Article Fifteen."

"I understand," Spell said. "I am sending Secretary RK June to meet with you in person to begin the proceedings."

Chief Justice Schleiff responded, "Thank you, Speaker. However, protocol dictates that the Chief Executive of ARRAY be present during any inquiry."

"Oh, how silly of me," Spell responded, "But Alex Detail has been dispatched on a priority ARRAY mission and has left the planet."

"Actually, Alex Detail's presence will not be necessary," Schleiff said. "Your executive order regarding the promotion of Alex Detail cannot be processed as its ratification would have been held until the formal completion of his promotion ceremony. Since that event was interrupted, Alex Detail cannot formally be recognized as the Chief Executive of ARRAY. Secretary Hiramoto continues as acting Chief Executive of ARRAY until Detail's promotion is ratified."

Spell exchanged glances with Guy Hiramoto and RK June, then replied, "Very well, Harry."

The call was discontinued. "How fortunate," Spell said. "RK, could you please deal with this?"

"Of course, Speaker," RK said. "But Guy, you're going to have to be there before we can get this settled and classified as a Level Five priority."

The speaker held up her hand. "RK, try to buy us a few days. Tell Justice Schleiff that Guy and I have gone away on vacation."

RK frowned. "Vacation?"

"Yes," Spell said. "Vacation. Taken a few days away from the city with our son. Doctor's recommendation. "

RK shrugged and left Madeline Spell alone in her office with Guy Hiramoto.

There was silence for a few moments, then Spell said, "Listen. I think we have to acknowledge that things have finally gotten beyond our ability to control."

Hiramoto nodded. "We have lost control of both George Spell and Alex

Detail. And I have a bad feeling one of them has something to do with the missing Reaper."

The missing Reaper.

After the destruction of the Harvester ring ships, the fleet of Reapers that George Spell's communications program had corralled around the sun had followed their motherships into the sun and were destroyed.

However, four Reapers remained.

Three had never left orbit around Mercury, and the Reaper that had pursued the *Cronus* had followed the *Virgin Mother* back into the inner system and remained in orbit around Venus.

Every admiral's uncle wanted to get their hands on a Reaper. Gut it, reverse-engineer its materials and weaponry. But that proved rather dangerous.

A drone had been sent to Mercury to see if the Reapers were still active. It was destroyed by a Reaper particle beam the moment it came within range of the Reaper weapons.

Madeline Spell had issued an executive order to destroy all the Reapers before some wayward group got it into their heads to try to go get one. Another drone programmed with the original George Spell command program had been sent on an intercept course with the sun. The three Reapers in orbit around Mercury followed it into the sun where they were all eradicated.

But the Reaper orbiting Venus never followed. It simply disappeared.

The New Africa Council claimed to have no knowledge of the Reaper's whereabouts, and the ARRAY monitoring network was unable to account for its disappearance.

"Well, I have formed some conclusions, Guy," Spell said. "It was no random act of kindness that President Innsbrook sent *UC One* to shuttle Ambassador JuneMary from Venus to attend Alex's promotion."

"So you think they are headed to Venus?" Hiramoto asked.

"Naturally," Spell replied. "And no, do not send the council a warning of our suspicions. It will be overheard by Innsbrook and tip our hand."

"What are our options?" Guy asked.

"It is time we regain some leverage," Spell said. "It is time we remind Alex Detail, President Innsbrook and Brother Lonadoon that we still have an ace up our sleeve."

"I was not aware that we had one," Hiramoto replied.

Spell nodded. "We don't, yet. But what is it that good poker players do when they don't have that ace up their sleeve, and they know all the other players are holding winning hands?"

"They bluff," Hiramoto responded.

"Yes," Spell said. "Then it's up to the other players to wonder whether or not to call that bluff."

Spell tapped a panel on her desk and phoned her assistant. "Please ready my flier. Secretary Hiramoto and I are going on vacation."

Hiramoto crossed his arms. "I'm guessing we're going someplace warm."

Spell placed a hand on Hiramoto's crossed arms, then locked his eyes with a look both defiant and mournful. "Guy, it is time we visited the Axiom."

The Axiom. The place George Spell had been created.

CHAPTER 5

•

FLAGSHIP SPACE RACE

Alex Detail had never enjoyed spaceships. His phobia of interplanetary travel was not well known to any but a handful of people, and he had cultivated an image that was just the opposite: Young Admiral Alex Detail at the helm of the *Cronus* and the *Virgin Mother*, fearlessly outwitting the Harvesters in pitched battles to save the world.

But this time Alex didn't need to take the usual sedatives to step foot on the *Virgin Mother*. This time Alex was awash with the euphoria of the Harvester chip, back in his thumb, enjoying his incredible good fortune of suddenly being in command of a ship.

There would be no attempt to rescue George. Whatever plans Innsbrook and Lonadoon had for little George Spell were of no interest to Alex. He simply needed to take command of the *Virgin Mother* as Chief Executive of ARRAY, and set course to the rings of Saturn where he would run the command program he had been working on for the past six months. Then the Harvesters would be under his total control, and they would serve him.

How presumptuous of the Harvesters to think they could terrorize the people they claimed to have created, to taunt them with the bliss of their universe, and to murder the very people they sought to save. Alex didn't much care for their moral code, and he had adjusted his accordingly.

If his attempt to drag the Harvesters from their universe to this destroyed them in the process, so be it. It was no less than the fate that had nearly befallen humanity when people did not comply with the Harvesters during the first two wars. Now, thanks to the Harvesters' blunders, Alex had the chip and the knowledge and his old mind back.

Retrieving the chip from Horace had been an interesting encounter. As they all left the ARRAY command center after their meeting with Madeline Spell, Captain Odessa had issued some orders to Horace to assemble a minimal crew and depart immediately.

Horace did not mention Alex's dropped admiral's pin.

Finally, after a few moments of watching Horace execute Odessa's orders as they marched to the flier port, Alex stopped Horace and said, "Excuse me, Vice Captain. Did you happen to find my insignia?"

Horace's eyes went blank for a moment, then he slowly reached into his pocket, brought out the pin, and simply held it without saying anything.

Alex reached out, expecting Horace to hand over the pin. But Horace was going in slow motion, his grip on the pin tightening. Alex had to snatch it from his grasp, and there was a curious longing in Horace's eyes as he finally let go.

Perhaps Horace could feel something. Perhaps his death experience and resurrection in the Harvester meadow had conditioned him to sense the link he was holding. Or perhaps he was only feeling a bit stung by his brief romance with Captain Odessa.

Either way, it didn't matter to Alex as he strode onto the bridge of the *Virgin Mother* as they prepared to break orbit.

Captain Odessa stuck her hand into the identifier and spoke, "Ship, recognize and authenticate."

The ship responded in the standard ARRAY voice, stern and vaguely feminine. "Recognized, Captain Odessa, House of Nations identification number four four eight eight, commanding officer of the *Virgin Mother*, House of Nation's mission two two six zero A dash two four."

Captain Odessa installed Vice Captain Horace Witaker as executive officer and Ambassador JuneMary as second officer.

The ship accepted Ambassador JuneMary's officer classification without dispute. Which was odd, Alex thought, since installing a non-commissioned civilian as an ARRAY officer would take the approval of ARRAY's Chief Admiral.

Which was Alex Detail.

"Ship, who approved Ambassador JuneMary's appointment?" Alex asked the ship.

The ship responded, "You do not have clearance to command program intelligence."

Odessa fixed Alex with a bemused smile. "Admiral, the order was authorized by Acting Chief Admiral, Secretary of Defense Guy Hiramoto. Apparently, your promotion has not been formalized due to the unpleasant interruption of your ceremony."

"Spell's using that formality to hold up my appointment?" Alex asked incredulously. "Get her on the com." His face turned red and he nearly yelled. "Get her on the com or I'll have the House ratify my appointment myself! I can get a two-thirds vote from them within the hour!"

The bridge crew stared at Alex. There was an awkward silence and Alex stood there feeling foolish.

"Perhaps you have forgotten that this a rescue mission, Admiral?" Odessa said, glaring at two large, empty consoles near the bridge that she had specifically ordered be laden with food. "ARRAY has enacted all standard wartime communications protocols. You will be unable to communicate with anyone without my authorization. If you feel your promotion is more important than recovering the speaker's son, then I suggest you disembark immediately."

Alex instantly regretted his display of anger. It revealed too much to Odessa, the last person who needed any more fodder for her suspicions. Immediately, he let his facial muscles relax and got control of himself. "Of course, Captain," Alex said calmly. "You know I am not, well, comfortable on these ships, especially when it's not my command program doing the driving." He chewed on a fingernail to add to his attempt at showing vulnerability. "Just let me know what you need from me."

Odessa huffed at him, turned to Vice Captain Witaker and said, "Vice Captain, calculate the shortest distance to the outer boundary of the magnetopause and lay in a course." Odessa looked again at the empty consoles. "And find out what the hell's taking so long with the food!"

"Coordinates calculated," Witaker said, sending the acceleration curve telemetry map to the main display. "Awaiting confirmation." Fortunately, Horace didn't need to answer Odessa's last question, as two officers entered the bridge with trays of food and began setting up a buffet. The mobile consoles that had been installed when Odessa took command of the *Virgin Mother* from RK June six months earlier had been left in place.

Alex moved over to stand next to JuneMary, who was rubbing her back and studying the display. "Daggest thing, we've got a buffet but no one got around to installing furniture."

Odessa turned and shot JuneMary a withering look. "Commander, I would suggest concentrating on confirming our vector so we may be underway."

JuneMary grumbled under her breath and checked Horace's calculations. The velocity curve was rather straightforward and showed their course to be seventy thousand kilometers sunward, the nearest point that would take them out of the Earth's magnetopause so they could begin tracking possible eddy currents left by Innsbrook's ship.

JuneMary confirmed their course. The *Virgin Mother* broke orbit and began to accelerate toward their target.

Alex frowned. Difficult though it was, he'd put the thought of being able to immediately take command of the ship out of his mind. But why was Captain Odessa setting a course that would not completely clear them of the Earth's magnetosphere? He didn't understand.

The layers of cosmic shielding caused by the Earth's rotation around its liquid core—called the magnetosphere—was actually not a sphere at all; rather, it was a tear-shaped field, shallowest on the side of the planet that faced the sun and longest on the opposite side where it was stretched several Earth diameters by the solar wind. The outer layers consisted of a boundary called the magnetopause, a further layer called the magnetosheath, and the exterior, called the bowshock, an area outside the magnetic field where the solar wind abruptly slowed as it collided with Earth's magnetic field. Alex had calculated the search pattern program based on mapping of eddy currents outside the field of ions and electrons, nearly ten thousand kilometers farther out than Odessa was taking the *Virgin Mother*.

"Captain, why aren't we taking the ship completely out of the magnetosphere?" Alex asked. "You need to clear the magnetopause by at least ten thousand kilometers if you want to get the best readings on the telemetry data."

Odessa already had her mouth full of something as she dismissed Alex's suggestion with a wave of her hand. "That would be remarkably wasteful and unnecessary," she replied. "And a violation of standard operating procedure to preserve conservation of a ship's q-field."

"I know," Alex snapped. "The damn rule is based on q-field modulation that I wrote!"

Odessa turned from the central display and faced Alex. "This is not a debate. I will take the ship to the outer boundary of the magnetopause. If we do not receive accurate readings, I will then spin up the q-field to max and take us into the bowshock. It is procedure. Not subject to debate. Not subject to speculation."

"Oh, really?" Alex said sarcastically. "So you want to risk getting trapped behind a wall of solar wind rather than use a minute amount of extra variable power for maximum q-field?"

"Getting trapped by what?" Odessa asked. "A space ghost? We are not authorized to use wartime propulsion protocols and you are not authorized to interfere with mission orders." She spoke to the bridge crew in a stern voice. "We will continue with variable power conservation procedure!"

Alex rolled his eyes at Odessa and turned his attention back to JuneMary's display.

It was then that Alex suddenly began receiving vivid images from within his mind: the red, white and blue flag of the United Countries of America, a mahogany paneled table, a deep blue carpet. The origin of the thoughts was unmistakable—they were coming from George Spell. But the degree of clarity and the volume were unusual this time. Normally, George guarded his mind much better than that. Which confirmed he was on board Innsbrook's ship and somehow incapacitated.

Then the images disappeared. It was as if George had somehow become aware of his lapse and put his guard back up. No images came through during the next few minutes as the ship approached the specified coordinates, but then one final image arrived: a coffee cup, and with it, the tail end of a sentence—four words, definitely President Innsbrook's voice, broadcast directly into Alex's mind.

Alex almost gasped, but quickly held a hand to his mouth.

"Don't be embarrassed," JuneMary said. "Something about this ship pressure makes my food repeat on me something powerful too."

Alex smiled at JuneMary. On the inside, he was both pleased and frightened. Pleased, because the words he'd just received meant that Captain Odessa's cocky command attitude was about to have a wrench thrown into it. Frightened, because of what those words revealed was about to occur.

Alex leaned against a console and watched as Odessa chewed on an enormous hunk of cheese. *Disgusting.*

"Approaching coordinates," Witaker reported.

"All stop on target," ordered Captain Odessa.

Five seconds passed. "All stop confirmed," Witaker replied.

Odessa walked over to JuneMary. "Are you ready?"

"Yes, sir!" JuneMary said, as if sensing the drama about to unfold. Did she have a gleam in her eye?

"Very good," Odessa said. "Outlay telemetry data and ping the system."

In a matter of moments, the glowing trail of trace gasses created by the ship's q-field lit the system. The program sorted through them, overlaid the eddy current data from the Kade Institute, identified the trail that was the least decayed, and displayed its trajectory.

Horace Witaker reported the findings. "We have confirmed the course of *UC One*. President Innsbrook's ship is on a standard elliptical course to Venus."

Odessa gave a curt nod. "Very good, Vice Captain. Spin up q-field to max and lay in an intercept course."

As Witaker carried out his orders, a self-satisfied Captain Odessa walked over to her buffet and shot a haughty look at Alex. "It seems I just might know how to operate an ARRAY vessel without the genius aid of Alex Detail."

Alex didn't respond. He watched Odessa grab a fork and reach for a piece of chocolate cake.

"Captain!" Horace Witaker suddenly shouted. "There is a Reaper dead astern!"

"What?" Odessa barked, whipping around with the fork still in her hand. "Where the hell did that come from?"

Alex could see Witaker wince as he answered. "It just emerged from a stream of charged particles." Horace then looked at Alex with something that resembled the awestruck respect he always effused at Captain Odessa. "It was in a blind spot—must have been hiding just ahead of us in the magnetosphere bowshock."

Before Alex had the briefest moment to enjoy Odessa's humiliation, the Reaper activated its forward weapon and fired.

CHAPTER 6

•

SEARCH FOR THE AXIOM

Madeline Spell had not taken a vacation in her entire sixteen years as Speaker of the House of Nations. As she walked alone along the cheerful streets of Gustavia Harbor on the tropical island of St. Barts, she felt completely out of her element.

It had been a long day.

Just six hours ago she was greeting guests at the planetarium, about to preside over the ridiculous charade of promoting Alex Detail to Chief Executive of ARRAY. Then there had been the unwelcome and unsettling appearance of her former spiritual advisor, Brother Israel Lonadoon, followed by the explosion and nearly being crushed to death by the planetarium. Cap it all off with the kidnapping of her son and sending the ARRAY flagship off to rescue him with the newly unpredictable Alex Detail . . . well, it was a full day even for the leader of the world.

Madeline Spell was tired, sweating under the sweltering afternoon sun. She sat down on a bench at the edge of the harbor and scratched at the itchy facial implants and hair exchangers that had been fashioned for her impromptu disguise.

Sitting there unnoticed by vacationing passers-by, Spell felt exposed and alone, though she knew her personal security detail was hidden among the tourists while cloaked ARRAY monitoring drones floated unseen far above the island.

A young couple strolled by hand in hand, and stopped to ask Spell to take their picture.

Startled, Spell reached out and took the pocket window the young man handed to her, careful to hold it by the edge just in case the screen decided to analyze her fingerprints.

They thanked her as she smiled weakly and returned the window. She could see they were not pleased with the picture, but despite her smile, new short-cropped black hair, false brown eyes and vaguely Asian cheeks and nose, her weariness clearly shone through and the couple didn't bother asking her to take another picture.

In the two hours since Spell and Hiramoto had arrived, they had split up and begun their search for the well-hidden Axiom. The exact location of the Generationists lab was never disclosed to Spell or Hiramoto; in the event their involvement with Alex Detail's early research was ever discovered, they would be shielded by plausible deniability. She doubted that even the government scientists in her employ, located in the classified offices at the House of Nations, were aware of the exact location of the people whose bidding they carried out on her behalf. The creation of George Spell had been a double-blind experiment, orchestrated by independent cells of compartmentalized information. There was likely no one who knew the exact location of the Generationist lab other than the three Generationist scientists she had secretly furloughed from prison.

It was nearly 5:00, and Spell's search of the small island capital of Gustavia had turned up no clues to the whereabouts of Dr. Willow Lastingday. Madeline had only met the man once, five years ago, and the 80-year-old geneticist had looked like a 20-year-old teen idol. It was hard to believe that Dr. Lastingday, with his surfer blonde hair down to his sparkling hazel eyes and perfect upturned nose was the man responsible for creating a highly specified rapid-age clone of Alex Detail. Knowing that the Generationists loved to push the envelope, Lastingday probably now looked like one of the local island boys who liked to torment the tourists by racing by them on loud monopeders.

Spell was about to return to her car and drive back to the hotel when Hiramoto called.

"Finally," Spell said, touching the implant in her wrist. "Guy, are you still out on that kayak? I'm famished and haven't found a place for dinner that looks good. I was about to go back to the hotel."

Spell and Hiramoto had worked out a shorthand code for their conversations. While her personal security was not officially monitoring her private communications, she had learned one could never be too careful. Their charade of an impulse vacation was to be followed, right down to the wife spending the afternoon shopping in town to the husband out hovering over coral reefs.

"Yes, actually I am still out on the water," Hiramoto replied. "I've found the most amazing coral in the bay on *Anse de Grande Cul de Sac*. You should come for a ride with me before sunset."

So, he had found it. Or some clue at least.

"That sounds like a wonderful idea," Spell replied, already in the car and recklessly tearing out of the small town in a decidedly un-tourist-like manner.

It was a brief ten-minute drive along the narrow winding streets of St. Barts. Spell had nearly careened off the side of a cliff, been honked at and told off in French several times. She imagined the cloaked monitor drones frightening birds as they repositioned above the island to keep better track of the speeding Madeline Spell.

She peeled to a screeching stop on the end of the bay road and walked to the rocky beach edge where Hiramoto sat waiting in his hovering kayak. She hopped into the rear seat as he handed her a sonipaddle.

Once they were a good fifty feet from shore, Spell asked, "Did you find it?"

Hiramoto shook his head. "No, but we're close. I wanted to get you before I got any closer."

"You think they will be difficult?" Spell asked.

"I have no idea how they will react," Hiramoto said. "But if I were to get close to the entrance I think they would be less inclined to go to lockdown or blast us with a daze horn once they realize I have the Speaker of the House of Nations with me."

Spell wondered what sort of genetic signature verifier Hiramoto imagined the Generationists possessed to read through their disguises, but it made sense to approach the facility together.

"Where exactly are you taking us?" Spell asked as they hummed above the slightly choppy water. An occasional wave brushed the hull, sprinkling them with sea water as they passed a tall outcrop at the end of the bay and headed toward open water.

Hiramoto made the slightest motion with his sonipaddle and Spell saw the island about a half mile ahead of them. "It's an island called *La Tortue*, about a square kilometer. Off limits to construction or people, as it is part of the nature preserve."

Well, that made a logical base for the Generationists, Spell thought as the kayak approached a small beach on the island's southern tip. But there must be something much more precise to lead Hiramoto to think this was the location of the Axiom.

Spell didn't bother asking. Hiramoto was obviously sure of himself. But as she swung her legs out of the kayak and pulled on a pair of gummy shoes to protect her feet from the sharp pieces of coral strewn along the shore, Spell couldn't help herself. "So, Guy, how do you know this is the place?"

Hiramoto didn't say anything, he just pointed down to the broken pieces of coral Spell was standing on.

Spell reached down, picked up a piece of coral and gasped.

In her hand she held a small piece of fragile sun-bleached coral.

It was in the perfect shape of an infant's hand.

CHAPTER 7

•

BUT NOT QUITE HUMAN

George Spell was unable to move or think as quickly as usual, and that really intrigued him.

Seated at a little mahogany conference table, George realized he was aboard a small interplanetary transport. A very fancy one with the United Countries of America emblem and flag printed on everything from the seats to the napkin next to the cup of coffee on the table across from him. *UC One.*

Across the table sat Brother Israel Lonadoon and the President of the United Countries of America, Jonathan Innsbrook.

George wasn't sure what they had done to him. He had no memory after being yanked off the planetarium and was not sure how long he had been sitting there or when he had regained consciousness. If George had ever been drugged with a sedative, he imagined this was what it would feel like.

They had been talking about something before he fully opened his eyes. They were saying something about a woman, and how she had created something that would keep Alex Detail from catching up to them. George was trying to remember more, but a movement of his eye caught Lonadoon's attention.

Lonadoon turned and stared straight into George's eyes, but he spoke to Jonathan Innsbrook, "Ah, there it goes now. It is increasing its epinephrine and norepinephrine output, searching for a way to become active and able to physically control the situation in which it finds itself."

Innsbrook's face displayed no emotion. He appeared to be staring off into space, not paying any attention to Lonadoon. But he did respond: "That only seems normal."

"Yes, a normal repose," Lonadoon replied. "However, it is not increasing output of dopamine and there is no activity in the precuneus region of its brain."

Innsbrook closed his eyes. "And you can tell this just by looking at him?"

"I can tell," Lonadoon said.

Innsbrook made a slight nod with his head. "Okay. What is this business about the precuneus all about?"

"Indeed. That is what is abnormal," Lonadoon replied, apparently referring to George. "It is not producing higher levels of dopamine, indicating an inhuman control over its sympathetic nervous system. There is no biological homeostasis or empathetic distress. Thus the lack of activity in the precuneus."

"That was a lot of words that made no sense to me," Innsbrook said in a monotone that seemed to be his version of irritation.

"Look me in the eye," Lonadoon said to Innsbrook. Jonathan lifted his head slightly and his eyes opened a crack. Lonadoon continued, "There is a higher meaning to life."

Innsbrook did not respond.

Lonadoon nodded. "Whether or not you agree with the statement, 'there is a higher meaning to life,' it just caused heightened activity in the precuneus region of your brain. We generally use that part of our brain to decipher the motives and intentions of other people. But it is also the foundation of spiritual curiosity. All humans, no matter how atheistic they profess to be, utilize the precuneus to process their experience of the mysteries of life—to occasionally overcome human conditioning." Lonadoon turned to George again and said, "It does not."

Innsbrook finally turned his full attention to Brother Lonadoon and asked, "Why do you call the boy 'it' rather than, 'him'?"

"Do not misinterpret my use of the article 'it' as a sign of disrespect," Lonadoon answered. "I regard all things with equal reverence. A rock is as perfect a creation as a human. I would call the rock 'it' and the human 'he or she.' George Spell is a pre-conscious human replica, and properly identified as 'it.' You understand, a conscious being is able to use even a small amount of awareness to overcome human conditioning. But George is simply a computer running a program. If we see evidence of humanity, I will properly refer to George as 'him.'"

Back to staring off into space, Innsbrook may have been pondering the matter or scrutinizing the wood paneling. "I'll say 'him.' Seems more humane."

Lonadoon tapped a finger on the table. "Very well. Take care, however, not to fall into the same trap Madeline Spell did. You may refer to a bomb as 'him' or 'her' but it will still act like a bomb, not a person."

"Yes, yes," Innsbrook said with a grand wave of one hand. "Please, not another lecture on the dangers of the two boys and the fact that humanity is at stake, and on and on. I got it." Innsbrook picked up a cup of coffee and took a sip. "I help you for the same reasons I helped Derringkite: The flow of natural events has put me in this place. Who am I to intervene with fate?"

Lonadoon cast a dubious look back at Innsbrook. "Oh now, Mr. President, let us not be too clever. You help me because New Africa wields considerable political clout among the House of Nations, and you are fond of collecting political leverage."

Innsbrook did not reply. He was back to gazing at the wood-paneled walls.

George thought it curious that they spoke in front of him, as they could clearly see that he was listening. Notwithstanding, the problem of why he was unable to respond or move was growing less intriguing and more troubling. As Lonadoon had said, George had indeed increased his adrenal output to counteract any sedative they may have given him. But doing so was not helping. He still couldn't move.

George had learned as much as he could about his particular physiology. It was important to know what he was vulnerable to, but without the Generationist files that contained all the information about his creation, George could only learn by experimentation. He had discovered that it was not possible to poison him. He had taken a variety of medications, each at increased doses. Even at lethal levels he was somehow able to neutralize their affects. So, if these people had put any toxin into his system now, it had already been neutralized. Whatever means they had devised to put him in this state was a mystery.

Obviously Lonadoon and Innsbrook knew enough about him to have found some other means to immobilize George. It was a curious sensation; he could feel his arms, legs and hands. It seemed like he could move his mouth and speak if he wanted. He just didn't seem to be able to make any of his other motor functions work.

George's first thought upon waking in this room was of the planetarium. He had stopped worrying about the fate of his mother when he overheard Brother Lonadoon and President Innsbrook talking about the planetarium's trip into Central Park.

"I think it is cognizant enough to understand if I explain some things to it," Lonadoon said to Innsbrook.

Innsbrook made a slight motion with his index finger that seemed to say, "Go ahead."

Lonadoon faced George and said, "George, I am Brother Israel Lonadoon. You met me only once, several months ago one evening when I visited your home. But I am aware that you have listened in on other conversations I have had with Madeline Spell during the Second Harvester War."

That was a strange admission, George thought. George had in fact twice eavesdropped on his mother and Brother Lonadoon, once in their kitchen when George's mother had admitted to Lonadoon that George was an enhanced clone of Alex Detail. George had eavesdropped another time when Lonadoon had conducted a tarot card reading for Madeline Spell. So, Lonadoon had known George had been listening in but had said nothing to his mother.

Lonadoon continued speaking to George. "I have placed you in a state called 'theta meditation.' It is a very deep form of mediation, similar to being in dream sleep. That is why you are unable to move or speak, but can hear and understand me. It is for your own safety as much as ours."

Placing his hands on the table, Lonadoon leaned forward and locked his eyes on George. "Now, listen very carefully. We have taken you because we need your help, and your mother was not cooperating. As you obviously suspect, Alex Detail is planning on doing something very dangerous and we need your help to stop him. However, your methods to interrupt Alex Detail's experiments were a danger to yourself and others, and ineffective, so now you are going to receive the proper tools and guidance. The first thing I need you to do is stop concentrating on moving, and concentrate on your thoughts. Alex Detail is in a ship in pursuit of us. We have devised a way to delay him, but that will not be effective if you do not regain control of your thoughts. You are currently broadcasting a very vivid series of images to Alex Detail."

This startled George Spell as he realized he was allowing his thoughts to drift into that area of his mind that Alex had access to. George quickly concentrated his efforts on mindful compartmentalization of his brain functions.

Lonadoon seemed to sense that George had regained control of his thoughts. "Very good," Lonadoon said, then gently tapped a finger on the back of George's right hand. He was suddenly able to move and speak.

"You want me to sit here and listen to you, so I will," George said. "What is Alex Detail trying to do with the Harvesters?"

Lonadoon smiled. "Thank you, George. We do not know exactly what Alex is attempting. We only know through the process of divinations the outcomes of certain events. If Alex is not stopped, there will be a large-scale catastrophe."

George nodded. "Okay. So what do you want me to do?"

"We are taking you to meet someone very important. She will be able to explain everything you need to know. For now, I need you to control your thoughts. In a few hours, you will have adapted to the theta state you are in and I will bring you to a more comfortable room. We will arrive at our destination in thirty hours."

George slowly nodded and realized that he was not yet able to stand.

Lonadoon and Innsbrook got up and left the room.

George stopped being intrigued and started to grow irritated. They were obviously withholding a lot of information from him, probably not trusting his ability to shield his mind from Alex Detail.

But George was very good at that. Alex had become increasingly lax as he experimented with his Harvester communications and George was able to study different ways to peek into his mind undetected.

As George sat there, he stared at the coffee cup across the table from him. He wanted to see what was going on inside Alex Detail's mind at this moment, and the price of entry was usually an initial exchange of images. The coffee cup seemed benign enough. He opened his mind, followed the tether that connected him to his genetic duplicate, and pulled an image from Alex's brain: The bridge of the *Virgin Mother*.

Outside the door to the conference room George heard the tail end of a sentence:

". . . trapped by the Reaper."

Which meant Alex Detail heard it as well.

CHAPTER 8

•

RETURN OF THE REAPER

The crew of the *Virgin Mother* was stuck dumb by the sight of the Reaper.

They had, of course, seen this particular Reaper before. It was the very same Reaper that had attacked the *Cronus*, killed Horace Witaker and destroyed the ship, many times over. It was well known that Alex Detail's ingeniously devised evasion program had saved their lives, holding their existence in the virtual stasis of quantum gravity until it resolved the infinite timeless, and returned the ship to a normal space-time in which the attack never occurred.

Ship_not_hit.

What was not well known was that Alex Detail's evasion program did not quite work as well as it appeared to have. The "events" occurring during the ship's shift to quantum gravity were too fast for the computer to calculate, so it was never able to fully select a timeline of *ship_not_hit* to take the *Cronus* back into normal space. The crew of the *Cronus* may have spent eternity getting blown up over and over again by the Reaper had Detail's program not been interrupted.

That little trick had been Captain Odessa's doing. She was the one who manually deactivated Detail's program. Captain Odessa was the one whose timing was a one-in-a-million shot at stopping the program at precisely the least likely outcome of *ship_not_hit*. (Odessa had later calculated it was actually a one in four hundred billion chance.) Alex Detail's evasion program had bought them time, but Captain Odessa's rare instinct had saved their lives.

And that's why I'm the captain, Odessa thought to herself at the time.

But now, staring down the nose of the Reaper, Odessa knew she didn't have time to issue orders, or contemplate the fact that if she had followed Alex Detail's advice to take the *Virgin Mother* clear of the magnetosphere in the first place, they would not be sitting face to face with the last existing Harvester Reaper vessel.

Odessa had one chance to save their ship—she had to be faster than the Reaper weapon. The second the Reaper activated its forward weapon, Odessa, fork still in hand, lunged at her com panel and placed her thumb, middle and ring fingers simultaneously on three keypads. The resulting instruction to the ship's computer would override any acceleration curve data confirmation algorithms and command program navigation controls and simply blow out the port thruster, sending the ship spinning away like a Frisbee.

If that somehow moved the ship away from the Reaper particle beam in time, and somehow the q-field was able to dampen the deadly g-forces that would result from the spin-jump, then there was only the problem of needing to avoid being hit by a second blast from the Reaper.

It was a reckless and ill-conceived course of action. But it was the only course of action available.

Odessa hit the three keys and the port thruster fired.

The Reaper weapon activated.

JuneMary said, "Here we go again."

Everything went blindingly bright and silent.

"What in the name of Mary and Joseph is going on?" JuneMary said, apparently the only one on the bridge not incapacitated by the blindingly bright light.

Alex Detail was feeling remarkably calm. Unlike their last encounter with this Reaper, Detail was not filled with the panic of imminent death. He did not feel compelled to take charge, like Odessa had attempted to do as he watched her dive toward the com panel. Alex did not know why, but he had a sense that carrying the Harvester chip in his thumb, as Derringkite had done, afforded him special protection from the Harvesters. After all, why would they destroy the last remaining physical link they had to this universe?

It didn't make any sense. It also didn't make any sense that President Innsbrook and Brother Lonadoon would have been able to track the Reaper and have some knowledge of its intent.

Somehow, for Alex, it all added up to a curious fascination about what would happen next.

The blinding light continued to fill the bridge. Horace Witaker was still at the helm and should have adjusted the q-field to polarize the light waves pouring through the windows and main display. But Witaker was probably in such a catatonic state at seeing the ship that had killed him that he'd be useless for a few more moments.

Alex squinted and tried to work his com panel.

The light was just too blinding.

JuneMary, accustomed to extremely bright light from her upbringing on Venus, didn't seemed bothered at all.

"JuneMary, make the q-field conform to a ten degree aperture," Detail said.

JuneMary keyed in a few commands and the light returned to normal.

Captain Odessa was up and examining her command console. "I activated the port thruster and the ship reads accordingly."

Huffing, JuneMary said, "Well, it ain't workin', mother, that's a cinch." She stood up straight and faced Odessa. "I don't know what all's been going on here, but Captain, if you still got any sense in you, stop being so darned prideful and listen to Alex when he's got something to say. Boy's saved our skin enough times he deserves a kind ear."

Wow, Alex thought, *that's going to make steam blast out of Odessa's ears.* Had there ever been a time when a subordinate had reprimanded the indomitable Captain Odessa in front of her crew? Technically, JuneMary was an ambassador and not the Captain's subordinate, but she probably would have spoken her mind regardless.

Good ol' JuneMary. The only person with enough backbone to stick up to Captain Odessa.

Odessa did not acknowledge JuneMary. "Witaker, report."

Vice Captain Witaker was scanning his display, but Witaker was obviously not going to be in any condition to report on anything any time soon. Last time he found himself staring down the nose of this particular Reaper, his head had been blown apart.

"First off, I think you better turn off the port fusion reactor before we blow up," Alex said.

Odessa terminated her bypass to the engine. "Why the hell aren't we moving?"

Alex was trying to make sense of the situation, but JuneMary was ahead of him. "Spectrometer readings in. And that was not an anti-matter beam like they usually use," JuneMary said, highlighting the glowing ray of yellowish-orange light beaming off the Reaper's front point.

"Try mapping the shape," Alex said to JuneMary.

Technically, Alex had just given JuneMary an order and he expected some sort of nasty rebuke from Captain Odessa. However, Odessa offered no objection. She simply took her place at the main display and waited for the results.

"There you go," JuneMary said. "I don't know what those old boys are up to but this is something new altogether now!"

This *was* something new. The tear-shaped Reaper vessel was using its hull like a giant magnet, sucking the solar wind into a narrow band and blasting it at the *Virgin Mother*. The result was a torus of charged particles whipping around the ship's q-field, creating two wide bands of radiation in front of the ship and two behind.

They were stuck in the middle.

"Wow," Alex said as he studied the display. "We're stuck."

"Stuck's better than dead," JuneMary said. "For sure!"

She seemed to be aiming her comment in the general direction of Witaker. Alex could see Witaker slowly confirming the spectral data. The vice captain finally nodded and highlighted the energy belts on the main display. "The Reaper has created a Van Allen radiation belt. And we do seem to be stuck in the center of it."

"A child's wagon could not get stuck in a Van Allen belt," Odessa replied. "Reversing the q-field polarity should be enough to regain propulsion."

"Possibly, Captain," Witaker replied, looking at Alex.

Alex could not disagree. But everyone was thinking the same thing—move and the Reaper would blow them to bits.

"I am not fond of having my ship stuck," Odessa said.

Alex raised his hands as if to say to the crew, *Who am I to interfere?* "So, go ahead and take us out of this, Captain."

All eyes were on Odessa. She had not taken Alex's advice earlier and was probably less inclined to do so after JuneMary's embarrassing rebuke.

Odessa shook her head. "I am less fond of having my ship destroyed. We are *stuck* here in a nonlethal trap meant to delay us. Spring the trap too quickly and we risk encountering a more deadly trap. Possibly a *boobied* trap. If the vicious Reaper wanted to destroy us, it would have done so already."

Interesting. Captain Odessa, displaying hesitation. Her response was likely as Pavlovian as it was practical: *Reapers respond to movement—try to escape and they shoot at you.*

"Vice Captain Witaker," Odessa said in a very stern voice, likely trying to pull him out of the slow motion state he appeared to be operating in. "Can we get a message to ARRAY?"

Witaker was a little slow in his actions, but he tried the com channels—with no success. "The ionic disturbance is too much. I doubt we even show up on any sensor as anything other than a plasma substorm caused by a solar flare or some other sort of coronal mass ejection."

"This is absurd!" Odessa yelled. "That this Reaper would accost *us* but allow safe passage of President Innsbrook's ship is outrageous."

"Are you suggesting that Innsbrook somehow has control over that Reaper?" Alex asked, truly curious what Odessa thought.

"Well, Admiral, I am not exonerating you of any malfeasance," the captain said, "but it is the only logical conclusion. This is the only Reaper left in the system and it mysteriously disappeared while in orbit around Venus—the apparent destination of Innsbrook's ship? Naturally, they knew we would be in hot pursuit and have laid this trap."

Odessa began pacing the bridge, stopping on each pass to viciously grab some food off the buffet. "Admiral Detail, do you think we would be stuck here if we dropped the q-field?"

"No," Alex answered. "But we'd be killed instantly by the radiation."

"And what do you further conjecture would be the outcome if we fired on the Reaper?" Odessa asked Alex.

"Well, every precedent of an ARRAY ship firing on a Reaper has resulted in the Reaper sustaining little damage and then it usually fires back, destroying the ARRAY ship." Alex paused for a moment before adding, "With the exception of the *Cronus.*"

Odessa clicked her tongue. "What a clever trap we have encountered." She stopped her pacing and looked up at Alex Detail. "It is a good thing that I have such a clever admiral on board to solve this peculiar puzzle."

Actually, Alex had already thought of ways to extract the ship from the Van Allen belt but had not figured out a way to get the ship clear of the Reaper should it decide to attack.

Well, there is one way: the last way we escaped this Reaper.

But Alex sensed this was a ploy by Odessa to see if Alex would immediately request access to the ship's command program—trying to find out right away what tricks he might have up his sleeve.

Furthermore, Alex was more concerned with the fact the he could not sense that the Reaper vessel was in any way receiving instructions from the domain the Harvesters used to communicate with him via the chip. It was a mystery to everyone, including Alex, why this Reaper had disappeared around Venus's orbit. Did a Reaper perhaps have some independent decision-processing capability? Previously, they seemed to respond to only two things: offensive activity against a Harvester ring ship, or other aggressive movement. The fact that the disappearing Reaper should suddenly reappear and launch this very un-Reaper-like attack on the *Virgin Mother* could mean only two things: somehow the Reaper had been tampered with, or someone else was now in communication with the Harvesters.

This was troubling and potentially threatening to Alex's ability to implement his Ultimate Plan. Had Innsbrook and Lonadoon figured out some way to talk to the Harvesters? Was that why they needed George Spell? Or was it Madeline Spell herself? She had always been behind the scenes of every significant event that had taken place since the Harvesters had first appeared. She had become speaker during the twenty years between the Harvesters' first contact and their arrival in the solar system.

At least Odessa was easier to understand. She just wanted two things: to successfully execute their mission, and to keep Alex from any mischief.

He could sense Odessa growing more anxious. She was at least four hours behind catching up to Innsbrook. But Alex was in no hurry. He had drawn his plans surely and carefully. He needed only to wait, commit no forced errors, and stay in the game long enough until he found himself in the circumstances necessary for him to take advantage. For now, patience would be key.

"Well, I will do my best, Captain," Alex said.

Five hours after the crew of the *Virgin Mother* first became trapped by the actions of the Reaper, the mood on the bridge had changed dramatically. The place could best be described as "homey." Fragrant aromas of cinnamon and apples filled the air. Soft, uplifting music with a quick beat and happy melody was being piped in throughout the bridge, and everyone was working nicely.

Odessa couldn't stand any of it. But she had asked for JuneMary's help, and this was what she got.

Shortly after asking Alex to help find a way out of the Van Allen radiation belt created by the Reaper, Odessa has excused herself from the bridge and summoned JuneMary to the room that had served as the captain's quarters on their last voyage.

"JuneMary, I am not one to overly concern myself with the emotional states of those under my command," Captain Odessa had begun. JuneMary smirked at her like that was a fairly evident fact. "But I fear there are interpersonal qualities manifesting that will be difficult to overcome using a standard command approach." Odessa paused for a moment, hoping JuneMary would get the gist of her highly convoluted statement.

Smiling, JuneMary said, "Oh mother, I never thought I'd see the glorious day you would let all that weight off your shoulders."

Odessa put her hand up to her mouth to take a bite out of whatever it was she was holding, but she had failed to grab some food on her way off the bridge. "JuneMary, I am simply asking for your guidance as a diplomat. I do fear that the quotidian operation imperatives have put us at a disadvantage."

"You mean your usual hard-nosed approach didn't work and got the mission off to an awful start?" JuneMary asked, still with that amused little smile.

"If you must put it so crudely," Odessa replied. "I would value your advice on dealing with the multiple emotional directives impeding my ability to work effectively with Alex and the Vice Captain."

"Whoo-ee!" JuneMary exclaimed. "You mean what are you going to do to get Horace out of the depression caused because he suddenly finds he ain't welcome in your bed, as well as his near-catatonia from looking at the ship that blew his head apart six months ago?"

"Yes," Captain Odessa replied, "That's exactly what I just said. And there is the other matter."

JuneMary rolled her eyes. "You mean that you don't trust the admiral, but if you had followed his advice in the first place we wouldn't be in this mess? Not to mention that your nasty attitude and shifty sneakiness has him darn near hating you?"

"Precisely what I keep saying to you," Odessa said. "Please stop repeating me and just tell me how to pamper these two infants so we can get on with the mission!"

JuneMary patted Odessa on the shoulder and made her sit on the small sofa. "Finally! Off my feet," JuneMary said with a sigh, putting her feet up on Odessa's coffee table.

"Let's break this down," JuneMary continued. "Sometimes, barking orders and being the boss doesn't get people to do what you want. Lot of times just the opposite. Right now, if it weren't for your reputation and the big stories about the heroic Captain Odessa during both Harvester wars, I think that the bridge pilot herself might have just up and quit, walked right out into space."

Odessa resisted the urge to tell JuneMary to hurry up and give her some pointers, but she remained silent.

"First, Captain, you have got to deal better with Admiral Detail," JuneMary said. "He is smarter than any of us about weapons and space, and he *is* Alex Detail. Everyone loves Alex, except you. And probably Madeline Spell. And maybe Hiramoto. And of course that little rascal George wants to kill him. But anyway, Alex knows Old Lady Spell's got you spying on him, waiting for the moment you see him turn into a Harvester and eat up the sun. Might as well just tell him and get it out there. I always liked that boy, no matter what he's up to. And let me tell you one last thing about that: Whatever he's cooking up in that big superconducting head of his, you ain't gonna be able to stop it. That's for the Lord Himself to decide."

Odessa squinted at JuneMary. "So, let me be clear. You want me to be honest and show Alex Detail the respect that I do not have for him given his selfish, narcissistic behavior and complete ineptness as an ARRAY officer?"

Sighing, JuneMary shook her head. "Yes, if that's the best you can manage, Captain."

"Very good, then," Odessa said. "I will attempt to be disingenuous." Odessa was less than enthusiastic. She was not finding this advice from JuneMary particularly helpful.

"Let me ask you a question," JuneMary said. "Captain, you ever been in love?"

Ridiculous! Why would JuneMary ask such a ridiculous question? Odessa had spent her entire adult life preparing to fight the Harvesters and then leading every major battle against them. She had undergone the proper psychological training to make sure her full capacities were devoted to her duties and not subject to the distractions of fruitless emotional flights. The notion that she was so weak that she would be overcome by love was as ridiculous as asking if she had ever been morbidly obese.

"No," Odessa answered.

"Well, that boy Witaker is in love with you, and you better deal with it," JuneMary said.

Odessa frowned as she heard JuneMary voice what she feared to be the case. She knew indulging in intimacies with Witaker following the war had been folly, but she had to admit she'd been weak in those confusing weeks after the Harvesters' destruction. *She* had regained control of her faculties. Why didn't Witaker?

"Just how exactly do I deal with that matter?" Odessa asked.

JuneMary waved a hand at Odessa. "Don't be silly. You're a grown-up. Deal with it."

JuneMary adjusted herself and crossed her arms. Apparently she was on a roll now and wasn't about to stop. "Now, about that sullen bridge crew of yours. Liven it up. Instead of flooding the air with tranix and kloptin and dopiates, try surrounding their senses with some nice things. The food's okay but you got some awful mix of things and it doesn't smell right. Did you know the smell of cinnamon can increases accurate motor task functions by up to a third?"

Finally, some useful information! "Really?" Odessa said. "What else did you have in mind?"

So, JuneMary had turned the bridge of the Virgin Mother into Odessa's idea of an old woman's kitchen. The dim emergency lighting was replaced with full spectrum imitation sunlight—an impractical waste of energy. The honey-glazed ham, the soy-steamed salmon, the deep-fried cheese squares and the chocolate-raisin cake had been replaced by a roasted turkey, steamed carrots and apple pies. And everyone was working nicely in little groups.

This is no longer a military ship, Odessa thought. *It's a kindergarten!*

But results were results. Odessa had apologized to Alex in front of the crew then quietly taken him aside and explained the difficult situation she had been put in. She did not explicitly admit that she had been ordered to spy on him for Madeline Spell, but she implied it, which seemed to surprise Alex. She then handed him a glass of cold maté tea, knowing his love of stimulants and his disgust for food.

Odessa had also done what she could with Horace. She explained to him that she was not pleased with her behavior in their personal interactions, and that she felt uncomfortable and unable to speak of them. It wasn't precisely true; she really wanted to tell Horace to mind his duties and snap out of it. But the former approach worked. He and Alex were now chatting away, working on several q-field modifications, defensive maneuvers, and whatever else would get them out of there.

Meanwhile, JuneMary was talking to Jacques L'Anu and Erika Mode, the two assistant lieutenants Odessa had chosen to serve on the bridge crew. Both had served aboard the *Cronus* and undergone officer's training from Captain Odessa before the Second Harvester War. As Odessa had stated in their last performance appraisals, they were the "least incompetent" junior officers under her command.

Every now and then, JuneMary would be forced to pause whatever story she was regaling, when either Assistant Lieutenant L'Anu or Mode was summoned to carry out some task that either Alex or Horace needed done.

Everyone seemed quite happy. But other than re-creating some idyllic workplace charade, they had made little progress. They were now nearly ten hours behind President Innsbrook's ship. While the *Virgin Mother* was theoretically capable of making the trip to Venus in under four hours given the planet's current apsis of just over forty million kilometers from Earth, it would have taken a running start from somewhere closer to Saturn's orbit to reach that velocity. By the time the *Virgin Mother* was spun up to its max inner-system speed and had to begin its deceleration curve, it would take nearly twenty hours to reach Venus. Therefore, Odessa's ship's greater speed compared to Innsbrook's would only make up a negligible amount of time.

Having gone off ARRAY's grid for so long on what was supposed to be a covert mission made every extra minute spent in the Reaper trap one minute closer to what would be considered the first failure in Captain Odessa's entire military career.

She had failed to authenticate the ship's beacon or provide an update on the heavily encrypted line Madeline Spell had provided for them. At some point, ARRAY would visually verify the location of the *Virgin Mother*, and Spell would be forced to pull two ships out of refit—one to take over their rescue mission to retrieve George Spell, and another to attempt a rescue of Odessa's crew from the Reaper trap.

The embarrassment of failure and the idea that she, Captain Odessa, would need to be rescued on such a mundane mission was infuriating.

But finally, Alex Detail reported that a solution had been found.

His explanation was long-winded and unnecessary. But a stern look from JuneMary kept Odessa from cutting him off while she listened to his brilliance.

Tests had confirmed the exact points at which the q-field's polarity needed to be shifted for them to regain maximum propulsion and attitude control. But then there was the problem of the Reaper firing at them.

"We were lucky that George Spell's Harvester program is still saved on the ship's nav-archive," Alex said. "I have re-written it to be transmitted on m-com tightbeam. That should be able to get it to the Reaper through the radiation without inverse beta decay."

Odessa was not pleased with this solution. First, Alex Detail was only able to understand the George Spell program while under the influence of Pluto's mind-altering properties. Of course it had also been conjectured that Alex Detail's mind was once again in top form, depending on his proximity to George Spell, but since George was quite far away, Odessa wondered what Alex was using to augment his mental capacities. Nevertheless, it was finally a way out.

"Very good, Admiral," Odessa said. "How will the modified George Spell program affect the Reaper?"

"Hopefully the same way it affected the Harvester ring ships," Alex answered. "It may follow the course we send it, to the center of the sun—or it may follow the earlier base instructions in the first George Spell program and simply follow us. It doesn't really matter. I have added an exponential code replicator algorithm that will take the Reaper at least twenty minutes to process. By that time we should be far enough away to maintain a safe distance."

Odessa did not like the sound of this plan at all. There was no way to know that the Reaper would process the program the same way the Harvester ring ships had processed it. And if there was the slightest data decay even on m-com tightbeam, it might trigger the Reaper to go hostile.

But there was one thing Odessa was sure of. Alex Detail was just as afraid of dying now as he had ever been. If he was certain this would work, then she was pretty sure, too.

"Make the necessary modifications," Odessa said. "And someone turn off that damned music!"

CHAPTER 9

THE TRICKY TRAP

Alex Detail and Horace Witaker were in the drive room making the necessary modifications. Alex was keenly aware that Witaker was making his best attempt to avoid eye contact with him. The last time the two were in this part of the ship they had talked of Derringkite's story of people not living their true potential. They had shared the understanding of a consciousness freed of physical limitations. They had made a silent pact not to activate the polar device that had been built to blow up Pluto. This was where Alex Detail and Horace Witaker had conspired to mutiny.

Alex doubted that the polar device they had built to destroy Pluto would have had any impact on the planetary body. After all, even a black hole had failed to destroy it. But now, Horace was keenly trying to hide both guilt and suspicion, something he had no problem doing while they were working on the bridge.

Horace was nervous to be alone with Alex.

As you should be, Alex thought. He was not going to waste this opportunity. But he had to be careful.

"Do you know how to synchronize the q-field and m-com for a tight-beam transmission?" Alex asked.

"Yes, I do, Admiral," Witaker replied, "but I think it would take me a lot longer than you."

Alex let out a slightly irritated sigh and shook his head at Horace. "Well, what the hell am I supposed to do if it needs an adjustment? I can't be here and on the bridge."

Horace appeared a bit stung. They had been working together for hours and this was the first time Alex had lost his temper. "I understand," Witaker said. "I will take care of it."

As Witaker removed the housing from the m-com, Alex made a show of being busy studying the q-field diagnostic panels.

Then he saw his moment. Horace had his hand on the internal m-com unit and was turning it slowly.

"Horace, it's a lot easier to keep the alignment if you turn the mobius counterclockwise ten degrees first, then turn it clockwise toward the new pole." Alex reached out and put his right hand on top of Horace's in an attempt to help him.

Alex's thumb touched Horace's inside the m-com magnetic field. The effect was stunning.

A wave of euphoria washed over Alex and he could see from Horace's sudden gasp and expression of rapture that he was experiencing the same sensation.

It was like they were back in the sunny meadow on Pluto. Their minds were able to conceive thoughts beyond the limitations of physical boundaries. The feeling that time had stopped and their bodies and minds existed as fields of energy that could process the intricate dynamics of multiple dimensions was overwhelming. The Harvester chip in Alex's thumb, processing the non-Euclidean geometric communications in the single dimension of the m-com field was stronger than Alex had anticipated.

Alex reached out with his left hand and tapped a code into a nearby panel that would mute the room's audio in the event that Captain Odessa was listening in on their conversation.

His eyes unfocused, caught in some mesmerizing thoughts, Horace stared blindly through Alex.

"Do you feel it, Horace?" Alex asked. "Do you remember what it was like? Do you understand now?"

Horace slowly shifted his line of sight to Alex's face, his eyes focused. "Yes," he breathed. "I feel it."

"They're not gone, Horace," Alex said. He knew he needed to speak quickly. "I have found a way to bring them back. There was never a need to go to the Harvester universe. We can have it here. They were trying to deceive us. The Harvesters reached a highly evolved state; they discovered a way to achieve the Omega Point. But something went wrong. They tore the very fabric of their universe and began to lose information stored in their universe's light cone. They needed our physical bodies to fill in the missing data. But I have figured out a way to stabilize the link they created to our universe and magnify it. We can change the laws of physics!"

With the magnifying influence of the Harvester chip, Alex could see Witaker needed no further explanation. He understood. "That's what your program does," Horace said. "There was a massive file uploaded to the *Virgin Mother* when we boarded. That's what it's for." Witaker paused for a moment, then shook his head. "But I don't understand how you will form a mobius of that magnitude to create that sort of amplification."

Alex was about to explain the simplicity of the final formula, but suddenly, he was unable to do so. Even with his mind augmented by the powers of the chip and the m-com flat space, he couldn't grasp the intricacies of the program he had been working on for the past six months.

In a flash, Alex realized his mistake. The localized omega field he was able to generate with the Harvester chip was too weak to re-create the magnitude of power he had been able to draw on while in the sunny meadow on Pluto. In order for his mind to function at the heightened state it had achieved at the age of seven, he needed access to the mind of George Spell. And for the first time since he had returned to Earth , Alex was too far away from George Spell for that to happen. He no longer had access to what he needed to hold the complex geometric instruction in his mind at one time.

And that's why George had been kidnapped. *Lonadoon must have known.*

Now, in order to achieve the great ascent, he would have to rescue George Spell.

"There's no time to explain," Alex said, knowing that Horace would be able to sense any deception he had in mind. "For now, we must follow orders and complete the rescue of George Spell."

Horace nodded weakly.

"Listen to me, Horace," Alex said quickly. "When the time comes, will you help me?"

Visibly struggling to reconcile his euphoria with his sense of duty, Horace said, "Please don't make me chose between . . ." The rest of what he was thinking went unsaid.

The audio mute had been activated too long. Odessa would notice by now. "Horace, you have free will. I cannot make you do something your consciousness does not agree with. I can only ask you, as the only other person who understands, that if I can make this possible, will you help?"

"I will not disobey orders," Horace said. "But if it is possible, I will help."

Alex removed his hand from Horace's. When he did, they both almost collapsed. Grasping the wall and each other's shoulders, they regained their equilibrium. Alex hurriedly turned the mobius to the correct alignment, then looked up at Horace. "That's it," he said. "But it is prudent to leave the room free of any unnecessary EM interference." Alex motioned to the audio mute. He hoped that would be Horace's answer when Odessa started asking her questions.

The searing glare from Odessa when Alex and Horace returned to the bridge was almost as intimidating as a Reaper. Alex could tell she knew the drive room had been muted, a private conversation had been had. Horace had such a stupid guilty expression on his face as he walked to his com panel he might as well have admitted to being a Harvester himself.

But Odessa never made the same mistake twice. She would not question Alex. She would allow him the opportunity to prove himself, save them from the Reaper trap. She'd give him control of the ship, and if he made one false move, she'd probably tackle him and throw him out into vacuum space.

"We're ready, Captain," Alex said.

Odessa kept staring at Alex as she put her hand into the central display. "Ship, transfer command program access to Admiral Alexander Detail, Captain's authorization *****."

JuneMary and Witaker authenticated the command and Alex put his hand into the display next to Odessa's.

The ship refused to comply. "Biometric signature for Admiral Alexander Detail does not match file specifications."

"Quite a memory," Odessa commented, referring to the fact that the last Alex Detail to command the *Virgin Mother* had been George Spell, and he had specified the ship to match his genetic imprint with physical characteristics to block Alex from regaining control of the ship.

Odessa instructed the ship to reset the default settings. Once the senior officers verified, the ship reported, "Access to command program has been transferred to Admiral Alexander Detail."

"Run Detail-Reaper program," Alex said to the ship.

The computer executed the program and the modified George Spell communications package was tightbeamed to the Reaper.

Everyone on the bridge held their breath.

The Reaper did not respond.

Witaker studied his display. "The tightbeam is being reflected back to us."

"That's not possible," Alex replied, looking at the same data Witaker was studying. "Reaper hulls are nearly absolute black. They absorb everything. It's impossible for it to reflect ..."

Odessa crossed her arms. "Try your q-field modifications. I'm quite done with being trapped here."

Horace put the reactors online and began to input instructions for a jump to minimal spin-up.

"Stop!" Alex yelled. "Don't fire the engines!"

Everyone on the bridge was looking at Alex like he'd lost his mind.

"The tightbeam! It's being reflected by heavy hydrogen." Alex waved his hands madly at the readout. "If you fire the engines you'll send a wave of gamma rays along the Van Allen belt!"

"Okay, just calm down now, we get the idea," JuneMary said, looking at the display, which showed the tightbeam's radar picture of a perfectly spherical object inside the Reaper. "That ain't no Reaper. It's a giant nuke."

CHAPTER 10

MADELINE SPELL AND THE GENERATIONISTS

Madeline Spell was sitting next to a giant wall of glass that separated her from the ocean floor. The last rays of sunlight were glistening in the ocean currents, casting a soft kaleidoscopic pattern of moving colors around her. Something large and dark glided past her on the other side of the glass, then with a sudden flick of its tail disappeared into the ocean depths.

"Don't worry, Speaker, the glass is stronger than the sharks," Dr. Lastingday said as he handed Madeline Spell and Guy Hiramoto each a dark blue glass of water.

Spell was parched, but she only took the slightest sip of water and then placed the glass on the table between her and Hiramoto. Dr. Lastingday had been rather calm when Spell and Hiramoto had slid aside a rusted old manhole and climbed down into a small dark room.

"We don't use that entrance," Lastingday had said by way of introduction, causing both Madeline and Hiramoto to jump. "There are two passways to the mainland. Had you told me you were coming, I would have made your trip less of a hassle."

Not likely, Spell thought. A personal visit from the Speaker of the House of Nations could only mean at the very least more work for the Generationists. At worst, it meant their dealings had been uncovered, and one or all were headed back to prison. *With me right behind them.*

After they were shown to the main room and seated, Lastingday had disappeared to get them water they didn't ask for. He was breathing heavily and probably trying to hide whatever he had been up to before their arrival.

"But you *were* expecting us," Spell said, pointing to the wall on the opposite side of the room. A curtain had been hastily drawn across the glass, its corner held in place behind a heavy chair. A dusty curtain that obviously didn't get much use.

Lastingday crossed his arms and shot a glance behind him. "I, uh, I only had a moment."

"I take it whatever's on the other side of that glass is rather gruesome?" Spell asked, holding up the tiny hand-shaped piece of coral she had picked up on the beach.

"Despite the lies so commonly told about the Generationists, we are humane. We applied the most rigorous scientific method before we ever experimented with humans." Lastingday looked earnestly at Madeline. "Especially with your project."

Spell didn't need Lastingday to pull the curtain aside to show her what was on the other side of the glass. She knew she would see the ocean floor covered with coral in the shape of young humans. It was their work with coral that made the Generationists ideal for making a clone of Alex Detail. When Alex first learned of the Generationists, it was not their cloning ability that had interested him. Replicating DNA and RNA had been perfected hundreds of years earlier. While cloning an entire person was illegal in most cases, therapeutic cloning—growing new tissue for replacement parts—was commonly practiced medical therapy until gene mutation had been eliminated by modern medicine. Once viruses could be fashioned to repair any part of the human body, growing organs through gene replication fell out of practice.

The thing the Generationists promised that intrigued Alex Detail was reversal of the biological aging of cells.

When fears of the Harvesters' return began to peak while Alex Detail's intelligence and cooperation declined, the need for a "safeguard" became obvious. Madeline Spell could not play dice with humanity, waiting for another savior to be born when there existed the ability to create a new and better version of Alex Detail to face the inevitable return of the Harvesters. What started as a theoretical inquiry became a necessity. The Generationists could reverse the aging process, unsuccessfully in most cases, but that was by design. They had not been allowed to continue their research in that direction. Once the accidents occurred, Madeline Spell had intervened, directing them to use their technology to accelerate the body's growth. The Generationists never had any idea that it was Madeline Spell who covertly interfered with their research. After the Generationist experiments had been linked with the death of three human volunteers, Spell had the necessary leverage to put the group at her mercy. She needed a fully functional clone and she needed it fast.

Spell imagined that if she looked through the curtain opposite her chair, she would see a pile of Alex Detail coral clones frozen in various stages of growth. The thought made her suddenly dizzy and nauseated.

Quick footsteps approached, and two people hurried into the room. They stopped short when they saw Madeline Spell and Guy Hiramoto sitting with Dr. Lastingday.

"They made it here before you, as you see," Lastingday said.

Spell recognized them as the couple who had stopped to ask her to take their picture. They must have called Lastingday and run here through one of the mainland tunnels.

"These are my colleagues," Willow Lastingday said. "Lexia and Nice."

The two did not say hello. They stared at Spell and sat tentatively next to Dr. Lastingday. *They're terrified of me*, Spell thought. *Terrified of my power over their lives, terrified of what I've made them do, terrified I'm here to ask them for some other monstrous project.*

For the accidents resulting in deaths, the Generationists had received sentences landing them in prison for life. The price for their furlough was to create George Spell.

"Yes, Lexia and Nice," Spell said. "I remember your names. Derivatives of Alexiares and Anicetus, the children of Hebe, Greek goddess of youth."

Amazing and tragic, Spell thought as she looked at three elderly people who could pass for teenagers. These people had discovered the secret of eternal youth, only to be condemned by her to a life of quarantine, forever maintaining their secret laboratory.

But as she stared longer at Dr. Willow Lastingday, she could see the way he moved was deliberate and somewhat slow. These were the movements of a man who carried a lifetime of experience, worry, and sorrow. No amount of genetic engineering could reverse that.

"You do realize," Dr. Lastingday said, "that your coming here violates every term of our agreement."

Guy Hiramoto stirred at this and angrily answered, "And you do know that your callousness, your carelessness, your disregard for your responsibility has caused us to bring a tortured and extremely dangerous person into the world. That, Doctor, violates every term of our agreement. We should have your sham of an operation shut down and send the three of you back to prison."

Spell held up a hand, then put it gently on Hiramoto's leg. "Calm down, dear. Their mistakes cannot be undone. No use in making yourself angry."

To gain their furlough, the Generationists had been less than truthful in their assurances they could create a clone of Alex Detail in the timeframe allowed. The documentation that showed how they would accelerate the growth of the Detail clone and upload seven years worth of data through rapid mitochondrial signaling had contained several areas of falsified data.

It hadn't surprised Spell. The Generationists had an incentive. She had the best minds review their studies. And there was a Harvester ring ship at the edge of the solar system and the probability of more on the way. There were risks involved in everything in life. Her job was to say yes or no and keep life moving. She had said yes, and George Spell had saved the world. From the Generationists' point of view, they had done their job.

But the manner in which George had saved the world alarmed even them. He was supposed to have respect for life and obedience to authority. But the way he saved the world . . . stealing a flier, poisoning the pilot, killing Derringkite. . . As Hiramoto had put it, George had gone "haywire."

Suddenly the girl, Lexia, began crying. "We tried so hard to make him human," she wailed to Spell and Hiramoto. "We watched him growing, so fast every day. He started talking to us!" She put her face in her hands and continued to sob while Nice gently rubbed his hand on her back.

Dr. Lastingday himself seemed to be holding back tears. "When I first met Alex Detail and he told me of his desire—well, his extreme request. . ." Lastingday paused, as if lost in reliving that meeting. "To take the human body in reverse through adolescence, well. . . The problem Alex Detail sought to correct was clearly psychological. But he believed in our research and he made us see we could truly achieve the technology to, well, give everyone a second chance at life."

Spell was staring curiously at Lastingday. She wondered what kind of man he was before he met Alex Detail, before he was forced to create a clone of his benefactor. As she looked at his youthful body, boyish face, all held with the sad posture of an old man, she could see he knew firsthand that youth is a once-in-a-lifetime experience. You couldn't get a second chance at it no matter how young your body's cells were.

Lastingday continued talking. "After the accidents, I was glad you had us separated from Alex Detail. His sadness was overpowering." He paused again, unable to continue speaking. Then he burst out, "But the mapping for George was perfect! We had perfected the mitochondrial signaling. We just didn't have—"

Guy Hiramoto cut him off. "You just didn't have time, so you falsified data and created one hell of a problem."

Nodding, Lastingday said, "I wish I had said we couldn't do it. I would rather have gone to prison. We perfectly understood the genetic defects that caused Detail's psychological problems. George's mapping was perfect. He was supposed to be happy. But—"

"But you wrote a program that was self defeating," Madeline answered. "In order for George to be happy, he cannot be responsible for saving the world. So his functional programming overrode his emotional programming and you created an automaton. You created an automaton, and none of the work you have done since, none of the packets you have sent to our doctors in the past six months have had any effect. You are unable to correct the problem."

Lastingday was about to rebuke Spell, but she rushed on. "I know what you are going to say. Yes, I love my child and wish I did not. Because George is not a child. He is not Alex Detail. Even a proper clone of Alex Detail would not be Alex Detail—just as identical twins separated at birth grow up to be different individuals. I came here in person because it is important for you to know that I have the same depth of feelings for George as you do."

Spell stood up, leaned her forehead against the now dark glass, the ocean beyond it cool and dark.

Spell continued, "I wanted you to know from me, just how painful this is." She pulled her head back from the glass and turned to face the Generationists. "I have come here to collect the Toolkit."

Lastingday stood and said, "But if you just give us more time—"

"No," Spell interrupted. "I have already given you too much time. It is time to stop the blind hope. I am here to take the Toolkit."

There was silence. The Toolkit was a last resort. A final solution.

Spell thought it important to be absolutely clear. "For the safety of humanity, it is time that Alex Detail and George Spell were incapacitated. Permanently."

CHAPTER 11

JUNEMARY'S WORLD

George Spell wasn't much interested in the view of Venus as they approached the planet, though he noted that Innsbrook and Lonadoon seemed very interested in looking at the bright yellow planet through the ship's small windows. It made little sense to George what information they could possibly be gathering. After looking once at the planet, in the main display rather than the window, he determined that its yellow plateaus, green oceans and thick gray-and-gold cloud clusters resembled pictures he had seen. George had all the information on Venus he needed in his memory, likely uploaded during his advanced growth stage, for he had never set out to study it. Staring out the window at it seemed a waste of time; if they required additional information, they could be gathering more accurate visual data through information files.

It appeared to be morning on top of the mountain where New Africa was located. As they boarded the lander and descended toward the Venusian surface, Lonadoon once again asked George if he felt well-rested. George had already answered the question. Yes, he felt well-rested. Lonadoon had then asked if he slept, which George had not, but that had nothing to do with the question. The entire trip had taken nineteen hours and George did not feel he required sleep. He felt well-rested.

"It conserves energy by compartmentalizing cerebral functions," Lonadoon was saying to Innsbrook. "It could probably go weeks without sleep."

Innsbrook didn't speak much. It also appeared he didn't listen much. Lonadoon was always making some observations, usually about George, to which Innsbrook paid little attention.

Much of Lonadoon's line of questioning had to do with George's mental state. Apparently, he was supposed to meet someone, be given a large amount of information, then required to perform some task. If he felt tired or not fully able to concentrate, Lonadoon said he would not be able to understand the information or perform the task. Since Lonadoon refused to tell George what the information was or what the task would be, how did he expect George to give him an accurate answer?

George was only interested in finding out what Alex Detail was planning to do with the Harvesters. If the information he was given explained that, and if the task he was given allowed him to stop Alex Detail, then he would be fully capable of carrying it out. If not, George would find a means to leave New Africa and return to New York City where he could continue to be more productive.

Having once stolen his mother's flier and taken command of an ARRAY warship, one under the command of the great ARRAY Captain Odessa, George felt confident he would be able to do the same with the much smaller *UC One*. As far as he could tell, there was only a two-person crew on President Innsbrook's ship. Both people were men wearing United Countries military uniforms, and oddly, both had the same name or classification that had to do with the ocean. George had noted President Innsbrook addressed each as "Marine." When one would say something to Innsbrook, he would often reply, "Very good, Marine," or "Thank you, Marine." They could, however, be differentiated by rank. Before the flier landed, Innsbrook told Lonadoon that the "'Assistant Commandant,' will accompany me when we land and the 'Major' will transport you."

President Innsbrook and the commandant were greeted by an important-looking group of people when they exited the lander. As George watched through the window, Innsbrook and the other man were handed cooling umbrellas. Apparently the heat was very uncomfortable to people not used to living on Venus.

George had wondered how his mother would react when she heard he'd been kidnapped. Whatever ship Alex Detail was on to "rescue" him was apparently very far behind. If his mother, the ruler of the worlds, had sent a message to the New Africa Council, George was sure that Innsbrook would have been stopped and taken into custody. But the President of the United Countries of America was being greeted the way George had seen his mother greet many heads of state at the House of Nations. No one acted as if Innsbrook were in trouble.

It quickly became clear that they either did not know George Spell was on the flier or did not care. George and Lonadoon remained on the flier while it was towed into a hangar. It was only then that the other person named Marine, the Major Marine, escorted them off the flier and into a car.

Perhaps Innsbrook and Lonadoon had convinced his mother that Alex needed to be stopped by George and she had called off her pursuit. It didn't really matter.

"Where is Alex Detail now?" George asked Brother Lonadoon.

"He is far enough away that he cannot access your mind," Lonadoon replied.

"I know that," George said. "But he is trying."

Lonadoon nodded. "Of course he is. You must continue to practice shielding him. He will eventually find a way into your mind."

George shrugged. "When I was first able to think the same things as him, he was very far away. Even before Pluto came to Earth, Alex wasn't really far away because he was always within the Harvesters' omegafield. After Pluto was destroyed, I was still able to think some of the things Alex Detail would think, but not real easy like before. It's like he always has a small omegafield surrounding him. Except when he was in the planetarium. The Harvesters don't like spheres for some reason and won't talk to him when he's in one. That's why I tried to kill him there. But you know that, because you have magical powers and that's why you were there. You wanted Mom to make me go home so I wouldn't hurt people. I don't understand why you keep asking me questions about myself when you already know the answers."

Lonadoon nodded. "Yes, correct deduction. I am simply verifying certain information. Why do you suppose redundancy troubles you?"

Another question with an obvious answer. But if Brother Lonadoon needed help verifying his magical information, then George would help him. "Because I could be doing other stuff. Why does President Innsbrook look upset when you call me 'it'?"

"Because he does not understand your true nature as we do," Lonadoon answered. "He is displaying a protective instinct called 'anthropomorphism.' It is the attribution of human characteristics to non-human beings and objects."

"I don't know if I understand my 'true nature.' I don't understand everything about myself," George said, surprised that Lonadoon didn't know this. "Like if I fell off the planetarium, would I die?"

"You would not have fallen," Lonadoon answered.

"I didn't think I would," George agreed. "But it would be good if I knew the things that could hurt me. Do you have the Generationist research that explains me?"

"You waste your time thinking about that," Lonadoon said in the sort of tone that indicated he was angry.

"Does it bother you that you can't read my mind the way you can read the minds of regular people?" George asked.

Lonadoon didn't answer right away. His facial expression was that of someone working on the answer to one of those word-box puzzles. It looked like he liked this question. "I cannot read people's minds," he finally answered. "The universe provides me with information about events and outcomes through processes I have learned. But the universe is no more aware of you than this car that we are riding in, and therefore I must obtain information about you in other ways."

"Like looking at my eyes and reading the minds of people around me," George answered.

This seemed to be a good answer, as Lonadoon nodded and said, "Yes, that is a suitable way of characterizing my methods with you."

"So you are taking me to meet a person with stronger magical powers than you," George said.

"In a way," Lonadoon said. "She is someone I have known for many years. Even before she was born."

That didn't make much sense to George, but then again, he didn't understand magical powers. "Why wouldn't my mother listen to you when you warned her that I was dangerous? Because of the anthropomorphism thing you said?"

Lonadoon smiled and nodded. "That is exactly correct—very well done! "

George had not seen Lonadoon smile before when they spoke. "Did you just anthropomorphize me?"

Ha! Lonadoon actually looked surprised, then frowned and put his hand to his forehead. The magician didn't say anything for a while, but as he sat there thinking, it seemed like he was getting sad.

Finally, Lonadoon looked at George. "I'm afraid I did."

This was disappointing to George, because until then, he thought Lonadoon was perfect like him. But apparently Lonadoon could be tricked. That was useful to know.

They had been driving for exactly fifteen minutes. George had made sure to memorize their route while he talked to Brother Lonadoon. After they left the spaceport hangar, they drove along a road that was attached to the side of a cliff. Street signs identified the road as Pallas Athena Pass. They drove by three other roads that led to clusters of rounded and pyramid-shaped buildings built into the side of the mountain. Pallas Athena Pass suddenly became very steep and as they drove up it, the driver made a sharp turn onto a fourth road with a sign that read Maxwell Center. They were now driving on the very top of the New Africa plateau, and it looked like pictures George had seen of the Grand Canyon, only everything was very smooth with lots of winding patterns. Most of Venus's mountains and ancient dry lava flows had been shaped by thick clouds and heavy rain before they changed it so people could live there. Even the tallest buildings had a curved triangular shape: It must still get windy, George reasoned.

They drove up to one of the taller buildings near the edge of the plateau and into a garage beneath it. The car stopped by a doorway where they got out of the vehicle. Major Marine drove away as Lonadoon led them down a hallway that looked like the kind beneath the House of Nations, except the ceiling, walls and floor were covered in the same sort of rusty-colored tiles. They came to the end of the hallway and stood on a raised platform. To their left was an exit sign above a door with another sign that indicated a stairwell.

George could hear the sound of footsteps. Someone was coming down the stairs.

George took a few steps to the edge of the platform, but Brother Lonadoon put a hand on his shoulder.

"Stand still a moment," Lonadoon said to George.

The footsteps grew louder, then the stairwell exit door opened.

A young woman, perhaps only a teenager, came through the door and took Brother Lonadoon's hand in a businesslike handshake. George noted that she was a very handsome girl with perfectly smooth dark skin. A braid circled her head like a halo.

"Very pleased to meet you in person, Brother Lonadoon," the young woman said. "I am Rosemary June."

"I am likewise pleased to meet *you*, Rosemary," Lonadoon said. "This is George Spell."

The young woman smiled at George, but quickly looked back at Brother Lonadoon. "She is ready," Rosemary said, placing her right hand on a wall panel.

A railing came out from the wall and surrounded them. The platform began to descend. George calculated that the elevator had gone down forty feet before it came to a stop in front of a door.

The railing slid back into the wall and the door opened into a very large, brightly lit room. It was bright because the sun was shining in through a wall of windows. Apparently, they were in a room built into the side of the cliff below the building.

As Rosemary motioned them off the platform, George saw a small animal running toward them from the direction of the windows. A cat.

The cat had orange and brown patterns that made it blend in with the rust-colored tiles on the floor. It immediately approached Rosemary, sniffed at her legs, then padded close enough to Lonadoon for a quick sniff at the edge of his trousers before coming to a stop at George's feet. The cat sat, looked up at George, and meowed. George had never encountered a cat in real life, and did not understand what it said. Before he could try to reply, the cat ran off.

As George's eyes adjusted, he could make out another person approaching them.

She had long brown hair and was wearing a pretty green dress and shoes that women wore to make them taller. George had never seen her before, but when she was close enough for him to see her face, he knew exactly who she was.

She nodded as George looked at her. "Good," she said to Lonadoon. "He recognizes me."

The woman standing in front of him was the powerful magician Brother Lonadoon had taken him to meet.

Alex Detail's mother.

"On behalf of the Speaker of the House of Nations, I demand to see

President Innsbrook," Captain Odessa was saying for the third time to Senior Councilman Hermes Retroguard.

"Again, I must apologize, Captain Odessa," Hermes Retroguard said. "Your visit here is unscheduled, and you do not have House Sanction confirmation. Unless and until we receive permission from the house or the speaker, I simply cannot help you."

The councilman looked disheveled and confused upon greeting the crew of the *Virgin Mother* at the New Africa Spaceport. Their arrival on Venus had caused quite a stir among the New Africa Council. ARRAY warships simply did not arrive at the planet without the population being notified through an official announcement. On this occasion, the council had been given no advance word from ARRAY that a ship was being sent.

Odessa had insisted they were on a priority mission and could not disclose any details. She was secretly furious that Speaker Madeline Spell had offered them no help or guidance throughout this entire ordeal she had sent them on. Captain Odessa wanted to just come out and tell the New Africa Councilman that Innsbrook had kidnapped George Spell; that someone, likely a citizen of his planet, had created a fake Reaper, turned it into a gigantic explosive, then set it to attack Odessa's ship. But talking that way would be an instant diplomatic failure.

At least Alex Detail had finally proven himself helpful there. Had Odessa fired up the engines once they freed the ship from the artificial Van Allen radiation belts, the fake Reaper would have exploded, likely causing heavy damage to the *Virgin Mother*. The nuclear bomb disguised as a Reaper had enough power to blast away a quarter of Earth's moon. Yes, ARRAY warship q-fields were designed to take much more punishment than that, so the actual explosive concussion itself would not have seriously damaged the ship or hurt its crew. However, the bombardment of nuclear radiation would have augmented the solar radial belts already surrounding the ship, and fried just about every external sensor. The thought of drifting in a crippled ship just outside Earth's magnetic field was the most humiliating thing Odessa could imagine.

Captain Odessa, the most decorated war hero in the history of ARRAY, unable to command the ARRAY flagship on the simplest mission? Odessa knew once they started raising those sorts of questions, the vultures descended and your career was over.

After Alex had successfully devised a way of inching the ship away from the fake Reaper by depressurizing the lander bay and main arch entrance to create non-electromagnetic propulsion, they were able to drift the necessary five kilometers clear of the Van Allen radiation belts to activate the engines without triggering the fake Reaper's explosives.

Once back on course to Venus, Odessa had finally authenticated the ship's beacon and waited to be contacted by Speaker Madeline Spell.

It certainly took her long enough to reply with a communication encryption key.

Odessa thought about waiting nearly an hour herself to reply back to the speaker, just to let her know what it was like, but then Odessa calmed herself. Who knew what the speaker had been up to since they had left Earth? So, Odessa sent the encrypted text detailing their discovery that Innsbrook's ship had gone to Venus.

Obviously, the speaker was highly suspicious of eavesdropping: She communicated via encrypted text. But her reply was rather surprising to Odessa.

"Continue mission covertly. Maintain all classified information. Update upon retrieval."

This was not a mother concerned for her son's safety, rather someone more concerned for her own safety, Odessa thought. Spell would not even put the words "George Spell" in an encrypted text.

And continue covertly? How the hell was Odessa supposed to continue covertly? The New Africa government wasn't going to just let her park an ARRAY ship in orbit without proper clearance, never mind letting her land. Captain Odessa realized that, as usual, Spell knew Odessa had just enough tools at her disposal to continue on without the speaker getting even her little finger dirty.

After assuming an orbit proximate to *UC One*, Admiral Alex Detail had managed to create a last-minute ARRAY command packet that seemed to satisfy the New Africa Council that their arrival was indeed official business—though it took some additional negotiations from Ambassador JuneMary before Odessa and her senior officers were cleared to land the ship's flier at the spaceport.

The walk across the tarmac to the spaceport terminal was unbearably hot even under the cooling umbrellas. Sweltering hot wind tore at them while blistering heat rose from the furnace-hot tarmac.

Unlike the rest of them, JuneMary had not opened her umbrella. "Glorious!"

she exclaimed, looking up at the extra-bright Venusian sun, soaking in the heat like a beachside sunbather.

Then a gigantic cloud engulfed them, pelting the crew with a fine warm spray. The Venus equivalent of a rainstorm.

"Drat," JuneMary said, fumbling with her umbrella as they ran the last twenty meters to the spaceport building.

Now, nearly nine hours after she calculated Innsbrook's ship had arrived at Venus, Captain Odessa, drenched from the unconventional rainstorm, stood with Alex Detail, JuneMary, and Horace Witaker, trying to explain herself to this New African council bureaucrat and a very nervous-looking spaceport manager.

Odessa was exhausted, aggravated, and had not eaten in nearly an hour. Wishing she could take out her hidden sidearm, Captain Odessa had half a mind to taser both men where they stood.

"Are you going to stand there and deny that President Innsbrook is even here?" Odessa roared. "Please, Councilman Hermes, my ship is orbiting two kilometers from *UC One*! I am not a senseless fool!"

Hermes Retroguard shrugged. "I am very sorry, Captain. I have really said all I can."

Odessa huffed and turned to JuneMary. "Some country you got here."

JuneMary held a wet towel. She was still drying the back of her neck when the sun lit the room. She looked wistfully outside as the raincloud sailed off the side of the mountaintop and the sun shone blindingly along the steaming tarmac.

"Oh come on now, Retroguard," JuneMary said. "If the captain here could tell you more, she would. It doesn't make a dag amount of sense that we'd be here like this if it wasn't an emergency." JuneMary then nudged him and winked. "Perhaps a personal emergency the speaker is unable to talk about . . ."

Retroguard frowned at JuneMary's suggestive comment. "Really now, JuneMary. I can't bend the rules without knowing what in heck's sake is going on here. You're the ambassador, so why don't you call the rest of the council and start doing some ambassadoring."

JuneMary signed. "Oh Hermy, since when did you get to be such a stick-in-the-mud?"

A muffled sonic boom came from the tarmac behind them.

They turned just in time to see President Innsbrook's flier disappear into the sky. It was clearly the same flier that had "rescued" George from the planetarium.

Odessa grabbed the spaceport manager by his collar and heaved the man who was almost twice her height against the nearest wall. "Was Innsbrook on that flier?"

Witaker and Councilman Hermes pulled Odessa away from the cowering man.

"Really now," Retroguard said.

"Now what?" JuneMary said, looking at Odessa.

Damn Madeline Spell! Why the hell hadn't she given them the proper clearance to get her son back? Odessa really wanted to ask this spaceport manager if he knew whether or not George Spell was on that flier, but if either he or the councilman was up on the latest fake news from Govnet, they'd think George had been rescued from the top of the planetarium yesterday and was at home playing with his toy dinosaurs. Mention George Spell's name and Odessa would be in violation of keeping her orders classified.

Odessa thought of sending Spell a message, but that would be the call of an incompetent officer. How would Spell have any way of knowing if George were on the flier going back up to *UC One*? Ground reconnaissance was Odessa's mission. *So, where the hell is George?*

Odessa looked at Alex Detail. "Admiral, I would say this is your call."

In the eyes of the councilman and the spaceport manager, this would look like a show of deference to a senior officer, but to everyone else it was a public acknowledgement that Detail had some sense of where the boy might be. Unfortunately, Alex looked completely confused.

He seemed to be straining, as if he were trying to remember something long forgotten. But he eventually shook his head. "I would say we should stay here and continue our mission," Alex finally said.

Well, that was certainly not the cocksure Alex Detail Odessa knew! *The whole trip he can't shut up and keep from poking his nose into all manner of spaceship operations and finally we get here and he goes mute. If he knows George is still here, why isn't he acting like a cat with a mouse? What's wrong with him now?*

"Glorious!" JuneMary said. "I'll call my brother to come pick us up, and we'll all go stay at the House of June. It's going to be high noon in a couple hours, and high noon on Venus is powerful glorious!"

CHAPTER 12

THE HOUSE OF JUNE

The House of June was located in the town of Oasis, an actual oasis of densely built homes among thick green vegetation and stiflingly hot humid air. The town was several miles long, built beside the first settlement domes that stretched along the western ridge on the summit of Maxwell Montes, the highest point on the planet Venus. Tall antenna towers lined the opposite western ridge creating a magnetic wall that helped protect the town's atmosphere from being buffeted by the strong winds and roving Venusian storm clouds.

While the majority of the twenty-five by two mile landmass that comprised most of the settlement on New Africa on the western mountain ridge was arid, hot and windy, Oasis was a tropical paradise. The temperature was a steady 105 degrees F for most of the 36-hour Venusian day, and 90 degrees F during the nearly 35-hour night. The homes were all three and four story townhouses built of indigenous composites mined from the central depression and slopes of Maxwell Montes.

The June family home was located at the southern tip of Oasis in the oldest part of town, about a two mile drive from the spaceport. Three stories high, surrounding a tropical courtyard full of palm trees, flowers, a large elaborately decorated pyramid, and a waterfall flowing into a triangular coy pond, the building was home to JuneMary, her Brother Jay'r June, and his wife and daughter. However, although the June clan was numerous, JuneMary assured her visitors that most of the twelve bedrooms were currently unoccupied, as most of the family was away.

As Alex and the others made their way into the house, it appeared that

Jay'r June had alerted his wife to expect visitors. The long kitchen that opened to the courtyard was overflowing with trays of freshly prepared food, mostly an assortment of chilled raw vegetables and fruits, topped and filled with soft cheese spreads and nuts. Jay'r's wife Kelen was standing next to a stack of plates. "Welcome, welcome," she said, waving them into the kitchen. "Can't believe you're back home so soon," she said to JuneMary, giving her sister-in-law a brief hug.

Is there a hint of sarcasm in Kelen's voice? Alex wondered. Was Kelen a wife all too happy to finally have the house to herself, expecting JuneMary to be away at the House of Nations for a long trip? There was something about the look Kelen shot her husband over JuneMary's shoulder that Alex could only identify as suspicious. JuneMary had unexpectedly returned, one day after a trip to New York City, on an ARRAY warship with *the* Alex Detail and *the* Captain Odessa, on an unexpected and unauthorized trip to Venus. And now, these strange members of the military were guests in her house. *Well, if I were up to something, and this gang arrived at my doorstep, I'd be suspicious too,* Alex thought.

As JuneMary was making introductions, Alex was suddenly hit by a sickening sense of déjà vu: Derringkite's kitchen on Pluto, filled with food, open to the sunny meadow beyond. He looked at Horace to see if he were experiencing the same thing, but Witaker was engaged in some small talk with Kelen and Jay'r. Why would this home and these nice people make him feel like he was back in that miraculous and tortuous House of Derringkite?

Alex heard the front door open and a young woman's voice call, "Hello?"

Alex turned in time to see a striking young woman enter the kitchen. Her smooth skin and intricately braided hair reminded Alex of the pictures he had seen of Generationist regenerative subjects, but this girl was naturally perfect. She looked even more radiant than the picture of her JuneMary had shown him yesterday.

"There's my Rosemary!" JuneMary exclaimed as she pulled her into a big hug. "Well now, we are gonna have to lock you up and throw away the key, else Alex and Horace aren't going to get a lick of work done!"

Odessa snorted in amusement.

Rosemary took the compliment with a small smile and a slight blush. "I'm sorry I'm late," the young woman said, "I got your message, Mom, but I was working late and then the busser was running behind again."

JuneMary made more introductions while Kelen bragged about her daughter being the youngest person in the history of New Africa University to complete a doctorate in Wave/Particle-Thermodynamics. "That was just six months ago, on her eighteenth birthday, just before the Pluto incident," Kelen was saying. "I believe you and Rosemary share the same birth date, Admiral Detail."

Rosemary smiled slightly at Alex. "Well, you don't look a day over sixteen," Alex said. Girls liked that kind of compliment.

Odessa, chomping on a beautifully filled and decorated celery stalk, said, "Well now, young lady, that is most impressive. I would be most pleased if you were of a mind to update Admiral Detail and Vice Captain Witaker about some of the more current practical theorems. They could use a brush-up with the whole quantum gizmo business."

While Alex wasn't surprised that Odessa took the opportunity to lob an insult at him, and perhaps one to cut down Horace in front of a potential object of attraction, he was surprised by Rosemary's enthusiastic response.

Rosemary took three quick strides and stood face to face with Odessa.

"The captain who speaks in dactylic hexameter. It's an honor to meet you, Captain Odessa."

Apparently delighted that someone so appreciated her ancient speech patterns, Odessa pursed her lips and nodded approvingly at Rosemary.

"Actually, I have studied you, Captain Odessa, more than any other ARRAY officer," Rosemary continued. "Theory is one thing, but command decisions in the field carry the most complex implications in the quantum wave."

Something isn't quite right about all this, Alex thought. He had met many people in his life, and no matter how hard they tried to hide it, no matter who else was in the room, it was Alex Detail who they were truly most eager to meet. *When people project on you that you're a legend, it really doesn't matter what you say. Just pretend to be a good listener and they walk away charmed.* Not only had Rosemary barely said hello to Alex, she was apparently completely disinterested in his presence here.

"Indeed, they do," Odessa replied, taking another vicious bite out of her celery. "And what have you learned from your studies of my storied command methods?"

"It's fascinating. By studying you, I was able to demonstrate that the reduction of quantum probabilities can be exponentially reduced by decision time," Rosemary said, still eye to eye with Odessa. "You have the fastest average response time of any field commander and the smallest delta in quantum field probability."

"A captain's concisely convincing cadence cuts cacophonous confusion," Odessa answered, now addressing the room more than carrying her side of the conversation with Rosemary. "In other words, don't think too much, or you'll screw it up."

Kelen seemed to be growing uncomfortable about her daughter's aggressiveness with the captain. She moved between the two and said, "It's just about mid-sleep. Let me bring you all to your rooms."

Mid-sleep was the first portion of the 72.1 hour Venusian day in which people slept in order to maintain the human circadian rhythm. The 72.1 hour day was divided into six sections of 16 hours and one minute of being awake followed by 8 hours and one minute of sleep, which almost exactly approximated the sleep and wake cycles of the 24 hour earth day. It conveniently kept everyone on New Africa on a common schedule, while "leap-hours" were subtracted every few cycles to synchronize daily life with the schedules of Earth.

Alex half expected Odessa to pull him aside and interrogate him on just how sure he was that George Spell was still on Venus. Instead, she grabbed a few more cream cheese and walnut filled celery stalks, then ordered them all to get a good "night's" sleep.

Twenty minutes after being shown to their rooms, Alex stepped out of the bathroom at the end of the hallway and nearly bumped into Rosemary June. She was carrying a shining spheroid with a small loop at its base, the kind Alex had seen in the ARRAY physics labs he'd spent so much time working in.

"Is that an MDM?" Alex asked.

Rosemary nodded and held up the silvery glob of moldable-metal that was used to display the real-world shapes of complicated mathematical equations. "Yes, I was working on a particular form of a Klein Bottle, but not having the best of luck with it as you can see."

"You trying to make a wormhole or something?" Alex asked, half jokingly.

Rosemary's eyes brightened. "Yes, well, not a real one but something that would approximate a local rift. Nothing self-sustaining, you know, like that hole they used to destroy Pluto."

Alex almost reflexively answered that the black hole New Africa had sent to destroy the incoming planet six months earlier had not destroyed Pluto, or at least not the "real" Pluto, but he stopped himself. "What's it for?"

"An internship," Rosemary said, "at the Kade Institute. You know how they are so obsessed with singularities there. Anyway, I can't get the derivative right. I either make the thing implode or end up with something several light years across. Which just causes this thing to blink, so you know you really messed up your math."

Alex laughed. "I know. I think they were intentionally designed to embarrass people. Here, let me." Alex studied the object a moment, then looked at the formula in the display. It was really like looking at a three-dimensional mobius, something Alex had a natural affinity for. He added a variable to one side of the equation, got rid of one on the other. The shape accepted the new formula and modulated itself accordingly.

"Wow, that was fast," Rosemary said with what sounded like genuine admiration.

As Alex handed the MDM back to Rosemary, he noticed a short orange hair on the base. "Do you have cats here?"

The question seemed to startle Rosemary. "What do you mean?"

Alex pointed to the orange cat hair.

"Oh, that, that, that's—" Rosemary stuttered. "I mean, yes. I think it was a stray one of the administrators took in."

When she reached up to take the shape from Alex's hand, she brushed his thumb, causing a mild sort of static between them.

Alex was mesmerized for a moment. Rosemary's eyes were so dark he could see his reflection in them. She had changed to a lighter sleeping dress and he couldn't help but notice the smooth skin of her shoulders and the sweep of slightly paler skin around the top curves of her breasts.

Their eyes locked as Rosemary took the MDM, and Alex found himself deeply relaxed standing there with her.

Suddenly, a tremendous snoring sound tore through the hallway.

Captain Odessa.

They both tried to conceal their laughter as Rosemary tiptoed over and gently shut the door to Captain Odessa's bedroom.

"Thank you for your help, Alex," Rosemary said.

Alex nodded and motioned to the Klein Bottle. "My pleasure."

"Do you want a heal-aid for that?" Rosemary said, looking at the cut on Alex's thumb.

Quickly pulling his hand away, Alex said, "Oh, this. No, it's fine. Just a small cut from the . . . stuff that happened." Why did he feel alternately guilty and sedated by Rosemary's presence?

"I better go to sleep," Alex said, turning toward the general direction he remembered his room to be.

"Yes, good night, and thanks again," Rosemary said, and walked down the stairs.

Suddenly, the last thing Alex felt like doing was going to sleep. He was just glad Captain Odessa hadn't seen any of that.

CHAPTER 13

GEORGE SPELL AND THE SORCERESS

Upon stepping off the elevator platform and seeing Alex Detail's mother, George knew that his other mother, Madeline Spell, had been tricked really good. He remembered months ago listening to his mother tell Brother Lonadoon that Alex Detail's mother had been sending Alex letters and emails for years, letters and emails saying she really wanted to see him, that she missed him. Madeline Spell had told Lonadoon she'd intercepted all of them, and made sure Alex never knew his real mother was trying to contact him. She had said she ordered people to keep Alex's mother away, that she made sure Alex believed his parents never thought about him.

But all along, Brother Lonadoon had known Alex's real mother, and he hadn't said anything about it to Madeline Spell. All this time, they had been fooling her and making her feel bad about taking Alex from his family.

George knew Madeline Spell, leader of the worlds, was smart. Zarena Detail must really be a powerful sorceress in order to fool her.

George's next thought was that Alex's mother had brought him here to kill him. But the first thing Zarena Detail did when George stepped off the elevator was not at all threatening. She held her hand about an inch over the top of his head. She then looked at Brother Lonadoon and said, "No indigo at all, Brother, but do you see the blue? It is very faint."

Brother Lonadoon looked at the space between Zarena's hand and George's head, and squinted. "No, I see nothing. No aura at all, Zarena. Perhaps you should make sure this very bright sunlight has not damaged your inner sight."

Now it was curious to George to see who was more powerful: Brother

Israel Lonadoon, or Zarena Detail? Zarena took Rosemary's hand and instructed George to hold it. "Now, Brother, again, do you see it?" Zarena asked.

"Ah, yes, indeed you are correct, Zarena," Lonadoon said. "It draws from the unprotected." He cast a glance at Rosemary.

Rosemary pulled her hand away. For a moment, George thought it seemed she was afraid.

"Nothing to fear, Rosemary," Zarena said, then handed Rosemary a silver shape. "When you find him, have him correct your mistakes."

Rosemary looked at the shape she was holding. "Mistakes?"

"Don't feel badly, it is beyond most people, even you," Zarena said.

Rosemary nodded, and left with the silver shape.

So, Zarena could see things that Brother Lonadoon could not, and Zarena could see mistakes that the girl Rosemary could not. George was eager to find out what else she could do. "How come my mother doesn't know about you?" George asked.

"The first thing you need to get straight, copy of Alex Detail named George Spell, is that Madeline Spell is not your mother. I am your mother," Zarena said. "As for the person you call your mother, Madeline Spell, the more she grows in power, the less she knows." Zarena motioned George and Lonadoon to follow her.

As they walked, George said, "Sometimes, people have two mothers, you know, like when they are adopted. How come my mother doesn't know about you? If you had had another son, would my regular mother have needed to make me? Or would he have been just like Alex, too? Do you and my mother not like each other? Did you have a fight?"

Zarena had led them to the center of the big room with all the windows. She turned on a big holo and scrolled through some files.

"Can I ask you more questions?" George asked.

Zarena shook some of her long hair away from her face as she worked at the display, and said, "Damn things, they make them so hard to use now. George, sweetheart, I'll answer all the questions you've got, but first we have to get to work on this thing."

That seemed a reasonable reply to George.

Zarena finally found out how to turn on the channel she was looking for. A display appeared. "Finally! Can you tell me what you see in this holo?" Zarena asked.

George assumed she was asking him, so he answered, "That is the ARRAY warship that I used to destroy the Harvester ring ships. Its name is the *Virgin Mother*. That is where I had to kill the man Peevchi Derringkite when he tried to stop me from saving the world."

Zarena touched a yellow circle in the virtual display and reduced the magnification. The image zoomed out. "Now, what else do you see?"

George studied the holo. He had taken many of these types of tests when he first remembered he was him. People were always measuring him, finding out how smart he was. He knew that when he looked at pictures to test his brain, there was usually something that looked one way but it was really another. If you answered too soon, it was usually harder to see what the picture really was. So, George looked at the holo and then realized that what he thought he saw was something else.

George pointed his index finger at what looked like a Reaper vessel face to face with the *Virgin Mother*. "That other ship looks like a Reaper but it's not. It's really the nose of a Poseidon Long Range Reconnaissance Drone modified to look like a Reaper. The shape and mass are an exact match. The modified Poseidon is collecting charged particles from the solar wind and using them to create a Van Allen radiation belt to trap the *Virgin Mother* against the Earth's magnetosphere."

"That's right," Zarena said. She pressed another virtual circle, and an equation appeared. "Can you solve this equation?"

George nodded. "Yup, but there's a variable that I think means there's some really big potential energy in the fake Reaper. The solution would make the radiation belts act like a fuse and make that ship explode. If you take the q-field force out of the equation then all you have to do is push on the ship."

Zarena turned the display off. "It took Alex nine hours to solve that equation."

"So, that means he'll be here in nine hours," George said. "Do you want me to kill him when he gets here?"

"No, of course I don't want you to kill my son!" Zarena scolded him. "Madeline Spell must have the most incompetent geneticists working on you."

George nodded. "They are trying to change things that can't be changed. Why can't I kill Alex here?"

George noticed Brother Lonadoon give Zarena a look that he didn't understand. It was interesting the way people could communicate like that.

Zarena waved a hand. "I am going to explain it to him anyway," she said to Lonadoon. "I don't give a crap about your methods, and I'm not using them on him."

Brother Lonadoon crossed his arms but didn't answer.

"Does my mother know about you?" George asked.

Zarena motioned to a chair, and George sat down. She pulled up another chair facing him and sat. "George Spell, do you understand what you are?"

"I am a modified clone of Alex Detail, constructed to defend the worlds from the Harvesters. My DNA has been modified from the original Alex Detail template, but I don't know how. Do you know more?"

"The only people who know more are Alex Detail, the Generationists, and the person who calls herself your mother, Madeline Spell." Zarena picked up a hand window and turned it on. "But you have never asked your mother for the Generationist research."

George shook his head.

"Why not?"

"Mom would have me killed if she knew I was looking for that," George said.

"Some mother," Zarena said. "So, you understand Madeline Spell knows that if she gave you that information you would be too powerful for her to control—and control is all she's really interested in." Zarena put her hand out and rubbed the side of George's head. "But I am your real mother, and I think you should have it."

Zarena handed George the window.

"Is this the Generationist research?" George asked.

"As much of it as I could get," Zarena said. "It's incomplete. Perhaps only ten percent of the entire file."

Brother Lonadoon lurched toward George to take the window from his hands, but he wasn't quick enough. George was out of his chair and across the room in a second.

"That was very unwise, Zarena," Lonadoon said. "Whatever means you used to obtain that, you are jeopardizing generations of work."

George was quickly reading the information. "Look at him," Zarena was saying. "Look at how he has desire, passion."

"Oh, for heaven's sake, it's simply trying to strengthen itself per its programming," Lonadoon said. "Do get on with it!"

George had read the entire file in under five seconds. It detailed only a small portion of the base pair DNA sequencing acceleration. But there appeared to be a mistake. There were two formulas that governed his growth acceleration. But only one was being used. The other would cause an almost instantaneous cellular retrograde. There was nothing to indicate what would activate that gene.

"You found it already," Zarena said.

George nodded. "Yes, and I want to know how that gene is turned on. It seems stupid to put that in me. What makes it go on?"

Zarena nodded. "Only Madeline Spell knows the answer to that, George. It is how she will end your life if something goes wrong."

"Can you get that information from Mom, without her knowing?" George asked.

"I will try," Zarena said. "But I think if you put your mind to it, you can figure it out for yourself."

George wasn't sure about that. He knew a lot about physics, more than he imagined he could have learned by himself. But he knew very little of biology.

Zarena stood and took George's hand. "Come with me. We have to start working."

The three of them walked toward a wall to the left of the elevator door. The cat jumped up from where it was lying and followed them. Zarena opened a door and flicked on the lights. The room was gigantic, the size of the hangar where they had parked the *UC One* flier. Like the room they had left, it had a wall of windows looking out over the edge of the mountain, but these were opaque. The only light was from lines of hanging utility lamps.

"You know what that is?" Zarena asked.

George nodded.

"My son will be landing on this planet in less than nine hours," Zarena said. "When he gets here, he will sense you, and perhaps me as well. Then, he will find us. I will keep him away for as long as possible. That will be all the time you have, to learn how to use this."

"What do you want me to use it for?" George asked.

"It is the only thing that can destroy the remains of Pluto still orbiting Earth," Zarena said. "It is the only thing that can finally close the door to the Harvester universe and save my son from killing us all."

That made sense, George thought.

In front of him, in the middle of the hangar, was the real Harvester Reaper.

CHAPTER 14

THE CAPTAIN'S CONCISELY CONVINCING CADENCE

Captain Odessa awoke after a good night's sleep: exactly five hours and fifty minutes. Her room was too warm, and sunlight was slicing in through the drawn shades. Five hours and fifty minutes was exactly the amount of time Captain Odessa allotted herself to sleep on any given night, and she regarded anyone who might take seven or eight hours as lazy and lacking in fortitude. The eight hour "first sleep" on Venus seemed remarkably excessive, but then, everything the New Africans did was remarkably excessive.

Odessa opened the window blind and allowed the sunlight to pour into the room. She peered out into the courtyard below, and saw Horace Witaker sitting by the triangular fishpond, eating an apple so large, it took two hands to hold.

One of the reasons Captain Odessa had chosen the young and unproven Horace Witaker as her first officer when she was given commission of the *Cronus* three years ago was that his ARRAY profile indicated he averaged four hours and twenty minutes of sleep. She often found Witaker exercising in the officer's drill hall before anyone else had risen, and she'd made a point of getting to know the young lieutenant. Odessa firmly believed in molding high-performance young officers rather than having to undo all the ingrained habits of older, more seasoned officers.

Horace had worked out perfectly as her executive officer. Though still young, he had gained the respect of his subordinates through his ability to execute Odessa's curt and hasty orders while buffering the more sensitive, longer-sleeping officers from her purportedly stringent command style.

Horace respected authority and revered the chain of command as a true ARRAY officer should. There was a war to be won, after all.

But that had all changed after Horace Witaker had been killed during the Reaper attack on the *Cronus*, stuck in that ridiculous quantum gravity command program Alex Detail had executed. The effects on Horace of surviving death had been compounded by the intoxicating effects of the illusions the Harvesters put in place. And if that hadn't been enough to ruin this perfectly fine officer, there had been the severe emotions everyone had experienced in the first days after the Harvester ships were destroyed. Captain Odessa did not blame herself for allowing the romance between herself and Witaker. Whatever wandering his mind had done after his near-death experience, whatever contagion had taken hold while in that sunny meadow on Pluto, and whatever lingering personal attachments he might still feel toward Odessa, she knew that eventually Witaker would snap out of it. Her finely trained vice captain would once again emerge.

Horace just needed a renewed purpose to reset his mind, and this mission provided the perfect opportunity to get Witaker back on track.

Before going to sleep, Odessa had asked Witaker to meet her in six hours. She was going to need his help. She did not fully trust JuneMary, and did not feel like dealing with Alex Detail's latest flight of treachery or teenage mood swings.

Kelen June was clearly hiding something, and not at all delighted to have the crew of the *Virgin Mother* as guests in her house. Captain Odessa could literally smell the woman's anxiety by the rising levels of fetaxemone Kelen was emitting as her sweet young daughter spoke to Odessa about her studies. The celery they had been served provided the most excellent palate cleansing, allowing Odessa to detect the more subtle female anxiety pheromone. Odessa had registered two clear spikes in Kelen's fetaxemone output—the first when Rosemary said she was late because the busser was running behind, and the second when Rosemary said she'd studied Odessa's command record.

The June family was well known to be deeply involved in the politics of New Africa. They had always aligned themselves with the more isolationist policies of the governing council. That had likely been the reason Speaker Spell had chosen RK June to be her head of intelligence some sixteen years earlier when he was the senior New African council member.

All of RK June's children held influential posts at either the Kade Institute or the University of New Africa, which collectively comprised the academic meritocracy that was the *de facto* governing force behind the New Africa Council. The Junes and the Romes, two of the oldest families on New Africa, had been brought together thirty years ago when Kelen Rome had married RK's youngest son, Jay'r. The Romes were notoriously extreme academics, deeply involved in the cutting edge covert science projects undertaken at the university. Kelen herself was involved in the creation of the project that had created the artificial black hole New Africa had used in its attempt to destroy Pluto.

Odessa didn't think it prudent to do any online investigating from the June house. She had asked Witaker to join her very early that morning so they could pay a visit to the Kade Institute under the guise of meeting with the astrophysicists who had provided them with the eddy current records.

But before going to sleep, Odessa accessed Govnet to check the New Africa busser schedules. While looking for the earliest transport from Oasis South to the Kade Institute, Odessa was able to check the busser logs from earlier in the day. They had all been running on schedule.

That explained Kelen's first anxiety spike. Rosemary had been lying about the late busser, and Kelen knew it.

Odessa, washed and dressed in under one minute, met Witaker in the courtyard, and the two walked the four blocks to the nearest busser exchange. Neither of them spoke for the first few moments of the walk. The sweltering heat of early afternoon on Venus was nearly intolerable even in Oasis, where the 105-degree air was nearly one hundred percent humidity and currently devoid of any wind. Captain Odessa pushed up the back of her tightly bound hair as far from her neck as possible. Had Horace just stolen a glance at her bosom? Most men did, of course. There was already a dark spot of sweat coming through the tight uniform clinging to Horace's broad back. Odessa chided herself for her straying attention. This must be what the hysterical Victorian women of old claimed to be vapors. Odessa finally broke the silence by sharing her suspicions of Kelen June with Witaker.

"Do you think Admiral Detail suspects Kelen was involved with George Spell's kidnapping?" Witaker asked.

Odessa shook her head. "That is difficult to determine. I do not like leaving Alex unattended, but no matter what, his only way out of here is on the *Virgin Mother*. Whatever maddening mischief our little admiral is up to, it's obviously contingent upon him becoming Chief Executive of ARRAY and subsequently being able to commandeer a ship." Odessa paused for a moment, then decided to give Witaker a small loyalty test by saying, "I assume Alex gave you some indication of his intentions when he cut the audio to the drive room."

Witaker nodded slightly. "As you suspected, he wants command access to run one of his programs."

This wasn't news. Odessa waved a hand. It seemed to go slowly through the thick Venusian air. "Alex Detail always travels with those massive half-baked command programs. Did he indicate which one or what it does?"

"No, he just wanted to gauge my willingness to grant him command access," Witaker replied. Little glistening specks of perspiration covered his face, but the air was too thick to sense any changes in his breathing or pheromones. Odessa was regretting her decision not to bring cooling umbrellas.

"And what did you say?" Odessa asked.

"I told him I would follow orders," Witaker replied.

That was too clever a response. *Full of ambiguity*—though whether aimed at herself or Detail, Odessa could not tell. She would just have to make sure if and when the moment came, that Horace remembered where his loyalties lay.

"Well it is up to us to recover George Spell and deal with Detail," Odessa said. "Spell was clear in her last text that she would not be forthcoming with any additional aid to us. Whatever backup plan she has, it must be solid. If George Spell is somehow spirited off this planet before we find him, she is no doubt prepared. But that is one humiliation I will not bear."

They reached the exchange a few blocks from the June house, where a busser stopped and picked them up. It was slightly cooler inside the busser, but not by all that much. As they were the only ones on the transport, Odessa adjusted the temperature controls as low as they could go, which earned her a stern warning beep from the busser. She assumed it was protesting the extra energy use.

Odessa and Horace knew better than to continue their conversation verbally. It was likely that cameras and security microphones were monitoring them. Odessa had hatched a plan to get the info they needed as quickly as possible, so she messaged instructions to Horace's window. The busser sailed silently, suspended above some underground track. It picked up speed, and shot out of the foliage onto the plateau road about half a mile from the exchange. The busser was instantly buffeted by winds, as six articulated wheels extended beneath them and sped along the barren highlands.

Ten minutes later, they arrived at the Kade Institute, a complex of over twenty glass buildings of various polyhedron shapes, part of the oldest structures on Venus. Another busser had arrived just ahead of them, and a number of people exited, but one of them stood under the main entrance awning, perhaps curious to see who was on the other busser so early in the morning.

When Odessa and Witaker exited, they were greeted by a tall, nervous young man, probably not even out of his teens, waiting under the awning.

"Wow, Captain Odessa and Vice Captain Horace Witaker," the young man exclaimed, eagerly shaking their hands. "I heard you were visiting but I can't believe I am meeting you here like this!" He held up his window and said, "Do you mind if I get an image of us?"

Odessa pushed his window out of the way. "I'm sorry, young man, but that is against ARRAY policy."

Apologizing, the embarrassed young man introduced himself as Morstan Talwitz, a student working as an intern at the Kade Institute Geological Society.

"An honorable profession, I am sure," Odessa said. "And yes, we are guests of the Junes, but the time change had us up early. We have business here in the Astrophysics Division, but it would be lovely to meet up with Kelen June after we have finished. Do you know where her office is located?"

Morstan did not know, but he walked them over to a directory and pressed his fingertips to it. After a few taps, he said, "Here it is. Her office is in the Natural Energy Division of the Stellar Cosmology Group."

"Naturally," Odessa said. "And where is that in relation to the Astrophysics Division?"

Morstan pointed to a building toward the center of the complex. "I think they also have offices over there," he said, indicating another building several stories high on the other side of the highway built into the side of the mountain. "You have to take the sub-passways to get over there to the Kade East complex."

As they left Morstan and walked along a covered corridor, Odessa felt a sense of unease. While still very early, there were other people about at the institute, people who clearly recognized the famous Captain Odessa. Whatever advantage she had gained by being the early bird was going to be quickly erased once word got around that she and Witaker were here.

Sure enough, by the time they arrived at the Astrophysics offices, the Senior Director was already waiting for them in the lobby.

The elderly man greeted them and introduced himself as Teddy. "I had no idea you were paying us a visit," Teddy said. "Is Ambassador JuneMary joining us?"

"Yes, but the ambassador is running a bit late," Odessa lied, expertly maintaining her pulse and her breathing, to prevent her thoracic spinal nerves from activating her adrenal medulla. She had a feeling this old fellow could smell a lie a mile away. "She is currently at the June residence with Alex Detail."

Teddy nodded and walked them over to a room. "I can pull up the telemetry data we sent you," he said, "but I will have to wait until you have been issued working clearances before I can allow you on the system."

"We understand," Odessa replied. "Is that a dectamic power collector?" She pointed to an ancient generator sitting outside one of the ground windows.

Teddy smiled, "You are very astute for such a youngster! Most people these days couldn't tell you the difference between a dectamic power collector and a sphericollider!"

Witaker was working on submitting the information to process their working clearances with the Kade Institute, but Odessa tapped him on the arm, indicating that he should hold off while Odessa worked her plan on Teddy.

"It must be nearly fifty years old," Odessa said.

"Just about," Teddy replied. "Lots of changes to this place in the past fifty years."

"Indeed," Odessa replied. "Perhaps you could give us a tour while we wait for the ambassador and admiral to arrive. Are there other models of dectamic power collectors still in use?"

"Indeed," Teddy replied, "Indeed so. Lots of 'em over in Natural Energy."

Odessa sent a text to JuneMary and Alex to come meet them at the Kade Institute when they got up.

Her line of questioning had Teddy bringing them on a tour of exactly what Odessa was looking for. As she was explaining her use of lighting on ARRAY warship bridges to Teddy, they passed by Kelen's office and an adjoining conference room. She was able to get Teddy to look up at the lighting fixtures long enough for her to drop two rain-drop sized spheres, and gently kick them under the doors to both Kelen's office and her conference room.

Having accomplished her mission, Odessa continued on the tour, and she actually began listening to Teddy's narrative.

She wasn't surprised when, twenty minutes later, JuneMary, Alex, and Kelen interrupted their tour.

"Why the hell did you have to get us up so early?" Detail complained upon seeing Odessa.

"You are well aware of my circadian patterns," Odessa replied.

Kelen handed Odessa and Witaker each a small metal strip. "I saw that you had not received your clearances, so I took care of it for you."

"Why, thank you, Kelen," Odessa said. *But it's too late to be giving us your spying devices; I've already bugged your offices*, Odessa thought to herself.

And that's why I'm the Captain.

JuneMary eyed Odessa in an all-knowing manner, while Alex scowled. They both knew she was up to something, but neither said anything. Odessa wondered just how close JuneMary and Kelen were, or were not.

"Well, mother, let's get a-going on that secret telemetry stuff," JuneMary said.

Kelen excused herself, and took Teddy with her, probably to interrogate the old man.

After they parted ways with Kelen and Teddy, JuneMary walked close to Odessa. "You got to be careful here, Captain," JuneMary said. "Showing up here without telling anyone has set off just about the biggest wave of gossip I've seen hit this planet in a dog's age. And people are already suspicious."

Odessa marched them toward their viewing suite in the astrophysics department. "We are on official ARRAY business, Ambassador, and according to the EVM Charter, I seem to recall this planet is under ARRAY's jurisdiction."

JuneMary grunted. "That's what the computers say."

Alex had his usual sour morning look on his face.

"Can you tell anything about where George is?" Odessa asked him.

Alex began rubbing his stomach and looked suddenly nauseated. "No, but I think I ate something bad."

"Nonsense," Odessa replied. "You seldom eat food. However, every time I query you about our quarry, you grow ill. Perhaps your young counterpart has gained some new skills to make you sick whenever you try to locate him."

Alex didn't reply, which indicated to Odessa that she was exactly on the mark.

Once inside the viewing room, Odessa called up the telemetry data, and ordered them to begin isolating particle signatures that could potentially lead to a means of tracking surface movement of anyone who had been on *UC One*.

"JuneMary, can you acquire visual data from the spaceport documenting Innsbrook's flier?" Odessa asked.

"Suppose I could call in a few favors," JuneMary replied. "But whatever you're up to, you better get it done. I hear Old Lady Spell isn't helping out much, and the council is not going to want big bad Captain Odessa poking around for long."

Damn Spell and her subterfuge. Why couldn't she just make a call and have ARRAY sweep the whole damned planet? Politicians had to do everything the most complicated way possible.

They spent the next several hours constructing a resonance program, a tedious task Odessa did not enjoy, particularly with Alex Detail complaining the entire time. Odessa had always been irritated by Detail's high-maintenance temperament and petulant mood swings. In the event that they finally did find George, and did take him back to Earth (assuming he and Alex were able to keep from killing each other), and then if Alex's promotion to Chief Admiral became finalized, Odessa was certain that neither his fame nor his tired hero persona would cover his incompetence for long.

ARRAY was an enormous bureaucracy, but it operated with all the elegant military efficiency of a well-run ship. The other admirals and department chiefs were accustomed to the decisive hard-nosed management style of former Chief Admiral Sevo and other lifetime military officers, who had devoted their entire careers to building a military complex designed to defeat the Harvesters through brute force and numbers. Once Alex Detail was forced to come out of the shadows of his plush science labs—an apartment full of holos and program assemblers—what then? Odessa could just imagine him spending a day dealing with the complex administration of ARRAY. How would he hold up under the constant haranguing by members of various House panels, and the scrutiny of lifelong soldiers turned commanding officers? Well, Alex would be eaten alive after people saw he was just a boy who liked to complain about his upset tummy and his uncomfortable sleep.

It appeared that even the saintly JuneMary was growing annoyed.

"Admiral, why don't you get a little sunlight," JuneMary finally said when Alex complained of a headache. "Nothing does a headache good like a nice face full of hot sun."

Alex looked at JuneMary with an expression best described as confusion mixed with reaction to a bad smell. "That's got to be the worst thing for a headache ever suggested."

"Sunlight is the best medicine," JuneMary replied. "Take a nice walk a couple buildings over, to the Radius Arboretum. Have a big glass of milk, and lay down under the Novus Ordum Pyramid. You'll feel fresh as a just-washed head of hair."

Fortunately for them all, Alex finally went for a walk, leaving them in peace.

Meanwhile, JuneMary had gained access to the spaceport closed-camera system, and obtained a visual record: Innsbrook exiting his flier together with one military officer, before the flier was towed into a hangar. Regulations dictated that at least two officers must pilot an interplanetary ship carrying a head of state. Obviously, any other crew members stayed on the vessel until it was inside the hangar. Not entirely unusual, but certainly logical if Lonadoon and George Spell were on the lander.

Finally, they were able to begin the painstaking process of resonance mapping. It was slow going, and Odessa was getting irritated that Alex had been gone for over an hour. At long last, he returned—in a much better mood. Alex claimed JuneMary's advice had made him feel much better, but Odessa suspected he simply found a bathroom and had a satisfying bowel movement.

The resonance program, finally complete, showed them exactly what they needed.

A vehicle had exited one of the spaceport hangars ten minutes after Innsbrook landed on Venus. The vehicle had driven straight toward the Kade Institute.

Which meant George Spell was very close indeed.

"Eureka," Odessa exclaimed.

Everyone looked at her with odd expressions.

Pursing her lips, Odessa said, "Vice Captain, magnify the last portion of the trail decay. See if you can pinpoint exactly which building that vehicle entered."

Right then, the entire computer system at the Kade Institute crashed.

CHAPTER 15

THE MAGIC AND DANGER OF FIRST SLEEP

Alex Detail was already awake before receiving the text from Captain Odessa requesting that he and JuneMary meet up with her and Witaker at the Kade Institute. He had just experienced the most remarkable six hours of sleep, entirely filled with dreams: colors and swirls, flying, being at large dinners with people and talking to them at great length, taking adventures to planets in other solar systems. It was like he lived five lifetimes during six hours of sleep.

He had woken nearly an hour earlier, just in time to hear Captain Odessa and Horace leaving the house. Normally, he would have wondered what they were up to, but his first instinct upon waking was to run to a mirror. There was a full length one hanging on the back of his bedroom door, and he could immediately see that he was younger. Usually, there was a small crease under his right eye, the side he slept on; the crease was always there when he woke up, and took a couple of hours to go away. Now, there was no sign of it. Had he slept on his back the entire night?

Looking closer, Alex ran his hand along the side of his face. He hadn't used a dermal wand since the morning of his promotion ceremony, and normally he would need to shave after a few days. But the hair on his face was barely visible: too fine and soft to be the beginnings of a beard.

After staring at his face for nearly thirty minutes, Alex ran his hand down his neck and across his chest and stomach. Everything felt newer, stronger, more firm.

There was something else much stranger going on. Alex did not feel like contacting the Harvesters. He did not feel like activating that chip in his thumb and experiencing the rush of super-sentience, the ecstasy he'd been seeking to bring back to all humanity again. He didn't even care about finding George Spell.

The last time Alex had felt like this was on the sunny meadow on Pluto. Well, this feeling was not so full of power and possibility, but it was certainly some sort of heightened awareness coupled with a deep sense of calm.

So, the rumors about Venus were true. *What the hell are these scientists up to here? Is that why Innsbrook and Lonadoon kidnapped George?* Not to stop Alex, but to be some sort of contributing member to whatever crazy science experiment they needed him for?

Alex found JuneMary's bedroom and bolted in without even knocking.

Yellow!

A blast of dazzling yellow light poured through JuneMary's bedroom. Alex squinted into the blazing light while his pupils shrank. How could anyone sleep like this? Every window shade was open, and the room had to be nearly a hundred degrees.

"Alex?" JuneMary said, sitting up in her bed.

"JuneMary," Alex said, shading his eyes. He made his way over to her bed. "Sorry to wake you, but I just had a bunch of dreams that were so detailed they would normally have taken weeks, and my face and body are getting younger. I'm actually getting younger in the way the Generationists promised I would, before they went and made that clone!"

JuneMary stretched her arms and yawned. "Yup, that'll happen to some people here. I told you high noon on Venus was glorious!" Swinging her legs out of bed, JuneMary put on a robe over her rather heavy sleeping gown.

"What do you mean that will happen to some people?" Alex asked. "And JuneMary, it's really hot in here! Aren't you roasting?"

JuneMary waved a hand at Alex then tapped her nightstand. Some cool air began circulating. "Look at you, running around the house in your underwear like a boy on Christmas morning. All it took was a little vacation to someplace warm."

"You don't look surprised at all," Alex said. "What do you mean that will happen to some people? What is up with this place?"

JuneMary was adjusting the blinds, as if any more light could possibly be let in. "I don't know what all we got laced under Oasis besides those thermworks and tripole-magnets and ultrafibers and pyranodes and a thousand other crazy notions people could think up in the past century or so, but when it hits high noon during First Sleep, bam!"

There was a sound in the hallway, and then a voice at the door. "Aunt JuneMary, are you up already?"

Rosemary stood in the doorway squinting into the light.

Realizing that he was actually sitting on JuneMary's bed in his underwear while Rosemary June's eyes adjusted, all Alex could think to do was wave hello.

"Oh, hi, uh, Admiral," Rosemary said, coming into the room.

She was dressed in a light, fitted suit, clearly ready to go to work, or school or whatever it was she did. Her hair was different today, Alex noted. The braid was gone. Instead, her hair was pulled back into a circlet that held it in a flowing tail.

"What are you doing off to work so early?" JuneMary asked. "Aren't there any nice boys around here for you to spend some time with?"

Alex couldn't tell if Rosemary's eyes had adjusted to the bright light, but if they had, she was now close enough to Alex to be able to see that he was blushing. She seemed to be looking down her nose at him, sizing him up somehow, as he sat there feeling like a little kid.

"I guess I got used to being the first one in to work," Rosemary said. "I never could sleep long; you know I take after Dad. Anyway, what was all the excitement I heard in here?"

JuneMary smiled as she tidied up the bed around Alex. "The admiral and I have a lot of catching up to do still! I mean seriously, I think he's more excited to see me than my own family!"

Curious, Alex thought. JuneMary was actually *lying*. JuneMary *never* lied. Never. A sharp chill went up his spine.

"Auntie! That's not true at all," Rosemary protested. "Anyway, you've only been gone for a day, really. Admiral, you look cold."

Alex tried to speak, but JuneMary was in front of him giving Rosemary a big hug and saying, "So, what's on the cooker at work today?"

Rosemary shook her head. "Oh, you know, the usual fifty different things. I better go though, Dad's giving me a ride. Mom's still here, though."

"Well, you have a blessed day, young princess," JuneMary said.

"You too, Auntie," Rosemary said. "Goodbye, Admiral, and thank you for helping me with my project last night."

Oh dear, that doesn't sound good, Alex thought. "Uh, anytime. Bye."

Alex didn't say anything, just watched JuneMary buzzing around her room humming until they heard Rosemary go out the front door.

Alex jumped up and pushed the door half closed. "JuneMary, what in the world is going on here?"

"Hush!" JuneMary said, peering out the half open door. "Of course, you and your big superconducting head couldn't make it through one night without getting caught up in the aether."

"Is that what happened? Because I don't know what that means. Why am I getting younger, and why did you lie to Rosemary just now?"

"That was for your own good," JuneMary said, more sternly than Alex had ever heard her speak. "All I know is that high noon on Venus is said to be revitalizing when you're in First Sleep. Some people feel it more than others. I don't know what causes it, and it ain't none of my business." JuneMary peered out her door again. "But be careful, because Venus is the goddess of love, and this planet can be too much for some to handle. People who get connected to the grid during First Sleep got to watch out. Because the more you go in, the more Venus takes back during Third Sleep."

"Wait a minute," Alex said. "What exactly happened to me?"

"I don't really know any more than that," JuneMary said. "We got a hundred years of people trying to pull some such energy out of this planet, and sometimes someone like you gets caught up in it too much. Doesn't surprise me."

"You're not answering my question," Alex said. "What's going to happen to me during Third Sleep?"

"Oh, nothing too serious, well, that I know about. But I don't have the answers, and it might take you more than a day here to find them. So if I were you, I'd try to get off this planet before you pay the price during Third Sleep. That gives you about fifty hours to find George Spell for mother, and then get out of here."

Alex was looking down at his hand, as if it might be aging again already. What was this price to pay that JuneMary was talking about? Alex had heard rumors about the mystical systems of Venus, of the different crystals in the planet's mantle created by the Radius asteroid impact, and of how everything from the shapes of the buildings to underground waterways were constructed to be in harmony with the planet's intrinsic geometry. But this was not science as he knew it: It was pseudo-science.

Like what he was trying to do with the Harvesters?

No, *his* quest had solid explanations based on physics. Whatever the Venusians had been up to for all these years, apparently there was a good reason they kept their society well-shielded. And JuneMary, for all her gossiping and all-seeing intelligence, wasn't about to start telling tales to someone from off-planet.

For his own good, she had said.

A chime sounded in JuneMary's window. "Well, there you have it," JuneMary said. "Mother's calling us to go meet her."

"I'd rather go back to sleep while it's still midday," Alex said.

"No, you better stay up. Get your stuff and let's go."

"You're not going to tell me why you didn't say anything to Rosemary about my First Sleep?" Alex asked.

"Darn right," JuneMary said. "Here on New Africa, everyone is allowed to go about their own business, and we don't ask questions. Rosemary is still young, and she shouldn't be asking certain questions. Neither should you. So, just keep this to yourself," JuneMary warned him sternly. "Do your business, and get going. Venus is a beautiful planet, like what everyone imagined for the perfect future. But some people have a reaction to the aether, and try to know too much. Then, this planet can be poisonous."

"Some people react to the aether?" Alex asked, puzzled by JuneMary's vagueness. "So, I'm like the Venus equivalent of a werewolf?"

"Well, that's one way to put it if you like," JuneMary said.

"You know, JuneMary, I can see why they made you ambassador," Alex said. "You must just drive them crazy with your circular answers. 'Where'd you get the black hole, Ambassador?' 'Why, there's one story about that, and another.' 'What do you know about the consciousness-altering grid under Oasis?' 'Well, there's one story about that, and another, too.' You're a pro!"

"Well, sometimes you just got to say 'hey'," JuneMary replied. "Can't try to know everything about everything."

Now Alex had gossiped plenty with JuneMary while on the *Cronus*. He knew there was a key to turning on her flow of gossip, and he decided to use it. "Boy, that sister-in-law of yours, Kelen—she wasn't so happy to see you home so soon. What's *that* all about?"

"Don't even go there," JuneMary said, shooting Alex a warning look.

"She's jealous," Alex continued, undeterred. "I've seen jealousy firsthand.

Lots of people are jealous of me, and I can tell that Kelen is definitely jealous of you."

JuneMary had crossed her arms and was frowning deeply at Alex. But, he noted, she didn't tell him to stop talking.

Alex paced a bit, probably looking silly walking around her bedroom in his underwear, tapping a finger on his forehead. "Now let's see, what could she be jealous of . . . big sister-in-law taking attention from her husband . . . no, that's not it. Pretty daughter spoiled by her famous auntie . . . no, that's not it." Suddenly, Alex stopped, like an actor playing the role of a very obvious detective. "By golly, that's it—you got famous during the war and they made you ambassador instead of her! She was up for it, wasn't she?"

"How many times do I have to tell you to keep your voice down?" JuneMary said. "A voice can carry powerful across that courtyard." She smirked in a conspiratorial way and whispered, "And darn good thing they kept Kelen out of that post, for now. Last thing we need is the Rome family pushing secession with the House of Nations."

"Secession?" Alex asked. "Is that even possible?"

"Not unless New Africa is willing to go make some big threat, which some here *are*," JuneMary said. "But don't worry about that, I got it all under control for the time being. Come on, go get ready. I'm sure Kelen will be happy to come with us to the Kade Institute when she hears mother and the vice captain are there."

As Alex was getting up to leave, JuneMary said. "And one last thing, Admiral, if I were you, I definitely wouldn't go poking around Kelen's files. Don't know that you could, even with your big brain and admiral's clearance, but I sure wouldn't try it. Just like you never broke into Captain Odessa's files on the *Cronus*."

Huh! *Just like* you *broke into Captain Odessa's files, too, JuneMary, and never told anyone until* I *did.*

So, it's Ambassador JuneMary vs. Kelen Rome June, Alex thought. Well, if JuneMary needs my help, she's going to get my help.

This was one feud he wouldn't miss for the world.

CHAPTER 16

ANCIENT CONSPIRACIES IN NEW AFRICA

After Kelen drove JuneMary and Alex to the Kade Institute to meet up with Captain Odessa and Horace Witaker, Alex began his whole sick and irritable routine. He needed an excuse to get away from the group, so he could go poke around and find out what Kelen was up to. Hopefully, JuneMary would take the hint and give him a clue to aim him in the right direction. Alex carried on about his upset stomach and terrible headache for almost two hours. He felt he was pouring it on a little heavy. He was even beginning to irritate himself with his whining, when JuneMary *finally* suggested Alex take a walk to the Radius Arboretum to get that *"face full of sunshine."*

Alex took the clue as he left the viewing room. *But why would JuneMary suggest I go to such a public place?* Alex wondered, as he strolled the brightly lit corridors of the Kade Institute. There were a lot of people milling around, and many of them clearly recognized Alex—which wasn't surprising, since news of his presence in New Africa was the top story wherever he looked. It wasn't clear if the people working at the Kade Institute were polite or suspicious, as they mostly smiled and nodded when Alex walked past them. No one stopped to get his image or ask to take a holo with him. Alex had read a number of stories in his window on the short drive to the Kade Institute. There was a lot of speculation as to why the ARRAY ship full of war heroes had arrived on Venus with no advance notice, and why it came on the heels of an official visit by the President of the United Countries of America, Jonathan Innsbrook.

But the news stories said things like, "The visiting ARRAY war heroes may potentially be creating an opportunity for the greater assemblies to consider alternative variables." There was no overt talk of secession, or references to conspiracies or differing political views in the government of New Africa. Alex suspected the newsgroup language was something between a local dialect and a code that would read to most off-worlders as the convoluted musings of elite scientists.

A directory showed Alex's current location and the route to the arboretum. Alex walked from the main lobby of the building he was crossing through, and into a passage that sloped down slightly, lit only by small windows in the ceiling. The walls and floor were a shiny orange tile that he imagined must have been fashioned from the Venusian ground nearby. The passage continued to dip until it was mostly underground, and the air was noticeably cooler by a few degrees. A plaque on the wall identified the tunnel as one of the first built, over a hundred years old, originally connecting the first ground-based shelters.

Not much interested in this bit of history, Alex hurried to the end of the tunnel, which opened into a bright, pyramid-shaped atrium that looked like the ancient glass structure attached to the Louvre museum. He guessed it was easily three hundred feet tall, and had lush paths of palm trees and exotic flowers. It reminded Alex of a shopping mall.

And it was hot. Whatever JuneMary wanted him to find in here, Alex hoped it didn't take too long. Odessa would probably call for him in less than an hour, and he didn't want to show up sweating, having to answer the requisite interrogation that would undoubtedly follow his mysterious absence.

A glistening, sparkling light was coming from the center of the atrium, reflected off the building's interior apex. Making his way toward the center, Alex expected to find a fountain or pool of water, but instead he found a gold pyramid, about thirty feet high.

It was the capstone to the Great Pyramid of Giza.

Well, not *the* capstone of the Great Pyramid. Rather, the capstone placed on the great pyramid during the year 2100 New Year's celebration.

Hundreds of years ago, travelers to the town of Giza in the former country of Egypt would visit the site of the ancient pyramids. Upon close inspection, those travelers could see that the Great Pyramid was missing its top stone, and that at the summit of the pyramid was a flat area about thirty feet by thirty. It wasn't known whether there had ever been a capstone. The oldest written records from visitors, as early as nearly 500 BC, indicated the absence of a capstone. Still, that was a good two thousand years after the pyramid's completion. It was likely that the original capstone had been made of soft limestone covered with a layer of polished gold, which would have been destroyed by the weather and occasional earthquakes over time—that is, if it escaped some of the earliest looters on Earth.

Whatever the case, the Great Pyramid of Giza had gone without a capstone for most of its five thousand year existence. A capstone had been planned to be put in place temporarily during the year 2000 New Year's celebration, but due to worries about everything from damage to the pyramid to terrorist attacks to all manner of conspiracy theories, the cap was never installed.

It wasn't until one hundred years later that a capstone constructed of a lightweight polished concrete covered with weatherproof gold plate was airlifted into place at 12:01 a.m. on January 1, 2100.

In the year 2200, when the African Federation granted autonomy to New Africa, an enormous celebration was held, and as part of its many highly symbolic ceremonies, the capstone from the Great Pyramid of Giza was removed and placed on the highest point of Venus—the summit of the mountain, Maxwell Montes, the place Alex Detail was currently standing.

Alex noticed a small plaque at the base of the pyramid capstone. It read: *Gift of Kofi C. and Elizabeth J. Rome, the Galactic Alignment Society.*

Alex pulled out his window and did a search on the names. It turned out Kofi and Elizabeth were Kelen's grandparents, both deceased some forty years earlier at the ages of 130 and 145 years of age respectively. They had been responsible for negotiating with the House of Nations to relocate the Giza pyramid capstone, pay for its transportation, and fund the construction of a new capstone to replace this one on top of the Giza pyramid back on Earth.

Alex wasn't about to query his window for a history of the Galactic Alignment Society, as online activity by his window was likely being monitored. But he had a good idea what the Galactic Alignment Society might be. There were a lot of pagan traditions that calculated the alignment of the earth and sun with the center of the Milky Way Galaxy. Many had been blown up to monumental cult theories way back in 2012, when the Mayan Calendar was erroneously interpreted as predicting the end of the world on the 2012 winter solstice. While the world didn't end, there was a lot of debate as to what exactly constituted alignment with the galactic center.

So what? The Romes were superstitious, big deal. That wasn't much of a lead, thank you very much, JuneMary.

It was mid-afternoon of the nearly 36-hour daylight period of Venus, and the slow-moving sun hung nearly forty-five degrees above the horizon, blasting directly into the atrium onto Alex, making him break out in a full sweat.

So much for the therapeutic effects of a face full of sunshine, JuneMary.

Alex walked around to the other side of the pyramid to cool off in the long shadow of its shaded side. It was there he noticed another plaque.

For some reason its inscription was written in Latin, but Alex was able to use his window to translate. It read: *May the All-Seeing Eye behold its antipode on the shores of Venus.*

Why did the term "All-Seeing Eye" sound familiar? Alex wondered. He was able to use the isolated omnipedia function on his window to do some research.

The first thing that came up was the Great Seal of the United Countries of America, adopted from the one used by the former United States. The seal depicted a pyramid, with the top portion, its capstone, floating above the base. There was a large eye in the center of the floating capstone surrounded by rays of light. The omnipedia article noted that the eye was also known as the Eye of Providence and in Egyptian mythology as the Eye of Horus.

How ironic, Alex thought. He'd have to tell Vice Captain Horace Witaker that he was named after a giant eyeball.

Alex read the plaque again.

May the All-Seeing Eye behold its antipode on the shores of Venus.

Antipode? It was curious Alex was running into that concept for a second time in as many days.

An antipodal point: the location on a sphere diametrically opposite another point. The previous morning, when Alex realized that George Spell had released a lethal particle from the Harvester chip in his thumb as he shook his hand, Alex had calculated his position in the planetarium at that exact time, as well as the antipode to formulate a model to predict when the particle would impact with his thumb.

So if the All-Seeing Eye was represented by the capstone of the pyramid, then what was its antipode?

Alex called up a map of Venus and calculated the antipode of his current location. It was a rather featureless basin in the southern hemisphere of Venus.

There was nothing there, though the satellite picture was probably over a year old. No one lived on any other place on Venus other than New Africa.

What if the antipode referred to Earth? What was the point on Earth exactly opposite the Great Pyramid of Giza?

Alex replaced his map of Venus with one of Earth and ran the calculations. The antipode of the Great Pyramid of Giza corresponded to the middle of nowhere in the South Pacific Ocean. There was nothing there.

Well, there was one volcanic island close by, but not really near the coordinates of the Great Pyramid of Giza's antipode.

But the pyramid was built over five thousand years earlier. Alex programmed in the time period and directed his hand window to account for five thousand years of tectonic shift.

In the center of his display, right on top of the coordinates of the antipode was an island.

Easter Island.

The one with all the big head statues. This was getting interesting.

So, JuneMary had sent him here to find out all this stuff. Stuff she already knew but couldn't talk about, or wouldn't talk about because of whatever Venus code these people obeyed that kept them from meddling with whatever they were all up to. What did this have to do with Kelen and why JuneMary was glad to keep her from becoming Ambassador?

Whatever the reason, Kelen was obviously deeply involved with a faction of Venus that had created the black hole they used to attempt to destroy Pluto. Maybe they were not being such great House of Nations patriots back six months ago when they produced that black hole, a violation of the charter of rules that were strictly enforced by the House and ARRAY. Maybe the presence of Pluto and the Harvesters had threatened more than their lives? Perhaps Kelen's faction of the New Africa government had been willing to go public with the illegal singularity and tarnish their good standing and independence for some bigger reason.

Alex wondered what the penalty was for such a huge violation of the law. Madeline Spell and the House of Nations were likely threatening the installation of independent inspectors to police the Kade Institute, and it was ironic that now Ambassador JuneMary was the diplomat currently engaged in the interplanetary relations surrounding the trouble New Africa was currently dealing with.

Alex decided it was time to use his position to open up an ARRAY reserved broadcast spectrum frequency from his window. ARRAY had very few installations on Venus, and Alex wondered just how long the proprietary communications buoys orbiting the planet would be allowed to continue operational now that the war was over. He was able to establish a connection, but the data bandwidth was so small it would take hours to download so much as a hundred words of text.

Fortunately, Alex had written most of the software on the satellites that relayed two-dimensional mobius communications, and he was able to put the m-com program into hibernation and open up some bandwidth.

The first thing Alex did was connect to the computer in his office back in New York. Its artificial intelligence would be able to covertly collect data undetected from the ARRAY house computers. Once that was done, Alex found the information he needed on Easter Island. Curiously, although the island was in the middle of nowhere in the South Pacific Ocean, it was classified as a territory of the South American continent, having been annexed by the country of Chile in 1888. As such, Easter Island was part of the United Countries of America, and therefore under the jurisdiction of President Jonathan Innsbrook.

The information Alex's computer sent included one news account of a recent archeological excavation a month ago, apparently the conclusion of some project that had been discontinued shortly before the Second Harvester War began.

There weren't any other public articles on the project, which was probably a trivial matter to most of the planet in the midst of global war recovery, but Alex had a hunch this was no coincidence. He sorted through flight plans and discovered that some very large object had been removed from the island just two weeks ago and transported to a museum in Buenos Aires.

May the All-Seeing Eye behold its antipode on the shores of Venus.

Apparently that prophecy was coming true, as Alex suspected that George Spell wasn't the only thing President Innsbrook was transporting on *UC One.*

It didn't take long for Alex to check the more public Venus transport logs that existed before the Second Harvester War. Following the first war, there had been several notable artifact shipments to Venus. They were listed under benign headers like, *North Altar Steps, Machu Picchu, Vault Casing, Chichen Itza, Interior Duct Column, Petra,* and a dozen others.

Alex wanted to use his connection to access a live resolution satellite in orbit around Venus, but that would likely set off some alarm. Instead, he found high-resolution images of Venus from the past several years. Using his current location at the summit of Maxwell Montes as the Venusian equivalent of the Great Pyramid of Giza, Alex superimposed the locations of the other Earth monument locations onto the surface of Venus, projecting their coordinates on Venus if they were placed on the planet relative to their locations on Earth.

Nearly ten thousand miles southwest of his current location, there was a cultivated area of land in the middle of untouched Venus surface. In the center of it stood a small gray pyramid. *The Venusian equivalent of Machu Picchu.* And just a few hundred miles from his present location stood a lone red column. *Petra.*

Alex called up locations across the entire planet, and found everything from replicas of Stonehenge to sites that corresponded to the pyramids of the Americas.

Finally, Alex called up the newest picture of his exact opposite location on the other side of Venus. The image was almost a year old, but once he zoomed in, he could make out a cleared area of land and a solid platform.

He was pretty certain that at that moment, whatever had been taken from Easter Island and transported on Innsbrook's shuttle was located on that platform on the other side of Venus.

So, apparently someone or some group was replicating all of Earth's ancient monuments on proximate locations on Venus. It didn't seem a very sinister plot, more like the eccentric hobby of someone with an archeological fetish, willing to trade favors with local Earth governments in exchange for harmless artifacts. But for what purpose? It certainly wasn't being done publicly; it wasn't some sort of tourist attraction on a planet that disdained outsiders.

But JuneMary knew about it, which was why she sent him here.

I definitely wouldn't go poking around Kelen's files, JuneMary had said.

Alex wondered what favor Kelen had traded with Innsbrook to get him to deliver the artifact from Easter Island, the apparent last piece of the project started by her grandparents sixty years earlier when they laid the capstone of the Great Pyramid at this very location.

Alex saved the file to his device then disconnected the line. It wouldn't do to have someone find out about the ARRAY channel. But just as he was closing out of his ARRAY application, his window displayed a message:

Spydrop network detected. Do you wish to connect?

Spydrop network? Those were top secret ARRAY devices, first developed to see inside a Reaper on the chance that ARRAY was ever able to penetrate the alien ships' hulls. Spydrops were small spheres the size of a pinhead, coated in an ultrathin human-made element called Cargyros-80, a combination of carbon and mercury that made the spydrop invisible to any visual or electromagnetic detection. The interior housed a camera that floated in a liquid electronic solution that allowed a 360-degree view and full spectral transmission of light and sound. They were very hard to come by, as only twenty had been successfully manufactured.

So *that* was what Odessa was up to, getting here so early.

You bet I wish to connect, Alex said to himself, and activated the connection.

Two fisheye image streams opened in his window. One was an empty conference room. The other was Kelen June, sitting at the desk in her office. She appeared to be talking to someone, though there wasn't anyone else in the room and Alex couldn't hear what she was saying. She was on the phone, and the lack of sound indicated there was an active audio mute in her office. Alex wondered if it would go off when she hung up the phone.

Alex zoomed in on Kelen's desk display, trying to see if he could find the display bar that would indicate the communication frequency modulation she used. Unfortunately, her display was polarized and therefore unreadable.

Boy, she sure took all the necessary precautions. This lady was good, and defiantly keeping whatever she was working on private.

Kelen looked up, then said something and ended her phone call.

Rosemary walked into her office. Despite the poor quality image, a more vivid picture of Rosemary's smooth skin against her night dress popped into Alex's thoughts.

Kelen said, "Rosema . . . sweethear . . . you. . ."

The phone audio-mute had been deactivated, but there was some other sort of dampening field interfering with the audio, and Alex could only catch a word here and there through the static.

Alex routed the audio through an enhancer function, and his window was able to clean up some of the sound. Now Rosemary was talking. ". . . let me go back . . ."

More static, then Kelen's voice, "Protect us . . . held up our part of . . ."

Now Rosemary was talking, but the sound had cut out completely. Alex strained to try to read her lips, but the visual distortion made the picture slightly blurred. The picture was only clear enough to see that whatever she was talking about, Rosemary was growing more and more upset. She seemed to be talking faster and at one point threw up her arms in frustration.

Kelen was now standing, and it looked like she was about to hug Rosemary, but instead she put her hands firmly on her daughter's arms and seemed to say something very stern.

Rosemary seemed to sigh, nodded, then walked around her mother's desk to look out the window. Alex could make out the tops of palm trees against some fast-moving clouds on the horizon. The sun was casting an orange-gold color on everything, making the landscape look like it was on fire.

Kelen was talking again, and Rosemary turned, then sat on the edge of the desk. Something about that caused the spydrop to pick up the audio again. Alex caught the end of a question Rosemary was asking, ". . . safe?"

"The only place . . ." Kelen said, before the sound dropped out. Then Alex caught three more words from Kelen, ". . . extinction level event."

That was the end of their conversation. The two hugged. Rosemary turned to leave, but spun around on her heel.

Alex saw a swirl of office furniture just before his window display went black.

It took Alex a few minutes to realize that the spydrop had been kicked up by Rosemary's turn, and landed in her shoe like a grain of sand.

Eavesdropping can quickly become addictive. Alex knew that having access to someone's personal conversations would increase dopamine output in a pattern similar to that of the brain's reaction to intermittent winning during gambling. It was a high, and Alex understood the psychology of it, which was why he allowed himself to continue to try to pick up some bit of word or sound even though the spydrop was muffled inside Rosemary's shoe. Wherever she was heading, there were too many different disturbance fields to adjust to, and it wouldn't have mattered. Alex wasn't going to be able to hear anything, let alone see anything, with the spydrop hidden in Rosemary's shoe.

Alex sat there at the base of the Giza pyramid capstone. He had just gotten a ton of information and none of it amounted to anything; he was no closer to finding George Spell. He had discovered a global network of tourist attractions, and overheard a fraction of a conversation between Kelen and

Rosemary—thanks to Odessa having planted the spydrops. Kelen had mentioned "extinction level event" and "only safe place"—and Rosemary had grown agitated then calm enough to hug her mother on her way out.

Whatever it all added up to, Alex had completely failed JuneMary. There was no way he could even attempt to break into the Kade Institute core without his usual bag of tricks at hand.

And if there was some clue here as to what had happened to cause him to have such intense dreams and to reverse his aging process, he didn't much care anymore. The effect had completely worn off. He was suddenly feeling old, tired, and irritated, not to mention incredibly thirsty.

George was here somewhere, still fully shielding his thoughts from Alex. That was more aggravating than anything. Alex and George always had access to each other's minds, like pulling aside a curtain with another person standing on the other side. You just pull the curtain back.

But now, other than the sense that George was just on the other side of that curtain, close by, George had managed to keep up the tight shielding on his mind for longer than he ever had before. Alex worried that it might be more than the strange energy fields on Venus. Someone on this planet had been able to make a Reaper disappear, construct a near-perfect duplicate, and load it with enough bells and whistles to obstruct the *Virgin Mother* and delay their arrival. Alex was pretty sure Brother Lonadoon wasn't up to that, which meant someone else was aiding George—someone who could be a larger adversary.

Alex contemplated all these things as he wandered through the arboretum trails. Suddenly, he heard someone crying. He stopped, and saw Rosemary sitting on a bench nearby, tears streaming down her face as she stared off into the trees.

"Rosemary?" Alex said.

Turning her head, she saw who it was, and wiped her face with the backs of her hands. Apparently, her conversation with Kelen had been more upsetting than Alex had been able to tell through the spydrop.

"Oh, hi, Admiral Alex," Rosemary said, trying to smile.

What were you supposed to do with a crying girl? She looked so sad behind her fake smile. "Is everything okay?" Alex asked, instantly regretting such a stupid question. "Um, that's a stupid question," he said before Rosemary could answer. "Of course everything's not all right."

Rosemary smiled again, this time for real. "Really, everything is fine. I just . . ." Her eyes welled up and she looked away, suppressing another wave of grief.

Alex sat on the bench beside her. She was wiping her face with the back of the same hand that held her window, and Alex noticed her tears had mixed with some glittery makeup, creating a glistening drip on the window display.

Rosemary successfully held back more tears, and looked at Alex with an embarrassed expression. "I guess I wouldn't make a very good famous war hero, crying like this."

War hero? Famous? So Rosemary had let her wall down, calling him a famous war hero. She must really be shaken by something. "Oh, well, you should see Captain Odessa. Constantly in tears."

Rosemary laughed and dropped her window. Alex caught it as it slipped from her hand. He gave it back, making sure she had a firm grip on it.

She pulled the window close to herself and said, "I was just talking to my mother, and all of a sudden it was like all the stress of life, and research, and expectations, just overwhelmed me. I mean, I never cry."

Alex wanted to say something comforting—like that he himself sometimes cried—but that wouldn't be true. In fact, he couldn't remember the last time he'd cried.

"I mean, this is what happens when we stop to think," Rosemary said. "We stop *doing*, and start *thinking* too much. The next think you know, you're crying in front of Alex Detail."

"Yeah, I think that's probably why I never cry," Alex said. "Boy, if I ever start, it's going to be like, a year straight, of crying."

"I can only imagine." Rosemary patted the back of her hair, pulling herself together. "I mean, I can't really imagine what you've been through your whole life. How do you deal with it? Do you just get used to it?"

Alex shook his head. "I'm sure you've heard . . . things about me . . . well, I keep my mind pretty tied up as much as I can, you know, like you said: Keep doing things so I don't think too much."

Rosemary was staring intensely at him now. She looked in his eyes as if she saw something she recognized.

Apparently realizing she was staring a little too closely, Rosemary abruptly stood up. "I had better get back to work."

Alex stood too, and gave a slight nod.

"And thank you for, well, helping me." Rosemary gave Alex a kiss on his cheek. Before she could move her head away, Alex turned to face her. Their lips brushed.

Rosemary's lips felt soft and warm, moist on one side from her tears. She looked down, blushing. Then she smiled quickly, and walked away.

Alex felt a rush of overlapping emotions. Two emotions, both very pleasant, were mixing within him. Alex was feeling a blissful lightness—something about sitting there with Rosemary had simply made him happy. But he was feeling another emotion: a shameful delight.

Shameful, because he shouldn't be enjoying the other emotion, the bliss.

And yet he was, because as he played back the scene in his memory, the glittery trail of tears that had streaked across Rosemary's window display led past the following characters: K R J 535.6 MHz.

Rosemary had just accidentally given Alex the frequency Kelen June used for communications.

Is it wrong to use ill-gotten information from a crying girl to break into her mother's files? Alex wondered, as he used the ill-gotten information to break into Kelen's files. He didn't have time to truly ponder the question because he had to work quickly. Kelen very likely automatically modulated her communications frequencies, so it was possible this one could change at any moment.

Then, there was the business of figuring out a way to decrypt her password. The communications frequency was only a way to locate her dedicated quantum-random-access files. If it wasn't actual data being moved, like sound over a phone or images in a holo, then it would be stored in a protected archive.

Passwords were a bit of a hobby for Alex, as they came with certain psychological pathologies. Some people used nostalgic things for passwords, like combinations of pet names or significant dates, usually birthdates. George Spell had gotten into Alex's dreams at one point, and was able to uncover his ARRAY command password based on the first letters of the names of his boyhood friends, who had appeared in the dream.

Some people used more random and meaningless series of letters and numbers for passwords, thinking they offered more protection. They were wrong. Such passwords were usually so complex, the people that used them seldom changed them, and the constant heavy use left traces of wear that could be more easily detected. Furthermore, once a small part of the password was discovered, it was usually easier to figure out the rest, because people followed universal patterns they weren't aware of. So, for Alex, figuring out passwords was no more complicated than doing a card trick, one in which the person drawing the cards was amazed by the magician's apparent ability to read minds.

It took Alex only a few moments to uncover Kelen's password, an obvious combination of family initials and dates.

Unfortunately, Kelen was better at changing her communications frequency than her password, as Alex was only able to use the decryption on files stored into memory on the 535.6 megahertz frequency. It appeared Kelen had about forty frequencies assigned to her, each set randomly every 72.1 hours.

Unable to spend the time to go back and download every file stored under the frequency he had obtained, Alex quickly took a snapshot of data created by Kelen in the past 72.1 hours and did a quick search.

The data contained communications with President Innsbrook.

That was all Alex needed. He would sort through the files later, but right now he needed to disconnect from Kelen's processing area and get back to helping Captain Odessa and the others. He had been gone for over an hour.

After copying her saved files, Alex took a quick look at what Kelen was working on that very moment. It was a directory called *Dream Induction Viewer*, tagged with a time index from six hours ago. Alex looked at the series of images moving through the holo on Kelen's desk. Strange images, seemingly from the point of view of someone climbing onto a tree branch.

The images displayed abstractly, like those of a person dreaming.

The tree is very high above a vast sunny meadow. There are no hills or clouds in sight. The person keeps going out farther along the tree branch. Some tigers and goats appear in the distance. The person goes out farther still, then suddenly falls, but grabs a large ring, and hangs on. The picture zooms back, showing a young man in a patchwork ARRAY uniform swinging from the disks of the planet Saturn.

Then it hit Alex. *Those are my dreams!* From last night.

So, *that* was a *dream induction*. That's why he'd experienced such a vivid and lively sleep. There was probably something in his bedroom in the June home that kept him asleep while stimulating portions of his brain related to recently stored memories and experiences: pulling up his recurring dream of being in the sunny meadow outside of Derringkite's house on Pluto; digging into his old phobias about aging; ferreting out the promises of eternal youth from his years working with the Generationists.

And Alex remembered what he had dreamed next: a vivid dream about the rings of Saturn. It was a visual representation of the unfolding of his plan to exact his revenge on the Harvesters—to steal their single-point consciousness and anchor it in this universe.

He had to shut this down. But how? He didn't have an invasive program that could be uploaded to corrupt Kelen's files. He couldn't even so much as cut off the power to her active display.

How could these people do this to him? How dared they go into his head and just invade him like that, teasing out his most private thoughts, activating areas of his mind to cause psychosomatic symptoms of having grown younger, until he ran around the house in his underwear, like a fool.

Alex grew so furious, he had the urge to storm into Kelen's office and smash her desk with his bare hands. But that wouldn't be wise. Someone had once told Alex: *"When you are experiencing success, you will overestimate your abilities, so be cautious. And when you are experiencing failure, you will underestimate your abilities, so aim higher. But when you are angry, you will overreact, so do nothing."*

But Alex had to do something.

That's when it came to him: A highly complex pattern that kept folding in on itself. Just release it into the Kade Institute ethernet, and it would be processed; it would uncap base files and cause a domino effect of file destruction, eventually crashing the entire system.

The shape was a gift from the Harvesters. They were protecting their asset, and they didn't like people taking these particular images from Alex's mind any more than he did. It was a threat to them. But if the Harvesters had the ability to see what he planned, to understand the images Kelen was seeing, then they would know Alex Detail was actually their greatest threat. Had Alex underestimated his ability to control the Harvesters? Had he grown so overconfident that he was becoming a mindless instrument like Peevchi Deringkite had become?

Overcome with anger, Alex was unable to follow his own advice not to act. He was unable to stop himself from using the destructive power the Harvesters had just handed him.

Alex created the paradox shape, uploaded it to the Kade ethernet, disconnected, then started walking back to the room where his little adventure had started just an hour earlier.

CHAPTER 17

THE DARK THINGS ON VENUS

It took nearly half an hour for Alex's Harvester-supplied irregular quaternion shape paradox to completely destroy the entire computer system at the Kade Institute.

He walked back to the viewing room and found Captain Odessa, Vice Captain Horace Witaker, and JuneMary all hard at work mapping the resonance trails left by the occupants of Innsbrook's ship.

As he entered the room and saw JuneMary working with her portion of the mapping project, it occurred to him that she must have pulled some fairly heavy strings to have gotten the Kade Institute to send them this file. Given the machinations, scheming, and distrust going on in this seemingly idyllic government, and given the apparent extremely powerful influence Kelen June wielded, JuneMary must have known the Kade Institute would send them incorrect or falsified information about the eddy currents.

Whatever faction of the government Kelen Rome June controlled had not only built a fake Reaper to delay their trip, it had also worked hard to throw off any rescue mission of George Spell by feeding false data to the rescue crew.

That explained why Kelen was so surprised and alarmed by their arrival on the planet. They were there far sooner than anyone had counted on.

So, what had JuneMary done in Madeline Spell's war room to obtain the *real* eddy current files from the Kade Institute? Her father, RK June, had also been in the room. Clearly, the information contained in the real files must not fall into the wrong hands—namely Kelen's. If it ever did, both RK and JuneMary could find their powerful positions seriously jeopardized.

Well, JuneMary didn't have to worry about that anymore. Within moments of releasing his malevolent attack on Kelen's files, the Kade Institute quantum-computing core stopped functioning properly. The effects spread to other systems until finally, every display and holo went dead. The power system failed, leaving them in the late afternoon sunlight and suddenly hot unconditioned indoor air.

The entire Kade Institute complex of ten buildings and over seventy thousand people was forced to evacuate.

Alex wasn't thinking clearly while the throngs of people were ushered out of the building. He didn't pay much attention to Odessa's virulent condemnation of their improper facilities. He just kept thinking about Kelen looking into a holo of his dream, and for some reason wondering if Rosemary had been in on it.

They arrived back at the June residence to find Jay'r waiting for them.

"I just spoke to Kelen," Jay'r said. "She told me about the system crash. Never heard of anything like that. Said she would probably be pulling an all-nighter helping to find out what went wrong."

"Is Rosemary still there?" Alex asked.

Jay'r gave him a quizzical look. "Why would Rosemary be there? She's working her assistant lab classes at the university."

Either Jay'r was a very good liar, or he was truly clueless about his wife and daughter's scheming. Alex guessed the latter. Otherwise, Odessa would have sniffed out the lie and called him on it.

Alex didn't find anything in his bedroom that looked suspicious enough to be the dream inducer. He suspected such a thing would likely be accomplished by some activation of all the underground gridworks JuneMary had told him about. It was unlikely there was anywhere in Oasis he could sleep without being monitored. Not that it mattered now. The destruction of the Kade Institute system was absolute. They wouldn't be processing House of Nation tax receipts any time soon, let alone dreams.

As the sun began its slow decent below the horizon, Alex sat in the gloomy solitude of his room. He was mad at himself for a lot of things. He'd been complacent, so complacent he'd thought he could land on Venus, quickly snap up George Spell, and be back to Earth easily. He'd let his guard down so far, he'd failed to consider the probable incursion on his mind and take steps to prevent it. And it bothered him that the Harvesters seemed to know what he was up to, yet continued to help him. Most of all, he was angry that so much of his attention was being taken by thoughts of the beautiful, smart girl he'd helped with a lab project in the hallway the night before, the girl he'd comforted after her anguish earlier in the day.

A quiet tap sounded on his door, then JuneMary let herself in. "Quite a complicated little planet we got here," she said.

Alex nodded. That was an understatement.

"They could have gotten to you anywhere on this planet," JuneMary said, patting Alex on the shoulder. "What you got in your brain is like gold to them."

"Is that what they're doing to George, too?" Alex asked. "Putting him to sleep and sucking everything out of his brain? Obviously, that's why I can't pull up his thoughts."

JuneMary didn't answer. She knew that just about any malfeasance was possible on this tricky planet, and all the warnings in the world would do no good. She was probably surprised he could be so vulnerable and naïve. What a foolish sight he must have been, running into her bedroom this morning all full of wonder, like a kid telling his mom he was just visited by the tooth fairy.

"I found all the monuments they're placing all over the planet," Alex said. "You know they just put up one from Easter Island on the other side of the planet?"

"Uh huh, Dad had just pieced that info together before we went to the planetarium," JuneMary said. "That's why he and I got to our people inside the Kade Institute and got back out here as soon as possible."

"What are they doing all that for?" Alex asked.

"Well, most of the people involved in that think it's our rightful place in the solar system," JuneMary said. "They believe life was meant to evolve here, and they think we need to transpose the historical monuments here, like all history happened on this planet."

"That's a stupid reason to come up with dangerous science experiments and sell them to Earth," Alex said.

Shrugging, JuneMary said, "One person's stupidity is another's dream."

"You think it's more than some history zealots?" Alex asked.

"Any world that depends on ARRAY for its defense is always bound to the House of Nations," JuneMary said. "They're messing around with some other sort of power to make a point."

Alex called up the Kelen June files he had managed to save to his window. The first file he queued up for decryption was complete. As he scanned it, he indicated to JuneMary to port her window with his so they could securely exchange files.

"I think you'll want to keep a copy of this one," Alex said.

It was a diplomatic agreement between the nation of New Africa and the United Countries of America, authenticated and sealed just one week earlier.

The undersigned parties hereby agree to the following:

1.The United Countries of America will obtain the Neverstruck Triangles from the pacific quarry of Easter Island, obtain clear title from the governing municipality, transport the Neverstruck Triangles to Venus, and transfer all titles and rights to New Africa's Galactic Alignment Society.

2. On behalf of the nation of New Africa, sanction shall be granted to the United Countries of America Chief Executive *et al,* in the event Earth is threatened by an extinction level event.

3. In exchange for recognizing secession right of New Africa from the House of Nations, New Africa will recognize reciprocal rights of secession for the United Countries of America, and will coordinate to form a new governing body, with immediate annexation of all respective House and ARRAY resources.

The document was signed by President Jonathan Innsbrook and his senior vice presidents. There were, as yet, no signatures from the New African Council.

"Looks like you've been busy with more than that black hole stuff," Alex said. "Is this for real?"

JuneMary made the sign of the cross, then nodded her head. "The Rome family has always considered New African independence to be manifest destiny. But this is a new trick."

"So, the United Countries of America and New Africa just create their own new government?" Alex asked.

"That's about the long and the short of it," JuneMary said. "But that ain't gonna happen now. Kelen was so heck bent on getting her family project finished, it looks like she negotiated this agreement before she actually got legitimate support from the council. Looks like she duped President Innsbrook and his country, but good."

"What are you going to do with this?" Alex asked.

JuneMary tapped the window. "Well, we wouldn't want to cause a big ol' scandal," she said with a little smile. "I'll just hold on to this, for now. If the time comes, I will quietly slip a copy of this to Retroguard, and Kelen will suddenly find herself out of supporters." JuneMary patted Alex on the shoulder. "Now, looks like I and the entire country of New Africa owe you a big favor, Admiral Detail."

Captain Odessa and Horace Witaker walked into Alex's bedroom. "New Africa owes Alex Detail a favor? What chicanery did Admiral the Great perform this time?" Odessa asked.

JuneMary explained the situation to Odessa and Horace.

Odessa pursed her lips and frowned. "Some family you have, Ambassador. And your brother just left to go check on his wife without so much as offering us dinner."

"By the way," Alex said to Odessa. "I found your spydrop network."

"Naturally," Odessa replied as she pulled a protocarb square out of a pocket and took a bite. "I presume you were able to obtain something more pertinent to our mission than this bogus treaty?"

Alex handed Odessa his window. "Well, I would have gotten something intelligible if you'd had the sense to add an anti-dampening filter to the spydrops. Instead, all I got was bits and pieces of some mother-daughter conversation."

Odessa handed Alex's window to Horace. "Add an anti-dampening filter? Why don't I just put up a large sign for the vision-impaired that reads, 'Warning! You are being recorded!'" Odessa shook her head. "Really, Alex, not only have you lost your youthful intellect, but I would say you have descended to the level of special-needs child." She retrieved the window from Witaker. "Thank you, Vice Captain. Your program works brilliantly, I see." She then turned to Alex. "The spydrops collect the corrupted data, and then we decrypt it on site rather than risk being detected by using an active anti-dampening filter. Do you understand this simple English I am speaking? Now, let us see what this conversation between celery-serving Kelen and your sneaky little girlfriend was all about."

Alex felt a sudden urge to defend Rosemary, but quickly thought better of it as it would only provoke Odessa into further innuendo.

Odessa tapped a code into the window, causing the entire conversation between Kelen and Rosemary to be played. The recording picked up just as Rosemary entered Kelen's office.

Kelen: "Rosemary, shouldn't you be at your classes, sweetheart? I didn't think I would be seeing you until tonight."

Rosemary: "I just wanted to see if they would let me go back one last time. He's really like a normal boy, and I just feel sad that he's seen as disposable."

Kelen: "The protocols are there to protect us, and we have held up our part of the bargain."

Rosemary: "But Mom, it's not right that he's being sent on this suicide mission! And I can see that it's not just me, but *she* wants him to find a way to survive, too. I can tell. And I don't care, I'm going back there tonight. I have ideas; I think I can help more than they've let me. How am I supposed to feel after he goes off and dies to save us?"

Kelen: "Remember, they are the ones sending him off on this mission, not us. And the only way we could even hope to survive is by giving our full cooperation. Our lives depend on that—your life, my life, and the lives of everyone else. Do you understand?"

Rosemary: "So, now that the last piece is in place, will we truly be safe?"

Kelen: "The only place in the solar system that *will* be safe is here, on this planet. Understand what we are dealing with—the final battle between Alex Detail and George Spell is foretold to be an extinction level event."

Hearing that conversation, especially the last little bit of it, jolted Alex.

All this time, Rosemary knew where George Spell was.

The second thing that processed through Alex's mind, he said out loud. "*I* cause an extinction level event?"

Odessa pursed her lips. "Poppycock! These people are full of nothing but ghost stories and superstitions. Now, where's the rest of this recording? Why does it simply stop?"

"Because Rosemary stepped on the spydrop and I think it's in her shoe or something," Alex said.

Captain Odessa smacked Alex on the back of his head. "You truly are a simpleton." Everyone looked at Odessa. "Oh, please! Horace—"

"Yes, I'm on it," Horace said without looking up from his hand window. "There she is."

Odessa grabbed the window from him, and showed Alex. There was a map of New Africa, with a small moving dot that indicated Rosemary's location. "This particular spydrop has a beacon, so go commandeer a car, because it looks like your pretty paramour is about to pay a visit to George Spell."

CHAPTER 18

•

THE POWER OF DETAILS

George Spell had been working for twenty-eight hours straight when Zarena Detail declared he was to stop so he could sleep for two hours. George was not tired, but Zarena seemed to know what was best for him, as she had demonstrated during her constant coaching while George Spell was learning how to use the Reaper. From using lighting that most people would find too dim to giving him the coffee flavored soy drink he never told her he liked, Zarena showed that she somehow knew George very well. She stopped him even though Brother Lonadoon told her that George did not require sleep, was fully capable of self-diagnosis, and would let them know when he needed rest.

"So, you know better than his own mother?" Zarena said with one lifted eyebrow.

Lonadoon did not argue further.

In the past twenty-eight hours, George had learned a great deal from Zarena, from how Alex Detail's genetic imprint could impact the Harvesters, to how Zarena had managed to take control of a Reaper, to the powers of the ancient pyramids of Egypt, Mexico, and China. But Zarena was always vague when talking about Madeline Spell. This seemed smart to George, as Zarena would want to protect whatever ways she kept herself hidden from the speaker's widespread intelligence network. But there seemed to be something else that caused Zarena to get quiet when the subject of Madeline Spell came up. George wondered if Zarena and his mother had once been friends but then had a fight.

George also thought Madeline and Zarena were a lot alike. Zarena had given birth to the savior, Alex Detail, and Madeline Spell had created the second savior, George Spell.

"How did you know to give birth to a savior?" George had asked. "Did Brother Lonadoon call you and tell you he needed one?"

This was apparently very funny, because Zarena laughed for a while. Even Brother Lonadoon smiled. Zarena finally said, "I don't know, and I wouldn't understand, but go ahead and ask Brother Lonadoon. Maybe you'll understand his gibberish."

George looked at Lonadoon, who said, "As Isis bore Horace, and Mary bore Jesus, so it was when Zarena bore Alex."

"Horace and Mary? Do you mean Vice Captain Horace Witaker and Ambassador JuneMary?" George asked.

Shaking his head, Lonadoon said, "Not them. Horace son of Isis and Osiris, born five thousand years ago, and Jesus Christ, son of Mary and Joseph, born nearly twenty-five hundred years ago."

George didn't know those people, but he knew that when he asked too many questions Zarena and Lonadoon would talk in their magic talk, talk that he didn't have the ability to understand—perhaps because he was not a real person. But George *could* do math: Whoever those people were that Brother Lonadoon was talking about, it was obvious that a savior was born every two thousand five hundred years.

He didn't have time to ask too many more questions, because he spent most of his time inside the Reaper.

The inside of a Harvester Reaper vessel was definitely not supposed to have a person in it, especially not a human. First of all, there was no door. Zarena or Lonadoon or someone had cut a hole in the side of the Reaper. The hull was solid metal of some sort, but had something that looked like a cross between wires and veins running along the inside.

Past the nearly three-foot-thick hole they'd cut was a hollowed spherical room about forty feet in diameter. There was no display and no console or means of interface. It was like standing in the inside of a hollowed-out pumpkin.

"So, how does it work?" George asked.

Zarena had touched a wall, and a shimmering field of energy became visible around them.

"That's all I can do," Zarena said. "Alex's tampering has created a recognition of my biometric signature, but I am only half of Alex's DNA."

"Is that how you got it here?" George asked.

"No," Zarena answered. "I used the ancient grid of pyramids. The Harvesters gave us this technology nearly five thousand years ago, to stabilize Earth's axis and bring together the necessary planetary alignments to prevent a cataclysm. There are similar systems, mostly buried on Venus and Mars. Course that was the first time they tried pulling us into their universe, and that ended up biting them on the ass. But the pyramid network has gone to hell; it isn't as strong as it was thousands of years ago. Only a few people even know a fraction of the capabilities built into that network. Brother Lonadoon is said to be the most well-versed. Anyway, it worked well enough to create a torsion guide field that coaxed this Reaper here, with my little bit of DNA confusing it into thinking Alex had called it. But the Harvesters learned their lesson the first time, so when they planted Pluto in our solar system, it was created to withstand any amount of destruction we could throw at it, including the pyramid torsion grid we used to kick their asses back five thousand years ago."

George realized that this was some of the big information Brother Lonadoon wanted him to absorb when he kept asking George about how he felt and his need for sleep while they were on *UC One.* But George had a question that he did not think it safe to ask. That was, if Zarena knew so much about the Harvesters and this ancient network they left behind, then why did she want to stop her son Alex from doing whatever it was that he wanted to do? George remembered something that Brother Lonadoon had said to him, *"All those who have power, fear threats to their way of life."* This seemed apt, but what power did Zarena have here, living in this old office building on Venus? What was she going to get out of this? Was it all about getting her son back? She didn't seem like she missed him at all.

"Place your hands on the wall," Zarena instructed George.

George did as he was told. As he placed his hands on the warm walls, an energy field visibly stronger than the one Zarena had created appeared. It was full of data, but so confusing it was like trying to read another language where you could only understand every tenth word. This was going to take a while.

"It thinks I'm Alex Detail," George said. "So it thinks I know how to use it?"

"Maybe," Zarena replied. "It doesn't think the way we do, so don't try to understand *why* it does things, just try to learn *how* it does things."

"I already know how it does things," George said. "I wrote the command program that made us able to talk to them."

Suddenly, Zarena looked very angry. "No, you used Alex's mind when he was on Pluto to write that command program that fixed the m-coms. Then, you went a step further and your program overtook the entire ARRAY fleet, killing hundreds of people in the massive acceleration g-forces! You have no regard for human life, and I will see to it that you don't kill another person as long as you live!"

Zarena must be confused. "But I saved everyone from the Harvesters. And after that I only had to kill one more person before the ring ships were all destroyed."

Zarena grabbed George by his arm. "Lonadoon says I should not waste time trying to reason with you. But I *will* keep you from killing even one more person. And then, when you have fulfilled the true Alex Detail prophecy and completely destroyed the last of the Harvesters, I will see to it that Madeline Spell is finally punished for the crime of creating you."

Letting go of George, Zarena sighed. "If you try to access Alex's mind, he will find you. This time, you have to do it on your own."

George wondered if Zarena knew what a paradox was. If it was a crime to create George, then why was she using him to stop Alex?

"So, what am I supposed to do when I figure out how to work this?" George asked.

"Just one really simple thing," Zarena said. "You will pilot this Reaper out past Earth, and pull the remains of Pluto out of orbit, beyond the asteroid belt. Then, when you have cleared the asteroid belt, you will use this Reaper to create a singularity and destroy what's left of Pluto."

"How do I create a singularity?" George asked.

"We're working on that," Zarena replied. "In the meantime, do what you can to get to know this."

So, George had spent nearly twenty-eight hours working, learning how to use the Reaper vessel. He had just figured out how to use the controls, when the cat suddenly darted into the Reaper, and Zarena arbitrarily ordered George to go to sleep.

George did not argue. He would be able to understand things better after a couple hours of sleep.

When he arrived at the small room in Zarena's apartment that was to serve as his bedroom, he noticed a curved silver cone shape at the foot of his bed.

"What's that?" George asked. "Is it the thing you gave Rosemary when we got here?"

"Yes, and it has been fixed," Zarena replied. "That is the shape you must concentrate on to create a singularity. You should take a good look at it, and let it process while you sleep. My son is nearby. I can't shield him from you forever."

Nodding, George pulled the blankets over him. He almost fell asleep before he could ask her one last question.

"Mom, if I create a singularity to destroy Pluto, the singularity will also capture me in its event horizon, and I will be killed. You said you didn't want me to kill one more person. But is it okay if I kill myself?"

Zarena looked at him, then slowly patted her hand along his hair. "Why did you just call me 'mom'?" she asked.

That was an odd question, George thought. "You are Alex Detail's mother, and I am also Alex Detail. By the transitive property, you are also my mother."

"If I am your mother, then what is Madeline Spell?" Zarena asked.

These questions were getting ridiculous, especially for such a smart and powerful sorceress who had given birth to a savior. "She made me, like you made Alex Detail, so she is also my mother."

At this, Zarena stood and turned off the lights. Before leaving she said, "Yes, the event horizon will catch you and kill you. I will do what I can to give you a chance to survive."

Exactly two hours later, George woke from his mandatory sleep. His mind had done a great deal of maintenance while he slept. Concepts that were difficult to grasp were now clearly fused into his brain's neurons. The shape at the foot of the bed had been translated into a mathematical formula he would think of while flying the Reaper. It would serve as the set of instructions that would create the singularity. After that, there would be nothing left for George to do.

As George lay there processing his thoughts, he felt a warm pressure, and a strange vibration on his chest. Opening his eyes he saw the cat lying on top of him, its eyes half closed. It seemed to be very happy.

"How come you're in here with me?" George asked the cat. It opened its eyes a bit more, made a small noise, then licked George on his chin with a very scratchy tongue.

"Zarena said she got you to eat mice, to keep them from getting into her stuff."

The cat's eyes were fully opened now, and it twitched its tail. It didn't say anything.

"I have to get up now, and go take the Reaper ship to destroy the rest of Pluto," George said. "So you're going to have to get off of me."

The cat licked George's chin again, then kept licking him, moving on to the side of his face like it was cleaning his cheek. That was very nice of the cat, but George had to get going, so he sat up.

The cat bounded off of him and ran out of the room.

George got out of bed, picked up the silver shape, and took it with him. As George walked into the living room, he could see that Zarena and Brother Lonadoon seemed to be arguing about something. They stopped abruptly when he entered.

"You are ready?" Zarena asked.

George nodded. He was ready.

"Did you think of a way to survive the singularity?" Zarena asked.

George had not. Zarena had told him he was not to kill any more people. He wondered if that meant himself too. He guessed not, since he was not a real person, so it was okay.

She handed him a small cube of plastic. "Take this. It is important that we recover your body, if possible."

Looking at the cube of plastic in his hands, George saw some graphic instructions on the side. It was an emergency pressure suit.

"Once you have activated the Reaper's primary weapon, you will have approximately thirty minutes until a singularity forms. Have you calculated the diameter of the event horizon before it collapses?"

"Yes," George nodded, calling up the formula in his mind. "It will be fifty-two point five kilometers, expanding and contracting over the course of forty-eight to fifty-four minutes. I cannot get the deviation below six minutes since there will be other things that affect it."

"Then, in order to escape the event horizon, you will have to exit the Reaper and achieve the proper escape velocity." Zarena handed him two pieces of something that looked like black rocks. "I would give you some sort of rocket to help propel you, but the Reaper does not allow complex machines inside it. But you can tie these to your shoes. After you have put on the pressure suit, exit the Reaper and kick off against the hull. These stones will have a negative reaction to the Reaper field, and they will propel you. You will only have once chance, so don't mess up. You will likely be in cold space for some days before a ship is able to retrieve you. Adjust your metabolism accordingly. The pressure suit will eventually stop working, so breathe sparingly. If you are not dead for too long and someone manages to collect your body, perhaps you can be reanimated."

Lonadoon suddenly jumped up and looked toward the door.

"I know," Zarena said, without looking at Lonadoon. "It is time for you to go, George."

"Thank you for helping me finally destroy the Harvesters." George held out his hand to shake Zarena's. Instead, she touched his hair and gave him a kiss on his forehead.

As George was about to leave for the Reaper hangar, the elevator door opened. Rosemary June stepped out.

"Rosemary, what are you doing here?" Zarena asked.

Rosemary quickly walked over to George and took the silver shape from him. "It won't be enough," she said, working her thumbs along a panel on the side of the base. "The event horizon is still too big, but I have been able to reduce the reaction temperature. I can get it so you have a smaller horizon by three kilometers."

Brother Lonadoon crossed his arms.

"Rosemary, you have done your best," Zarena said.

Rosemary's eyes were beginning to get red. George noted that this was likely because she was trying not to cry.

"But if it's just a matter of meters, and he can't—" Rosemary did not say the rest of the sentence. She was obviously being sensitive. Rosemary finished her adjustment to the singularity model, and handed it back to George. "Here you are. I'm certain you will be successful."

"Thank you for helping me," George said, taking the model from Rosemary.

Suddenly Zarena and Lonadoon's eyes widened.

Lonadoon put his hand on George's shoulder and said, "Go, now. Hurry!"

"You were followed," Zarena said to Rosemary.

The last thing George heard as he ran into the hangar was an unlikely mixture of sounds that he had heard just two days ago.

The sound of Captain Odessa's voice, and gunfire.

CHAPTER 19

•

APPROACHING THE TERMINATOR

The sun was down by the time Alex, Odessa, Horace, and JuneMary reached the building across the highway from the Kade Institute. The spydrop in Rosemary's shoe was glowing on Odessa's window display, indicating that the girl had just exited a subterranean tunnel beneath the highway, and was now walking through an underground parking structure.

Because the entire Kade Institute was on emergency power, it was eerily dark. All exterior lights were out; what little light there was came from dimly lit offices in the towers above them.

"She's on an elevator," Odessa reported, "but going down. Approximately four stories below us."

A wave of nausea swept over Alex. He could feel some sort of warm, dizzying energy coming from beneath them. The feeling was familiar; it was connected somehow to George Spell, but not only to George, to someone else who felt more alive and familiar than George—a sensation like some scent from the distant past that had lost all physical association but still carried a vague emotion.

They followed Odessa as she crept softly down a dim hallway that ended at the elevator Rosemary had taken.

"I don't think we should try to take the elevator," Horace said.

"Obviously not," Odessa said. "I'm sure it makes a fine trap for the feeble-minded." She walked over to a door under an exit sign. The stairway appeared to go up only, but Odessa waved them toward her. "Do you smell that? Lemons." She placed her hand straight into a holographic wall. The instant she stepped through the projection, the wall disappeared. Odessa smiled grimly, then started leading the others down a hidden flight of stairs.

As they stood on the landing, they could hear a voice. Rosemary's.

Odessa held up a finger for silence, then pulled out her gun.

They were standing adjacent to the elevator shaft, but could not see past the second holographic wall that hid the stairs. Odessa motioned the others to follow as she burst through.

George Spell was already on his way through a door in the back of the room, but he stopped and looked over his shoulder. It was as if he needed to make eye contact with Alex.

Alex had no time to ponder the strange look, because he was focusing on the back of Rosemary's head, pausing a moment to wonder if she might look back. Rosemary and another woman were both running full tilt toward the same doorway through which George was exiting.

Captain Odessa yelled, "Stop, or I will shoot!" But she didn't actually give anyone time to stop before she opened fire.

Odessa was a perfect shot, the best in all ARRAY. George was to their left, just through the wide doorway when Odessa started shooting, while Rosemary and the other woman simultaneously ran through the right side of the exit. If Captain Odessa had wanted to hit George in, say, the sole of his shoe to knock him off his feet, it should have been easy for her to do so.

Instead, her shots flew wide, ricocheting off the wall, and shattering the glass windows. Something was causing her to be wildly inaccurate.

George and the women were through the door. Odessa turned her gun on Brother Lonadoon.

"Don't move!" she shouted.

Brother Lonadoon froze, just five feet short of the exit.

"Turn around and put your hands in front of you!" Odessa shouted as she marched toward Lonadoon.

He looked strangely calm for someone who had the enraged Captain Odessa bearing down on him, showing him the business end of a deadly weapon. There was a gleam in his eye; he held his hands out in front of him, then made a small twitching motion with his fingers.

Odessa's right arm jerked in pain, and her gun went flying. Lonadoon darted out the door.

Odessa was grasping her arm as Alex and Horace rushed after Lonadoon. It was too late. The door slid shut with a loud, echoing bang.

"Dammit!" Odessa yelled.

JuneMary was by Odessa's side, examining her arm and making the sign of the cross.

Alex watched as Horace worked on the door mechanism. He saw Odessa brush JuneMary aside as she retrieved her gun from the floor.

"Stand aside!" Odessa yelled.

Horace Witaker jumped away from the door.

"Oh come on, don't shoot the door pad!" Alex shouted. "That never works; it's just going to jam—"

The sound of gunfire cut him off, as Odessa emptied an entire round of super-heated crystalline-tipped thermal bullets at the door mechanism. The volley of iridescent ammunition blasted the door pad through the wall, igniting the surrounding metal into a glowing magma. In seconds, the housing surrounding the door-lock burst into flames.

The locking mechanisms melted away.

Well, I guess she showed me.

When Alex and Horace tried the door, they were able to push it open. But as soon as they did, a sound filled the room, as if a musical note were being played too loudly through a bad speaker, the low bass vibrating the air. The sound had a paralyzing effect. It reverberated though Alex's bones and felt like it was tearing at his eyes, causing them to water and fill with pressure. He had a sudden vivid image of his eyeballs exploding out of his head.

Odessa was the first to steel herself against the strange force coming from the hangar and step through the door. Alex and the others followed. A large dark shape was rising above them. As his eyes adjusted, Alex could see it was a Reaper. The last of the Reapers—the very same one that had attacked the *Cronus*. The Reaper that had fired on them, and not fired on them. The same ship that had killed Horace, and not killed Horace.

Odessa opened fired on the Reaper, but the bullets didn't even bounce off the ship's hull. Rather, they appeared to be absorbed by a strange dark blur surrounding the ship.

As the Reaper rose higher, Alex could see a small circle of dim light coming from it. It appeared there was a hole in the side of the ship, a hole covered by the same dark blur. Maybe it was a trick of the light playing across the ship's shifting energy field, but Alex could have sworn he saw a cat looking out of the hole at them.

The musical note jumped an octave, and the Reaper majestically accelerated in an arc through the open hangar roof, then shot off into the dark Venusian sky.

Absolute silence ensued. The only sound they could hear was their heavy breathing echoing off the walls of the dark hangar.

Horace Witaker was holding Captain Odessa's window. "Rosemary wasn't on that ship," he said, looking at the window's glowing schematics. "She went off that way, into the building above us."

"We have to get to the flier, and get out of here," Alex said, his panic over George escaping overcoming his last thoughts of Rosemary.

Odessa grabbed Horace's window. "For once, I agree with Detail. To hell with her, to hell with this planet, and to hell with their foolish regulations and do-nothing populace." Then she added, "No offense, JuneMary, but I had a feeling something like this would happen. We have no time to go to the spaceport and deal with their nonsensical disembarkment procedures."

"I can operate the flier on remote," Witaker said. "I might have to fly it through a hangar door, but I can get it here."

Odessa waved a hand. "Nonsense. We'll do nothing of the sort. A colossal waste of time; I've already taken care of it. And that's why I'm the captain!"

With that, the roar of engines filled the air as the 500-foot-long hull of the *Virgin Mother*, still glowing hot from its rapid entry through the atmosphere, crashed through the sides of the open hangar roof to land on the concrete pad.

The ship's weight was causing large cracks in the floor, and its roaring engines were making the entire structure crumble and fall apart.

An emergency heat-shield chute unfolded from the side of the *Virgin Mother*, opening up in front of where they stood.

Moments later they were on the ship, watching as its tidal forces destroyed the hangar and tore cracks in the side of the mountain, sending large boulders and rockslides plummeting beneath the building down the steep slopes of Maxwell Montes.

Alex noticed JuneMary looking at the rear display as closely as he was, making sure the main building, the one where Rosemary and the others had fled, was undamaged.

As the *Virgin Mother* accelerated through the atmosphere and spun up to max on an intercept course with the Reaper, Odessa took a moment to turn to JuneMary and say, "Please relay my apologies to your government for the damage to the hangars." Then Odessa shook her head. "On second thought, disregard that order."

CHAPTER 20

•

MADELINE SPELL'S SHOCK AND AWE

Madeline Spell stopped on the south lawn of the White House and took a moment to enjoy the early spring air and warm morning sun, looking wistfully at the place she had lived for almost eight years before becoming Speaker of the House of Nations. The first of the rosebuds were beginning to bloom; a few bees buzzed through the air, hovering above the flowers.

Other insects were also buzzing around the grounds, not only pollinating the various flora, but also serving double duty killing aphids and other pests that would otherwise overrun the meticulously manicured grounds. Of course, the flying drones were not real insects, rather they were large nanosects, small flying robots that monitored the health of plants and flowers, helping do the work that had been the domain of bees, beetles, and other insects, before the mysterious loss of two-thirds of the planet's bee population in the past two and a half centuries.

Spell missed the sound of buzzing bees, and the smell of fresh cut grass. During her terms as President of the United Countries of America, Madeline had literally never stopped to smell the roses, but she had, on occasion, left the windows open. It was almost impossible to believe that just six months earlier, the Harvesters' rapid attack on the sun had made the thought of walking outside to take in the beauty of nature seem like it was part of some distant past, a history long forgotten, as humankind floated through dark vacuum space in dry sterile shelters.

But that bleak future had not come to pass, thanks to Madeline's Spell's ultimate crime of creating a clone of Alex Detail. It had been the right thing to do. If anyone questioned that, all they had to do was go outside and look around, then consider the alternative. Unfortunately, humans had a tendency to revert to old habits. That would never change.

Peevchi Derringkite, Admiral Sevo, President Innsbrook, and the other conspirators had sought to save people from the brutal rule of nature by taking them into the Harvester Universe. But survival of the fittest was still the one constant law of life. Ironically, ignoring that first rule of nature had been the downfall of those conspirators, when they were all bested by George Spell.

All but President Jonathan Innsbrook.

Not only did he escape the conspiracy unscathed, Innsbrook had apparently been the one whom Brother Lonadoon turned to when Madeline Spell ignored Lonadoon's warnings of impending doom. Lonadoon had been adamant: If Madeline did not take more drastic measures to neutralize the protective instincts within George, which were building ever higher as Alex Detail continued his Harvester research and positioned himself to take control of ARRAY, an extinction level event would befall humanity. While Spell could no longer ignore the dangers of her super-human clone after he had unleashed his powers in the planetarium, she was determined that Innsbrook would not get away with kidnapping George.

"Are you all right?" Guy Hiramoto asked, gently grasping Spell's arm.

Realizing that she had stopped walking and was lost in a daydream, Spell quickly nodded and continued walking to the entrance of the White House.

"It brings back a lot of memories, doesn't it, Guy?"

"Don't start reminiscing," Guy said quietly. "You'll just make yourself melancholy."

He was right, of course. Not that her time here was all that blissful or idyllic. Most of it was spent plotting and politicking her way to the chief position of the House of Nations, years of convincing people that her predecessor was not the person who could lead the worlds through the impending first encounter with a hostile alien force.

Madeline Spell slowly turned the platinum ring she always wore on her left hand. Today, she was wearing the ring on her right hand. It had a newly added feature that could be used only once. Spell wore a new watch, too—one that not only told time but also could detect certain airborne antibodies to a particular virus. Both the ring and the watch were from the Toolkit she had retrieved from the Generationists.

As they stepped onto the south portico, Spell smiled at Hiramoto and quietly said, "Let's go get 'em."

President Innsbrook's personal secretary greeted them, and led Spell to the Oval Office while Hiramoto went off to visit with the senior vice presidents.

Etiquette required that the Speaker of the House of Nations be shown to the president's office without delay. But that would mean Spell would be immediately ushered into the oval office, and probably find Innsbrook lounging on a sofa staring off into space.

Madeline Spell needed to create a reason to shake the president's hand.

So, before being led into the oval office, Spell took a seat outside the office and said to Innsbrook's secretary, "When I was president, the last thing I needed was the Speaker of the House of Nations barging in on me. You let the President know I'll be here when he's ready."

A few moments later, Jonathan Innsbrook opened his office door and said, "Speaker, please come in."

Spell stood, as did everyone else in the office, and said, "Thank you Mr. President." While everyone was looking, she held out her hand.

Innsbrook was probably thinking, *Since when does the Speaker shake my hand?* But the social reflex kicked in. Innsbrook took Spell's hand and returned her handshake.

Spell locked her gaze on his, giving his hand one final aggressive squeeze, bearing down as forcefully as possible, making sure the ring on her right hand made full contact with his palm.

Jonathan motioned Spell into the oval office. She walked into her old haunt and took a seat on one of the sofas in the middle of the room. Surprisingly, Jonathan did not go fiddle with something behind his desk, or stare off into space. He promptly took a seat across from her.

"Well, I know it must be serious if you've come to see me in person," Innsbrook said.

Spell smirked. "Just a courtesy on my part, as I imagine you must be fatigued with the kidnapping of my son and the long trip to Venus and back."

Shrugging, Innsbrook replied, "I got to spend some quality time with your old guru. Fascinating man, that Lonadoon. He seems to think that by keeping George on the same planet with Alex Detail while this chunk of Pluto still orbits us, they will have some sort of war that will kill everyone. It's all the rage in the prophecies, you know."

"Oh, since when did any of that interest you?" Spell sneered. "Why did you take George to Venus?"

"They've got a Reaper there, and they needed him to use it to destroy the remains of Pluto."

"And your reward for this?" Spell asked. "Sanction on their magical world if things go terribly wrong with George and Alex? Support for your secession from the House of Nations? Perhaps a statue or two named after you?"

Innsbrook shrugged. "All of the above, I suppose."

"The eastern federations would never support secession and they might just be a match for you and your friends on New Africa, so we know that is not going to happen." Crossing her arms, Spell leaned back into the sofa. "It's not such an easy job, Jonathan. Are you sure you want to continue down this path to oust me and take my job? How do you think you would have done in the war against the Harvesters?"

"Whatever was meant to happen would happen," President Innsbrook replied, leaning into a pile of pillows at his side. "I doubt, however, that I would have created a terrorist clone of Alex Detail, and let him run loose blowing up buildings in New York City."

Madeline Spell looked at her watch. An orange light on the display blinked, indicating that Jonathan Innsbrook was now exhaling antibodies to a certain virus he'd picked up from Madeline Spell's ring. "Captain Odessa reports that the Reaper is slowing as it assumes a parabolic approach to Earth. I presume this means George is on the Reaper, as you say. Of course, I cannot have a Reaper on the loose near Earth, so I have deployed a fleet to rendezvous with the *Virgin Mother*."

"Launch as many ships as you want," Innsbrook said. "You can't destroy a Reaper."

"True," Spell said. "But apparently, someone else can. Apparently, your friends on New Africa can pull a Reaper right out of the sky and retrofit it so that a child can drive it."

"Apparently," Innsbrook replied dryly.

Spell smiled. "Well, I do hope they are concerned with your good health."

"Why?" Jonathan asked. "Are you going to kill me?" His tone lacked any trace of humor.

It's almost like he knows, Madeline thought.

"Jonathan, if there is any means of getting my son back, you are the most direct path."

"Events have been set in motion, Madeline."

Madeline Spell stood and said, "When Captain Odessa arrives in orbit in one hour, I want you to board her ship and use whatever influence you have to retrieve George off that Reaper."

"What makes you think I am either able or inclined to do so?"

"It will be a pity for you if you are neither," Spell said. "You may have your personal doctor check you. While you were away, I activated certain safeguards built by the Generationists. I have just now infected you with a virus that will be lethal to you within three days, though with these things it is quite impossible to be exact."

Jonathan stood, his eyes drawn to his right hand. A rash was spreading from the spot where his hand had come into contact with Spell's ring.

"Fortunately, there is a cure," Madeline Spell said. "It is rather specifically tailored. The virus that has infected you can be killed only if you breathe the same air as George."

Innsbrook went over to his desk, pulled out a small panel, and spat on it. Spell went over and stood behind Innsbrook as he waited for his self-diagnostic to complete. As she suspected, he was having his saliva tested for foreign viruses. He found one. He had his computer check the DNA virus polymerases template against all known genetic imprints on file. Only one came back, thought it was not an exact match.

Alex Detail.

Innsbrook did not look angry. Perhaps he had heard that mothers would go to any lengths to save their children. Perhaps he was in shock that he could be dead in three days. He simply nodded at the results on his screen. "I would ask if you thought this was a bit extreme," Innsbrook said, "But then, I have learned the hard way that everything you do is a bit extreme."

"You had best be on your way, Jonathan," Spell said. "If George dies, you both die."

A few moments later Spell and Hiramoto had crossed back across the south lawn. They boarded their flier for their return journey to the House of Nations in New York City.

As the city came into view over the horizon, Guy Hiramoto said, "He'll have every geneticist in the hemisphere working on this by now."

Spell nodded. "Dr. Lastingday assured me it would take a long time for anyone to discover the true nature of that virus. By then, our two biggest problems will be solved, and if Innsbrook somehow does return, he will be the chief suspect in a double homicide. Then, our final problem will be taken care of."

"If you are having any second thoughts, now is the time to do something about it," Hiramoto said.

Spell hoped that Hiramoto could not see her face in the dimly lit flier cabin. She hoped he could not hear the quiver in her voice. She wondered how she would live with herself for the rest of her life. It would be torture. But she was doing what had to be done. Lonadoon had warned her, but she had not listened—and now it was too late. Whatever had gone wrong with George was beyond repair. And for as long as Alex Detail lived, he would work to overtake ARRAY and bring the Harvesters back into this universe. The combination, as Lonadoon had warned, would lead to a war between the two boys that would result in an extinction level event.

It would take weeks for Innsbrook's scientists to learn the true nature of the virus, but he would find out soon enough that the virus actually did the opposite of what Madeline Spell told him it did. It was just as specifically tailored as Spell had indicated—but it was actually quite harmless to Jonathan Innsbrook.

However, the moment Innsbrook came into contact with Alex Detail and George Spell, the virus would kill both boys.

CHAPTER 21

•

THE ADVENTURES OF GEORGE SPELL AND THE CAT

George Spell was just getting used to controlling the Reaper with his mind, processing the acceleration formulas and plotting a curve to scoop little Pluto out of its orbit around Earth, when he heard a sound. He saw something move near the hole in the side of the Reaper; it was that cat he liked!

Nice of the cat to come along with him! George didn't think the trip should take too long, but he was happy to see the cat. It seemed to want to walk over to George, but the air inside the Reaper had a thickness to it that prevented either of them from moving.

"You have to wait until the acceleration curve isn't so steep," George said to the cat. "Then we can walk around."

The cat stopped trying to pad its way over to George and sat still, its ears back slightly. George turned his thoughts to reducing the thickness of the air. By using his powers of concentration, he was able to diminish the thickness in a small area between the cat's face and its paw. The cat always liked to lick its paw; doing so seemed to make it feel better.

The cat's ears perked up as the field thinned a bit. It licked its paw.

There were no displays inside the Reaper. But as long as he was touching the wall, George had full control over all the ship's functions. He also had a view outside the ship in any direction, at nearly any magnification, all of it processed through his optic nerve.

"Alex Detail is in a ship behind us, chasing us," George explained to the cat. "So I have to drive fast. And there are six ARRAY ships in orbit around

Earth, so when I stop to get Pluto, there will probably be some shaking if they fire at us."

A few hours on course, George was able to thin out their internal stabilizing field. The cat walked over and sniffed his shoes. It seemed pleased with that, and sat down, curling its tail, tucking the tip between its paws.

"I'm a clone of Alex Detail, in case you didn't already know," George told the cat. "He used to be good, but then he got tricked by the Harvesters like everyone else. Now, he won't stop. He wants to be able to do what he could do when Pluto was a Harvester outpost, before I killed Peevchi Derringkite and wrecked the big Harvester ring ships. I'm not sure if you were in the room when Zarena was explaining it, but I guess that in the Harvester Universe they got to the omega point by using baryon tunneling. They actually wanted to make their universe collapse, if you can believe that. But anyway, I guess they made a mess of it. They're losing all the information they stored, you know, like you and I store memories in our brains. So they used one of their baryon tunnelers to get to our universe. They told Derringkite they created us, but Zarena didn't believe it. Brother Lonadoon, though, seemed to think she was wrong about that.

"Anyway, so the Harvesters made that hole to us, and tried taking us to their universe so they wouldn't keep losing their information. But they got beaten by us the first time they came around, about five thousand years ago. Eleven years ago, they tried again, but they were beaten by Alex Detail. Six months ago, they were beaten again—by me. Now, I just have to close the hole."

The cat looked up at George and let out a big yawn.

That meant the cat needed more oxygen. George made a mental adjustment to increase the breathable air mix. The cat had listened very carefully to George, and must have found the story interesting, since cats were said to be curious. It didn't move at all, just sat by his feet, leaning slightly against his leg.

George asked the cat if it had eaten a hydrip, because Zarena had made sure to put plenty of them in the ship so he didn't dehydrate in the very dry air. The cat didn't answer. Maybe, it was just being strong like George. To be safe, George picked up a hydrip and held it to the cat's mouth. After sniffing it a bit, the cat took the hydrip in its mouth, then dropped it to the floor where it batted it with a paw until it popped open into a thousand drops of water. The cat jumped.

George Spell giggled at the cat.

George had never laughed before.

"I think that was funny," he said to the cat. "You are supposed to eat it."

The cat sniffed around the floor and lapped at a drop of water here and there, shifting the energy field as it wandered.

After a few more hours, they were close enough to Earth to get Pluto.

But Alex's ship was right behind them, and there was a fleet of ARRAY ships deployed between him and Earth.

George looked down at the cat before thickening the stabilizing field. "This is going to get a little bumpy, Cat."

CHAPTER 22

LIVING IN THE SHADOW OF ALEX DETAIL

Horace Witaker had spent his life following orders, doing what he was told to do, and excelling in every way possible. He was the youngest vice captain in all of ARRAY, and the youngest officer to be awarded the House Medal of Valor (well, not including Alex Detail). He had survived having his head blown up and being thrown back into this life by Alex Detail's evasion program. He had experienced transcendence on Pluto, only to have it torn away from him again when George Spell destroyed the last Harvester invasion.

Horace Witaker had had enough.

Horace did not shield his emotions from the torments of the past or the taxing demands of daily life by fixating on total obsession to duty the way Captain Odessa did. He did not comfort himself with faith in a loving God like JuneMary. And he did not keep himself from going mad by calming his mind with the cocktail of sedatives Alex Detail favored.

Horace wasn't like any of the people he had grown so close to in the past year, and he had never felt lonelier. If people thought his despondence was the result of the manner in which Odessa had put an abrupt end to their brief romance, let them. It kept people from asking him questions.

Horace found himself in the middle of events that were unfolding rapidly, and this time he was not going to trust his fate to anyone other than himself.

The *Virgin Mother* was in pursuit of the Reaper purported to be piloted by George Spell. It amazed Horace to see none of them had learned their lesson. All of them, driven by whatever belief system they held, were simply blinded by their egos. No one could stop George Spell from doing whatever he was going to do. Why couldn't they see that?

Alex had grown more agitated and simultaneously elated, the closer the ship got to Earth. Horace knew it had something to do with the Harvester chip stolen from Peevchi Derringkite's body. At first, Horace hadn't understood the euphoric sensation he felt when he had retrieved Alex Detail's admiral's insignia and held it while waiting outside the ARRAY war room. He thought perhaps there was some nuero-inducer built in to the insignia, to keep the admiral in an elevated mental state.

But when Alex had put his hand on Horace's inside the drive room within the mobius ring, and flooded Horace with the same power he had felt on Pluto, it had become clear that Alex Detail had turned himself into a second Peevchi Derringkite—yet another pawn to be used by the Harvesters. Alex might believe himself too strong or too smart to fall into the same trap, but he wasn't.

Odessa had given Witaker access to the massive processing area of the ship's computer that stored command programs. He had been given orders to study the files Alex had uploaded to the ship, and tell Odessa what Alex planned.

But the program was beyond Horace's ability to understand. He could see that part of the enormous program involved a logarithmic expansion of an ARRAY warship quantum field, but the rest of it dealt with two-dimensional physics far beyond Horace's comprehension.

Fortunately, Alex could not run the program without the captain and her officers transferring command to him. And Odessa would never do that, which meant Alex would need Horace to relieve Captain Odessa from command.

During the Reaper chase back to Earth, Odessa had given them each two-hour sleep shifts during the nearly twenty-four hour voyage. A chime sounded in Horace's quarters, alerting him that he was due on the bridge in ten minutes. Horace was just pulling on his jacket after a quick sonic when another chime sounded.

When he opened the door, Alex Detail walked in.

"You've been poking around my files," Alex said. His eyes were bright and wide but had dark circles under them. Whatever he was using to keep himself awake must be taking a toll.

Horace didn't answer.

Taking a step closer to Horace in the small room, Alex stared up at Whitaker, peering into the taller man's eyes. "Whatever Odessa thinks you're going to unravel would be pointless to explain to her. She never felt what we did. She never understood the possibilities." Alex stared at Horace's hands, frozen where he was about to fasten his jacket. "She certainly never cared what you felt."

Despite being fresh from the sonic, Horace suddenly felt stiflingly hot in his small room. A bead of sweat formed just below his neck and slowly slid down his chest.

He fastened his jacket while trying to hold Alex's menacing stare.

"You have only one choice to make, Horace," Alex said. "Keep living the life you are living, or finally fulfill your destiny."

With that, Alex turned and left.

Horace had let Alex talk him into going along with his last plan to help the Harvesters, and it had nearly led to total annihilation.

Not this time, Admiral, Witaker thought to himself.

But the essence of the Harvesters had been stirred inside him once again. Alex had grown far more powerful than Witaker had imagined.

This time, maybe Alex Detail is right.

The bridge of the *Virgin Mother* smelled putrid. The ship had been poorly stocked when they left for Venus, and JuneMary's bridge buffet makeover had pretty much depleted the larders. Without any restocking on their stopover at Venus, Odessa was forced to ask the food processors to mix together molecules that were never meant to form ham, or chocolate cake, or whatever it was she was in the mood for. Now, there were piles of steaming glop Alex doubted would qualify as actual food.

As if Odessa needed anything more to spoil her mood.

The second thing to hit Alex as he walked onto the bridge was a slightly menacing glance from Horace Witaker. He might doubt himself now, Alex thought, but Witaker was the only one who understood what it was like to die.

Alex felt time stalk him every day of his life—that dark void of hell that had driven him to sponsor the Generationists; the deep gnawing hunger for serenity and control that had caused him to help the very race he had nearly eradicated in this universe a decade earlier. So, Alex was quite sure that when it came time to remove Odessa from command, Horace could either do it voluntarily, or Alex could make him. The chip in his thumb was humming with life as the Harvesters felt their day fast approaching, and Alex believed they would soon be lending him all their powers.

The central display showed Earth, glowing blue, magnified to fill the entire center of the bridge. Superimposed over the image was the acceleration curve of the Reaper, still over one hundred fifty thousand kilometers ahead of them. Odessa was approaching at maximum speed.

She turned to the crew. "This time, let's not muck it up!"

Six ARRAY ships were forming a blockade between Earth and the Reaper. "What's their plan?" Alex asked, stepping between Witaker and Odessa in front of the main display. "How do they think they are going to stop a Reaper?"

"Stop it?" Odessa asked. "Why in the world would they try to stop it?"

Alex held his hands up. "Because it's a REEE- PERRR." Alex drew out the word as if talking to a mentally compromised person. "They usually end up blowing up ships."

Odessa ignored Alex's theatrics. "The fleet is there to protect Earth if something goes wrong. The Reaper's intent is unknown, though the speaker believes it aims to be the destruction of Pluto."

"Yes," Alex said. "We know what George Spell is capable of when he wants to destroy something. A few days ago he wanted to destroy me. He could have ended up killing you and a lot of other people in that planetarium."

"Indeed!" Odessa agreed. "It seems young George Spell has not developed a refined sense of acceptable collateral damage. The fleet is maintaining an anti-proton grid proximate to the Pluto fragment."

"They seriously think the Reaper's anti-matter weapon would have any impact on Pluto?" Alex asked.

Odessa said, "I seriously hope so."

Alex watched Odessa calibrate the *Virgin Mother's* reactors to help power the anti-proton grid as they approached Earth.

Odessa hailed the lead ship, the ARRAY warship *Ulixes*, contacting the captain on encrypted m-com. "Captain Hazel Sanchez, this is Captain Odessa. Lock channel and stand by."

"Copy, Captain Odessa," Captain Sanchez replied. "Confirm Reaper coordinates."

"Confirmed," Odessa replied. "We will track—"

Odessa was cut off as the Reaper unexpectedly emitted six beams of energy, creating a constellation that looked surprisingly like a cat. The display went blank for a moment, then reappeared, but the long range tracking had lost the Reaper. It was as if the ship had disappeared. The *Virgin Mother* automatically displayed an estimated location for the Reaper as it searched its tracking sensors for a new way to reestablish a lock.

"Captain Sanchez, what just happened?" Odessa asked.

There was a moment of hesitation, then Sanchez replied, "The Reaper just created six explosions proximate to each ARRAY ship. It appears to be attempting to disrupt our sensors. We went blind for a few seconds."

"Can you lock on to its new course?" Odessa asked.

Another moment of hesitation, then Captain Sanchez answered, "Stand by."

Odessa shook her head. "Vice Captain, forward them the projected coordinates so they are not blind."

"Thank you, Captain Odessa," Sanchez replied. "But we have reestablished contact. We are pursuing a new intercept course."

Odessa activated the audio mute. "Captain Sanchez is a rather poor choice to command the fleet, don't you agree, Vice Captain?"

Horace nodded. "I agree, sir."

"Hiramoto really should have consulted with me before making that decision. Now, Captain Gallo, there's a man who can—"

"Captain, look at this," Witaker interrupted. The new course the fleet was following was significantly different from the *Virgin Mother's* course based on their own estimated location of the Reaper. The coordinates Sanchez forwarded showed the Reaper on an altered vector, crossing Earth's orbit, headed away from the Pluto satellite.

Odessa frowned. "Oh, now really, even Captain Sanchez couldn't possibly be foolish enough—"

JuneMary made a throat clearing noise. "Ahem . . . did anyone ever tell them about that?"

Odessa watched in horror as the ARRAY fleet closed in on the Reaper they were tracking. She immediately opened the com and said, "Sanchez, order all stop and reverse course! The ship you are following is—"

Odessa didn't get a chance to finish her sentence.

The Reaper burst into a blinding thermonuclear explosion.

CHAPTER 23

•

GETTING TO THE OTHER SIDE OF THE BOARD

George Spell had an issue with the six ARRAY ships on the other side of Pluto. They were too close for George to activate the gravimetric vortex he was going to use to take Pluto with him to the asteroid belt. If he activated it, he'd end up dragging all those ships with him. They'd all get sucked into the black hole he was going to create.

The only other option was to shoot them down, but Zarena had instructed him not to kill any other people, so he couldn't do that either.

"So what do I do now, Cat?" George asked his feline copilot.

The cat was curled up by his feet, sleeping. He thought he saw it open one eye, then close it and return to its slumber.

"That's a good idea," George said.

There was nothing about the Reaper that would allow George to communicate with the other ships. Not that they would probably listen to him. But the cat had given him a good idea; it was the only way he could think of to get the ships away from Pluto without destroying them.

The fake Reaper ship that Zarena had constructed to fool Alex Detail was still circling Earth in a highly elliptical orbit. It was packed with thermonuclear explosives that, if detonated, would create a shockwave strong enough to push any ship out of the way without compromising its q-field. The resulting explosion would emit so much EM radiation that the ships would go blind for a few minutes while they spun out of control.

George just needed to create an illusion, confuse them.

If he could get them to lock their sensors on the fake Reaper, then he could turn his own ship off, and they wouldn't be able to see him. He could ride in on inertia, let them get close enough to the fake Reaper, detonate it and blow the other ships out of the way, then scoop up Pluto and be off on his way.

There was just one problem with turning the Reaper off: It had a hole in its side. He'd lose all his air once the containment field was down. There was a good chance both he and the cat would get blown into space. There was nothing inside to hold on to.

George looked at the black stones Zarena had given him. They reacted with the Reaper's anti-field, Zarena had said. George held one up to the side of the Reaper. It stuck.

George quickly put on his pressure suit, then strapped the stones to his shoes as Zarena had instructed. He picked up the sleeping cat. It meowed at him, but then nuzzled him and tried to curl up in the crook of his neck.

"You have to go in here for a minute," George said, pulling the suit around the cat and sealing it. The cat squirmed momentarily, but George held its head to his chest and quickly slowed his heart rate from 80 beats per minute to 40. The cat stopped squirming and seemed to fall back asleep.

Turning his attention back to the ships, George noted a lot of junk orbiting Earth. Mostly old satellites and waste dumped by early space flights, along with a few errant rocks that hadn't burned up in the atmosphere yet. George located six objects, one near each of the ARRAY ships. He targeted his weapons.

Bracing his feet against the wall, he fired, then turned the Reaper off completely.

A rush of air tore past George and out into space, buffeting him with a gale force wind, but his shoes remained firmly stuck to the Reaper wall. As the air rushed out, it carried off what little there was in the Reaper: bits of dust and dirt that had been tracked in by him and Zarena during their work, as well as the supply of hydrips, blowing them all into cold space.

Then it was absolutely quiet as George stood in the vacuum space inside the Reaper. He could sense the ARRAY ships adjusting their course, but he couldn't use the Reaper to double check. Even the tiniest energy readings would put him back on their radar.

George just had to keep his calculations in mind, and fly blind.

After counting down what he figured was the optimal position to grab Pluto, George activated the forward weapon. He sent a microburst of radiation to the fake Reaper. It instantly exploded, its shockwave catching the ARRAY fleet in its wake and sending the ships spinning.

After only a few seconds, the ships were far enough away.

George turned the Reaper back on, activated the gravimetric scoop, grabbed the small chunk of Pluto in tow, and accelerated as fast as he could go.

By the time the *Virgin Mother* arrived in orbit around Earth, Pluto was gone.

Six ARRAY ships were adrift nearby in various states of disrepair.

Odessa was getting tired of this wild goose chase. George Spell had somehow managed to get control of a Reaper. By all appearances, he was trying to rid them of that last piece of Pluto that still orbited Earth. It was the one problem that still plagued Madeline Spell. She had actively enlisted Odessa in her undercover plot to spy on Alex Detail and find out what he was trying to do with the remains of Pluto.

But George Spell was one step ahead of them. If he was indeed going to get rid of Pluto for good, why stop him?

None of this was adding up, and Odessa was tired of following orders that made no sense. So, when she arrived in orbit around Earth and suddenly received the message from Madeline Spell to pursue the Reaper and continue their attempt to retrieve George, she refused.

Odessa stood on the bridge of her ship, arms crossed, and waited.

It didn't take long.

Vice Captain Witaker informed her that there was an incoming message from ARRAY Command.

Finally.

Odessa went to her quarters to take the message in private. She found Secretary Hiramoto on the com.

"Captain Odessa, why have you disregarded the order to pursue that Reaper?" Hiramoto asked.

"Because it is an illogical order," Odessa replied. "You are sending this ship into an adversarial situation with a Harvester Reaper that is towing Pluto across the solar system."

"It does not have to make sense to you, Captain," Hiramoto said firmly. "It is an order. Follow it."

Odessa snorted. "Under what authority do you issue this order?"

Secretary Hiramoto said, "Captain, I am the acting Chief Executive of ARRAY, as you well know."

Oh, Odessa knew the rulebook like JuneMary knew the Bible. She'd written half of it herself. "Perhaps you are unaware, Secretary Hiramoto, that what you are asking me to do is likely to be seen by George Spell as a hostile act, resulting in a combat situation. As a civilian commander, you are not an enlisted officer of ARRAY. Therefore, you do not have the authority to issue direct combat orders. Only the enlisted officer serving as Chief Executive Fleet Admiral or the Commander in Chief of ARRAY can initiate such an order."

"The orders have been authenticated by the Speaker of the House of Nations," Hiramoto replied.

Odessa sat down on the small chair in her quarters, putting her feet up on another chair. *Who does he think he is?* She had served the House of Nations and ARRAY her entire adult life, building a reputation as one of the most successful commanders in recorded military history. If Madeline Spell was going to send the *Virgin Mother* on a suicide mission, she could have the decency to tell Captain Odessa herself.

Captain Odessa wasn't saying another word to Hiramoto.

A few moments passed, then the code on Odessa's com changed, indicating she was now in communication with the Speaker of the House of Nations. "Captain Odessa, I really don't understand your refusal to follow these orders."

"Speaker," Odessa said, "you have asked me to monitor Alex Detail's activities with regard to the remains of Pluto. I have done so, and reported all my findings to you. It seems that with the removal of Pluto, we no longer have a problem. So why are you sending my ship after him? It would seem prudent to stay clear until we have reason to do otherwise."

"Captain, I do not explain myself to you. Proximity to the Reaper is paramount." *Paramount to what?* Odessa thought. Why wasn't Spell just coming out with whatever it was she wanted Odessa to do?

"Captain, there is a flier on its way to your ship. I can relieve you of duty if that is what you wish," the speaker said.

"Really now, Speaker?" Odessa said sarcastically. "There is no one on this ship or in service in ARRAY who would dare take command of my ship away from me, regardless of the origin of orders."

"There is one person," Speaker Spell said. "I have only to press my index finger onto a document, and the ratification of Alex Detail's promotion will occur. He will be Chief Executive of ARRAY, and the ship will be his. I doubt he will have any qualms about taking command."

This was madness! Put in charge the person whom she had been trying to stop all along from being in a position of power?

Odessa now knew she was dealing with someone desperately afraid. *My mistake*, trying to reason with an irrational person.

Odessa had followed Spell's covert plant to spy on Alex Detail. She had conducted a clandestine operation outside the sanction of ARRAY Command. She'd done it because it had made sense. But this did not.

Madeline Spell had now shown Odessa just how she repaid loyalty. *It is easy to sit behind a desk and send people off to die when you think it's* you *who's saving the world.*

There was nothing else Odessa could do. What was left? She could sit there and wait until one of the other ARRAY ships straightened itself out and got sent off to provoke George Spell—or she could do her best to keep more people from being killed.

"Very well," Odessa said, and cut her com.

What odd turn of events had occurred to allow Madeline Spell to threaten to put Alex Detail in command? He'd be more than happy to go try to destroy George and the Reaper with one of his inane quantum command programs.

The disturbing thing was that it all began to make sense to Odessa. Madeline Spell was going to take advantage of a unique situation. The war between Alex Detail and George Spell would never end. It would continue to escalate, no matter what. So, while Alex Detail and George Spell were far enough away from Earth, Spell was trying to create a situation where George Spell and Alex Detail both ended up dead.

Moments later Odessa returned to the bridge, announcing, "We're going after it."

She paced around the buffet, picking at the food. "For the record, the pursuit of that Reaper is a direct order from the speaker, and the mission is classified as covert MOOTW." The acronym stood for Military Operations Other Than War. "Also for the record, according to House of Nations Resolution 161, a MOOTW must provide officers with clear guidelines regarding what can and should be done to achieve their missions. As of this point, I am not able to delineate either goals or guidelines as we venture into hazards of unknown potential. Therefore, I am ordering all junior officers to report to the escape lander and disembark. I would give you the courtesy of leaving on a flier, but we left ours behind on Venus."

A lesser trained crew would have gasped at this. Captain Odessa was publicly stating that she did not believe in their mission. If there was ever a schism between ARRAY Command and Captain Odessa, she would certainly not air that dirty laundry in public.

Captain Odessa looked at the two bridge assistant lieutenants, Jacques L'Anu and Erika Mode. "Have you two suffered damage to your hearing?" she asked.

The assistant lieutenants stood at attention. "No, sir!" They saluted and ran off the bridge.

"Ambassador," Odessa said to JuneMary, "I strongly suggest you disembark with the rest of the crew."

JuneMary smiled and placed her hand on the captain's shoulder. "Captain, thank you. But it'd be a cold day on Venus before I abandoned my captain."

While Odessa appreciated the loyalty, she did not think it was necessary for JuneMary to accompany her reply with physical contact.

JuneMary gave the captain's shoulder one last squeeze before letting her go.

Odessa waited until the eight junior officers signaled they were safely in the emergency lander. She now had a crew of just four people: herself, Vice Captain Witaker, JuneMary, and, of course, Alex Detail. Under any other circumstances, Alex Detail would have been the first person on that lander, probably pushing everyone else out of his way. But he had a look in his eye like a cat with a mouse in its sight.

"Vice Captain, once the lander has ejected, lock on to the Reaper and spin up to max intercept course," Odessa said.

"Yes sir," Witaker said. "Lock established. Ready for spin-up." Then Witaker abruptly said, "Captain, a flier is approaching us."

"What?" Odessa exclaimed, looking into her display. A message alert suddenly appeared. Why was Spell still sending someone to her ship after she had agreed to follow orders?

Then she read the flier's passenger manifest.

"What the devil is *he* doing here?"

Odessa transferred her personal display to the main holo. "Orders from Madeline Spell, authenticated. Open the lander bay."

The display showed the configuration of the flier, and the boarding orders from Madeline Spell.

The *Virgin Mother* was being boarded by President Jonathan Innsbrook.

"That old boy sure does get around," JuneMary said.

Odessa thought of a fitting message to send Madeline Spell and the rest of ARRAY Command who had not learned the lessons of war in the past twenty years.

"Vice Captain, have the junior crew transfer from the emergency lander and return to the White Plains Spaceport on President Innsbrook's flier," Odessa said. "It would be a waste of equipment if it were to get destroyed along with this ship."

Odessa left President Innsbrook locked in the flier bay for nearly an hour while she personally supervised the ship's spin-up. It was unheard of for an ARRAY ship to cruise at this excessive speed without a drive officer. While the ship's computers monitored the q-field and counteracted the inertial forces created by the massive acceleration that would otherwise turn them to pulp, accidents had been known to occur.

Maximum speed protocols were different once outside the orbit of Mars. In this unpopulated area of space, a ship was allowed to use the Simmons Fission Engines. The fusion reactors that powered all ships between the sun and Mars provided sufficient speed on the relatively smaller scale of travel needed between Earth, Venus, and Mars without leaving radioactive waste behind.

To really get going at anything approaching the speed a Reaper was capable of, the lighter, stronger fission engines were brought online. The Simmons Fission Engines simply split the atoms of fissile material inside a spherical chamber with a valve that released the energy. In crude terms, it blew the ship forward to speeds that quickly approached tens of millions of kilometers per hour.

Odessa had initiated max spin-up a littler earlier than regulations stated. The last time she brought the fission engines online this close to Earth was when they were being pursued by the very Reaper vessel she was now pursuing. She enjoyed being the pursuer this time. *Although, I feel a little too much like Ahab after that whale.* Odessa imagined the Reaper with a harpoon in its side, dragging her underwater.

Now for the matter of President Innsbrook. He had been very quiet in the flier bay. After the junior crew took his flier and left, and the ship initiated its pursuit of George Spell, all Odessa had said to Innsbrook over the ship's com was, "We'll be with you when we can."

Usually, these high and mighty types didn't take well to not getting their way. They would start whining, complaining, and making demands and threats that revealed everything an adversary needed to know.

But Innsbrook hadn't said a word. He just stood patiently in the lander bay, waiting.

Naturally, Alex wanted to go interrogate him, but Odessa was not allowing that. She would deal with Innsbrook herself.

Odessa stood outside the bay door, typed a code into the panel, then held her hand in front of it to allow the ship to check her biometric signature. While Odessa doubted Innsbrook was dangerous, she held her trusty sidearm at her hip as the door slid open.

"President Innsbrook, what the hell are you doing here?"

The President of the United Countries of America stood calmly in the empty bay, dressed in his usual blue suit and dark tie, looking a bit overheated. He answered, "She made me."

That took Odessa by surprise. How could *she* make *him* do anything?

"How?" Odessa asked. "How could Spell coax you into joining this suicide mission?"

"Does it matter?" Innsbrook asked.

"Yes, it matters," Odessa replied. "You kidnapped George Spell, conspired with the radical factions of New Africa's government, and led us on this wild goose chase."

Innsbrook shrugged. "All true. But I don't intend to interfere with you."

"Then what do you want?" Odessa asked.

"Does it matter?" Innsbrook asked for the second time.

This was quickly becoming a ship of the dammed. Whatever threat Madeline Spell had used against Innsbrook to get him here must have been quite a shock to him. Odessa could smell his genuine fear of death with every breath he took.

However Madeline Spell had done it, she had accomplished the near impossible. Now, one ship held all the people in the world who knew her secrets, while the Reaper they were chasing held her biggest secret. How convenient for Madeline Spell if one or both ships were destroyed. No more Alex to worry about. No more Innsbrook to worry about. No more George to worry about.

It was then that Odessa vowed she would commit herself to her last breath to doing the impossible. She was going to keep Alex from activating whatever horrible plan he had been working on for the past six months. She was going to make sure George survived whatever horrible plan they had programmed into him on Venus. And she was going to make sure that Innsbrook lived to answer for everything he had done.

Madeline Spell, you picked the wrong day to tangle with Captain Odessa.

Odessa took a vow: Everyone was going home alive.

CHAPTER 24

FULFILLING A SHORT DESTINY

When George arrived at the specified coordinates beyond the asteroid belt between the orbits of Jupiter and Saturn, he saw a nice view of Saturn through the hole in the hull; the hole was now sealed again by the force field protecting him and the cat from being torn out into space.

George didn't remember enjoying views of things before. When everyone said how beautiful Pluto was when it first arrived to orbit Earth, George had just found it irritating that Pluto blocked the sunlight.

But the tens of hours that had passed on this trip with the cat had been the nicest time of his life. George had expected he and the cat would have to stay inside the pressure suit in order to keep breathing, because they'd lost their air out the hole. Once he turned the Reaper back on, George had concentrated his thoughts on the idea of replacing the air. But although the Reaper's protective field was in place again, the ship didn't seem to know how to re-create the lost atmosphere inside its hull.

George had some hydrips in his pocket. He adjusted his rebreather's electrolyzer then wrapped it around a hydrip before allowing it to explode in the vacuum. After a few drops, he had a nice thick humid environment, and the warm walls had chased away the chill of near absolute zero. Once they could breathe again, George allowed the cat out of the pressure suit, which made the little animal happy. There were some tasty protocarb squares left in his pocket, which the cat was eager to eat. When it was full, it would usually prop itself up on George's legs while he sat on the floor. Sometimes, the cat would sleep on his lap.

The Reaper was easy to drive; he just had to think of certain vectors and shapes to control their course. Alex Detail was far enough behind them to allow for plenty of time to destroy Pluto before the ARRAY vessel caught up.

The Reaper's control interface was sort of like looking in a mirror. George had been able to see his own thoughts as he looked back through the filing cabinet of his life.

He remembered the first three people, the ones who grew him. They smiled at him, talked to him, and uploaded information into him the way a parent would read a storybook to a child before bed. He'd been surrounded by water and fish, and warm flickering sunlight.

He remembered seeing his mother, Madeline Spell, and his father, Guy Hiramoto, in some sort of sterile medical suite in their townhouse in New York City. Madeline Spell would come into his room every day after work, sometimes late at night, and just look at him for a long time as he stared blankly at the ceiling while millions of neurons absorbed the data streams pouring into his quickly growing cells. His mind had been filled with information, memories and experiences, all offered visually, aurally, and synoptically.

He recalled the first time his mother had spoken to him. She was reading an industrial manual on historic battle strategies. It must have bored her, because she had tossed it aside and started telling George her own stories of the great world leaders that had come before her. Although he was still in a rapid growth stage, lying on a warm wet sponge that fed his body and accelerated cell replication, he was able to move his eyes in response to what his mother was saying. It was their first communication.

Soon, George was living in a normal bedroom, following an advanced home schooling program, and playing strategy games on the holo tournaments. His mother had stopped teaching him about politics and war. Instead, she had started asking him about schoolwork and his favorite tournament games. Upon reflection, George could see that there was a time when Madeline Spell had nearly forgotten the reason he had been created, simply allowing herself the pleasure of having a son. And why not? If the Harvesters had never returned, then she could have indulged that maternal fantasy for the rest of her life.

By that time George had learned enough of human emotions and motives that he could easily discern the difference between how Madeline Spell felt towards him and how his "father," Guy Hiramoto, regarded him. He recalled overhearing conversations between Guy Hiramoto and Madeline Spell about her imprinting too strongly on George. Hiramoto was careful not to spend too much time with George. However, he did seem to be growing more and more concerned with Madeline's deepening maternal connection to George. That had been the first instance of George feeling an instinct to protect: He could be capable of harming someone who would harm his mother.

Those times together had ended with the Second Harvester War. George remembered the day his parents presented him with a broken m-com, and asked him to fix it. That was when George learned his true origins and discovered the reason he'd been created as well as the person he was created from.

George had ultimately fulfilled his purpose, sending back the Harvesters when Alex Detail could not. And now he had but one task to complete before his entire existence potential would be maximized. Then, it would be okay for him to end.

As George took a position outside the asteroid belt, he once again marveled at the beauty of Saturn and its glimmering rings. Zarena was very clear that this was where he was to create the singularity to destroy Pluto. Once destroyed, the Reaper would enact some sort of auto-destruct that would result in sealing the black hole. But in the time it took to create the black hole and totally eradicate Pluto, a lot of other stuff could get sucked in. Zarena wanted to make sure it was useless stuff, like asteroids. And, if things went really wrong, giant gas planets like Saturn were there to overwhelm the black hole with more mass than it could handle

"Well, Cat, here we are," George announced, slowly standing as the sleepy cat made a few squeaky mews.

Checking the display in his mind, George noted that Alex Detail's ship had accelerated to a velocity he did not think possible for an ARRAY ship. He would be here sooner than George had planned.

George deactivated the scoop, allowing the Pluto chunk to float freely while he turned the Reaper 180 degrees. He slowly closed the distance between the Reaper and Pluto until the Reaper was moving just millimeters per second. The Reaper's nose very slowly closed in on the tip of what once had been a mountain range on the former planet Pluto, now a mountain with its side blown away, the entire extinct volcanic interior exposed like an autopsied body.

Using the exterior interface to look very closely down a chasm in the side of the mountain, George could see a dim yellow glow, a patch of green, and the charred entrance to an old house.

That was where the Harvesters maintained their link to this universe. It was what they were using to protect their last hold on humanity. It was how they still talked to Alex Detail.

And it would end now.

George locked the Reaper at all stop as its nose brushed the frozen methane crystals coating the mountainside. He picked up the cat, placing it against his chest in the pressure suit. This time the cat was more agitated than before, struggling to get out. As George tried to hold the cat down, it kept pulling itself up, scratching him through his shirt and reaching one of its paws up to gouge the side of George's face.

As trickles of blood slid down his cheek, George held the cat's forelegs, firmly pushing them down into his pressure suit. "You have to calm down, Cat. I know the end of things scares people."

George could feel Alex Detail getting closer as he spent precious time to calm the cat and safely get it inside his pressure suit. Once done, he put the rocks back on his feet and stood by the hole in the side of the Reaper. Before exiting the hull, George issued his last instruction to the Reaper. He thought of a shape, the shape of the object Rosemary June had given Zarena, the shape that Alex Detail had helped create, the shape Rosemary had adjusted at the last minute so George would have a better chance of survival.

The moment he focused on the shape, the Reaper began to glow. A glittering golden energy swirled around its nose, spreading across the frozen surface of shattered Pluto.

With that, George stepped outside and pulled himself to the side of the Reaper opposite Pluto. He had to be exact—he would get only one chance to escape the soon-to-form black hole.

Placing his feet squarely on the hull, George slowly pulled them up until he was floating just a few centimeters above the hull. Then, he quickly kicked his legs down. The rocks hit the hull, nearly exploding in a blast of sparks. The explosive force blew George off the side of the Reaper, shooting him into empty, quiet space.

The cat was struggling again inside the pressure suit. George understood it couldn't see what was going on, so he kept his arms crossed, holding the cat still. It was unlikely the cat could tear the fabric of the suit, but it might not understand it couldn't walk around in space like it could on a planet or in a ship, so George kept a firm grip until the cat settled down.

George could see a pinpoint of nothingness surrounded by the glowing, glimmering gold energy coming from the ship. The black hole's event horizon was beginning to grow. It would expand to fifty kilometers in twenty-seven minutes. If George was going to survive, the explosive reaction that propelled him off the side of the Reaper needed to push George into a speed of 111.1 kilometers per hour—escape velocity.

George pinged a beam of light from his suit's arm panel at the Reaper falling away beneath him. The light bounced off the hull and returned to George's suit, allowing him to calculate his speed relative to the Reaper.

106.6 kilometers per hour.

He had not reached escape velocity.

In twenty-seven minutes, the black hole's event horizon would reach him, suck him in as it collapsed, and that would be the end of his life.

George felt the cat under his hands, nestled in his suit, calmed once again by the steady beat of his heart. George did his best to pet the cat the way it liked, through the thick fabric of the pressure suit.

"I'm sorry," he said to the cat.

There was no air to carry George's voice. The cat never heard him.

CHAPTER 25

•

REVENGE OF THE HARVESTERS

JuneMary was watching Alex Detail stare into the main display when Odessa returned from her meeting with President Innsbrook.

"What'd he say?" JuneMary asked Odessa.

Odessa ignored JuneMary and stood directly in front of the drive display. "Mr. Witaker, uncouple the Simmons regulator."

"Captain, regulations state that I must warn you uncoupling the Simmons regulator will exceed hull strain and flood us with dangerous levels of radiation." Horace said.

"I am aware of the risks," Odessa said. "Do it."

"Holy crap!" Alex yelled, rushing over to the display as the Simmons engines were allowed to split enough atoms of fissile material to fill the release chamber. Alex quickly input a safety formula and sent it to Captain Odessa for approval. She hit OK without even checking.

As the ship speed-jumped, the formula Alex designed moved the q-field shape to a precise balance that diffused some of the radiation while creating a strong forward gravitational force just before the jump would have smashed them all to bits against the walls.

JuneMary decided she was going to have a little talk with Innsbrook. She left the bridge and found the room Captain Odessa had put him in. When she chimed the door, President Innsbrook's voice came over the com, "It's locked."

"No kidding," JuneMary said. "What code did mother punch in?" President Innsbrook might come off as completely distracted and disinterested in anything around him, but JuneMary knew he paid attention to every little detail and had a perfect memory.

"It doesn't matter," Innsbrook said. "She's sealed the lock biometrically."

"I know, just tell me the code."

"She typed in C-A-T-O-N-I-N-E-T-A-I-L-S."

JuneMary shook her head. Were all the captain's codes ancient torture devices? JuneMary removed a small square blue metal chip from the inside of her jacket. It was featureless except for a tiny etching of the triangle from the House of Nations seal. JuneMary waved the chip in front of the door's lock. The door slid open.

President Innsbrook was sitting in a small junior officer's quarters, a room about six by eight feet. He perched on the edge of a shelf-bed attached to the wall. "How'd you do that?"

JuneMary placed the metal square back inside her jacket. "I understand you're friendly with my sister-in-law, Kelen Rome June."

"You pretty much understand everything, Ambassador," President Innsbrook said.

JuneMary nodded. "People like to talk to me, and my dad too. So do you have some code or something?"

President Innsbrook raised an eyebrow.

"Oh, come on now, Mr. President. Let's put all our cards on the table, I mean for real now. Old mother up there has this ship going so fast it's liable to come flying apart any minute, and Alex Detail has a look in his eye like the devil sat down and gave birth to the baby Jesus."

Innsbrook didn't so much as raise an eyebrow or turn a corner of his mouth. "Yes, I have a code. It was part of the deal."

JuneMary nodded. "Well, I suggest you get ready to use it."

"Have we created an extinction level event?" Innsbrook asked.

JuneMary sat down next to Innsbrook. "Well, let's see now, you got A.D. up there, scheming to teleport the Harvester magic back at us, then you got the other one out there in a Reaper pulling little Pluto, and seems he's been taught how to create a black hole, courtesy of the Rome family's little hidden research facility to which you have been so kind as to donate." JuneMary shifted, put her foot against the wall. "I'd say whatever that torsion network does, we're going to need it soon."

"But it only protects Venus," Innsbrook said.

JuneMary patted Innsbrook on his back. "Oh, come on now, father. We both know high and holy Brother Lonadoon wouldn't be helping out with something so trivial. Now, if I were a betting woman, which Lord bless me, I'm not, I would say you got yourself plugged in all throughout the solar system."

Innsbrook laid his head back against the wall. "A lifetime of work, scuttled."

"What's that supposed to mean?" JuneMary asked.

Innsbrook smiled. "Oh, finally, something you don't know."

"Well, out with it!"

Innsbrook sat up. "They made it pretty clear to me that George would not survive the destruction of Pluto." He smiled, adding, "And I even heard that your niece Rosemary went running in at the last minute with some extra help for little George." Innsbrook stood and stared out the small porthole at the blur of space. "But I doubt I'll be sending Kelen any passwords. It's embedded in my synaptic uplink, and unfortunately doesn't work if I'm dead."

"Then you need to not be dead," JuneMary said.

"That would be nice," Innsbrook said. "But Madeline Spell is a whiz with her geneticists. It seems I've got a little bug. And if I don't see George Spell soon, I will die."

That's an inventive way to get rid of an adversary, JuneMary thought. *Compel him to go on a rescue mission he's likely to die on, or stay home and face certain death.*

JuneMary stood to leave. "Well then, father, I'll just have to see what I can do about that."

Alex Detail's life as the savior of humanity had all started with a circle.

One day he was taping together strips of paper into hoops, then looping them together, making the Christmas Tree paper chain just like his mother showed him. But that wasn't his first experience with circles.

The Detail house was filled with circles.

At the time Alex was born, it was still six years until the Harvester ring ship would reach them, still six years away from the first war.

Back then, some people didn't think the Harvesters intended any harm. Before they had attacked the sun, sucking its energy away and deploying the deadly Reaper ships, the Harvesters weren't even called the Harvesters. Most people referred to them as the Ring People.

There was never any fear of the Ring People in the Detail house. But sometimes when Alex went to play with friends, he could tell other families were suspicious of the Detail family. Other families were fearful of the Ring People, and construed the Detail's cult-like reverence of the circle as something akin to demonic worship. Zarena Detail, however, had always seemed to regard the Ring People as some kind of vengeful gods, to be emulated for their beauty, and feared for their horrible powers.

After the Harvesters attacked, Alex watched the news holos show how slow ARRAY ships were compared to the Reapers. It was then he realized that the rings were a clue. His mother had, perhaps unconsciously, surrounded Alex's early life with circles, conditioning his mind for the times ahead.

Alex went back to the strips of paper, and gave a strip a half turn before taping it together, creating a mobius.

The contemplation of the mobius led to the m-com, faster-than-light communications. Alex remembered that time in his life as one of incredible growth in his mind's abilities to create and process information.

To this day, Alex Detail was the only one who completely understood how the m-com worked. That was partially because the mobius was at once an amplifier and a de-amplifier. When the m-com took three-dimensional electromagnetic information and sent it into two-dimensional space, it was trading volume for speed. The amount of mass was reduced, transformed into tachyon-like particles, received by another m-com almost instantly; the information was decelerated and mass was restored. Some physicists insisted the m-com was a particle time machine, sending information to the receiver's past relative to the sender. But Alex understood time had nothing to do with it.

There was a very tenuous link in the last remaining bits of Pluto, a small link through non-Euclidean space that kept this universe connected to the Harvester universe. In their original plan, the Harvesters had thought big: Remove the sun so the planets could be moved through a singularity at the center of the solar system.

But Alex was thinking small. Take the permanent link the Harvesters had installed in Pluto and apply the principles of the m-com; trade speed for mass. If he could make a big enough mobius, Alex could create a localized field of Harvester physics. This solar system would truly become heaven, just as it had been when Pluto first arrived to orbit Earth.

The problem was, there was so little energy coming through the remains of Pluto, by Alex's calculation it would take a mobius nearly 300,000 kilometers across to generate the type of amplification he needed.

It would take more material than the planet Earth itself was made of, to create a ring 300,000 kilometers across.

Alex had just about dropped the idea altogether when it suddenly hit him that there was just such a ring mysteriously hanging around the solar system.

The rings of Saturn.

Alex immediately got to work writing his biggest and best program yet. From the rings of his youth, Alex was about to bring life full circle.

The *Virgin Mother* was decelerating at such a dangerous rate, the q-field was not able to completely dampen the inertia. Odessa had them all run the calculations to take the ship to the quickest all-stop in the location of the Reaper. The resulting deceleration curve would create g-forces beyond the q-field dampening powers of nearly nine gees for almost thirty minutes.

During that time, the four crew members were required to lie in horizontal g-force emergency crèches. They were administered a drug that would prevent any veins or arteries from bursting under the greater pressure. While still locked in his room, Innsbrook was ordered to follow the same instructions.

By the time the *Virgin Mother* had reached all-stop, the ship's claxons were going wild as it detected a space-time disturbance. "Reverse Course," said the ship, "Reverse cour—"

Odessa cut the audio.

That's when Alex watched with horror what George Spell was doing with the Reaper. The display showed an event-horizon expanding around the Reaper and the remains of Pluto. It was currently ten kilometers across and growing.

"Calculate critical mass," Odessa said.

The computer carried out the calculation: fifty kilometers. When the event horizon reached fifty kilometers, a black hole would blink into existence for a fraction of a second, eating up everything in the surrounding area.

"Back away, Mr. Witaker, nice and slow," Odessa said.

"Wait!" Alex said. "We—" This was the moment he had been waiting for, but something held him back.

This was the time when he was supposed to invoke the Harvester powers and initiate his massive q-field command program. But something was stopping him.

He realized what it was. George Spell was attacking his mind. But it was a new kind of attack, something he had never experienced from George before. Alex felt George flooding his mind with sorrow.

No, George doesn't feel sorrow, doesn't have empathy. It must be some sort of trick.

Before anyone could respond to Alex, Horace Witaker said, "There is a body accelerating away from the event horizon."

There was no question whose it was.

"Ping it," Odessa said.

The display showed the ping results: human male, three to six years old. Then a surprise: Feline, male, three to six years old.

"He has a cat with him?" Alex asked.

Witaker magnified the image, displaying it on all light frequencies. "He's in a pressure suit, and he has a cat in the pressure suit. Vital signs are suppressed but both are alive."

It was a disquieting image, a boy in a pressure suit with a small lump on his chest, lying flat, floating through space.

Well, not floating, Alex noted. George was traveling at a velocity of over one hundred kilometers per hour.

"Is someone going to go out there and get that boy?" JuneMary cried. "I mean, I know there's some bad blood between the two of you, but let's be for real now."

"That's not going to be possible," Horace Witaker replied. He superimposed the expanding event horizon with George's speeding body. It showed that within twenty-one minutes, George would be enveloped by the event horizon and killed.

Alex wondered what had happened to George on Venus. Somehow he had gotten control of a Reaper, taken a pet, and been outfitted with this feeble attempt to escape a black hole. George knew he was going to die, and he felt sorrow. That was it.

A cat?

Alex knew he had to take the action that fate had been calling on him to do ever since the destruction of Pluto. "I know how to stop the black hole from forming," he said.

"How?" Odessa asked.

"I have a command program."

"Of course you do," Odessa replied. "The one that makes you king of the universe."

"Do you have a better idea?" Alex asked.

"Oh, please," Odessa scoffed. "You would ask me to believe that you have a command program that can save the very person whose existence is a constant threat to your life?"

Alex didn't bother answering, but he could see that Odessa was tempted to let him have a go at it. Surprisingly, she turned to Horace Witaker and asked, "Mr. Witaker, would you recommend transferring command control to the admiral?"

Horace Witaker turned around, looked Alex squarely in the eye. The chip in Alex's thumb was pulsing with life. It was like some drug had been injected, and his mind was suddenly crisp, clear, and open to the visions beyond mortal sight. What he saw in Horace's mind and body was something surprising. Pure, blinding rage. He saw someone who had followed orders his entire life, lived by other's rules and never made a decision that put his own wishes before others. He was looking at a man who had never done a thing he wanted to do in all of his life.

Horace squinted his eyes in a look of hatred and said, "If you transfer command authority to Alex Detail, there is absolutely no way I will comply." Horace crossed his arms and stood like a man braced for impact.

Odessa seemed a bit surprised by his manner, but it was the answer she expected. "Well then, there you have it."

Before Alex could respond, JuneMary stepped forward and stuck her hand into the ship's main display. "Not so fast," she said. "Ship, transfer command to Admiral Alexander Detail."

To everyone's surprise, the ship did not refuse, did not so much as ask for a password. It simply said, "Command transferred."

"What the hell is going on?" Odessa screeched.

JuneMary waved a finger at Odessa. "I can't believe you're going to stand by and let that boy die!"

The ship suddenly moved. Alex was already at the controls, his command program active.

"What treachery is this?" Odessa demanded.

JuneMary said, "Ship, inform Captain Odessa of command structure, historical record."

The ship replied, "The ARRAY warship Eleven-A prototype was originally the commission of Secretary RK June via executive order, House command badge issued on August 3, 2259. This vessel was renamed the *Virgin Mother* on August 20, 2259. Subcommand was granted to Captain Odessa, House of Nations identification number four four eight eight on the same date. Secretary RK June retained the executive command badge and mission command veto authority. On March 25, 2060, Secretary RK June transferred title of the executive command badge to ARRAY Commander JuneMary, House of Nations identification number currently classified."

The look of scorn on Odessa's face was as menacing as any of them had ever seen from her. "What a bunch of sneaky conniving cohorts you Junes are."

Alex was barely processing the conversation. He didn't have much time. He was pushing the ship into a massive acceleration curve and calculating the exact point at which he would transfer the entire fission/fusion energy potential to the q-field. He had originally designed this program to be run by four ARRAY ships. It would have been a simple matter of taking a small fleet out under some pretense after he had been made Chief Executive of ARRAY.

But that had never happened. And then suddenly Alex found himself on the *Virgin Mother*; he had to make do the best he could. Fortunately, the ARRAY flagship was capable of producing the massive energy needed.

As Alex concentrated on aligning the ship with the axial equator of the plant Saturn, he could hear Odessa and JuneMary continuing some argument. Then out of the corner of his eye he caught something, too late. Horace Witaker was charging at him.

Alex had half a second to brace for impact. Horace was taller and more muscular by about six inches and fifty pounds. The force of Horace's impact pitched Alex clear through the central display. The two landed hard against the corner of the wall and floor. The harsh impact with the wall and slamming weight of Horace on top of Alex nearly caused him to lose consciousness.

Horace grabbed Alex by the front of his jacket, tearing it in the process, then raised his fist to punch Alex square in the face. Alex had an image of his scull being fractured by the imminent pummeling. As Horace's fist was bearing down on Alex's face, Alex thrust out his right hand. A jolt of energy arced from his thumb, slamming into Horace, knocking him on his back.

Horace was back up on his feet in a second when Captain Odessa grabbed him in a paralyzing chokehold. "Get control of yourself, Vice Captain!"

Before either of them could move another muscle, JuneMary exclaimed, "Holy Mary, Mother of God!"

The ship was on a collision course with the edge of Saturn's rings.

Seen from another perspective, it might have been a beautiful sight: the *Virgin Mother* slicing through the plane of rings encircling Saturn's equator. But the view Alex and his crewmates had was terrifying. Not only was the q-field being pummeled by the frozen debris that made up the rings, the ship was caught in Saturn's gravity well, diving nose-first toward the planet's surface.

It was hard to tell whether the terrible tremors tearing at the ship were caused by slicing through the rings or entering Saturn's gravity well at such a high rate of speed.

But it was over in a moment. Alex dragged himself up from the floor. He watched as they passed through the inner ring, then reached a panel and slammed all the energy to the q-field, bouncing the ship off the planet's atmosphere.

"What the hell are you doing?" Odessa yelled, a hand still firmly holding Witaker's arm—either to keep control of him or help her stay upright; it was hard to tell which.

Alex had a beatific smile on his face and said simply, "Look. . ."

Pulling up an image of Saturn from a nearby satellite, the crew could see their ship, the *Virgin Mother*, had cut a clear path straight back through the plane of Saturn's rings. They were now speeding along the outer circle of the rings.

An astonishing sight greeted the crew: Saturn's rings were collapsing in on themselves, coalescing into a more solid shape! Then, they began to buckle and turn in, forming a hoop, like a strip of paper floating around the planet.

But one end of the hoop did not turn. The portion of the rings that had been cut by the *Virgin Mother* stayed in place on one end while a ripple passed through the length of the ring. As the ripple reached the other end of the circle, the edges connected.

The rings of Saturn were now a mobius.

The rings majestically tilted on an axis. In a flash they moved at a near light speed then stopped fast. The gigantic mobius had compressed space-time in a dizzying effect.

The rings of Saturn, now a mobius, were encircling the remains of Pluto, the Reaper, the growing event horizon, and George Spell.

The feeling that flooded the *Virgin Mother* was familiar to its crew. They had experienced it first in the sunny meadow in the backyard of Peevchi Derringkite's house on Pluto. They had experienced it again in the days that Pluto orbited Earth.

"*This* again," Odessa said with a less than convincing sound of disgust.

The effects of the Harvester universe were unexplainable. They delivered not only a sense of euphoria or omniscience, but also a knowingness that time could be altered: moments could be slowed to their true essence, experiences held in mind for as long as one needed to savor and enjoy every aspect and essence of life.

The event horizon surrounding the remains of Pluto froze in time, then began to shrink.

Horace Witaker had a hand to the side of his head as he watched the *Virgin Mother* approach Pluto and the Reaper. "How are you doing this?" he asked Alex.

"There has always been a rift in space buried inside Pluto. It was how Derringkite first established contact with the Harvesters. That rift was nearly destroyed by the black hole launched by Venus after the ring ships were destroyed. But its mass was larger, so it consumed the black hole before the singularity consumed *it*. Now, someone has instructed George Spell on just the right size singularity to simultaneously destroy the rift *and* the hole created by the Reaper."

Alex shook his head. "That is no matter anymore. I've created a steady state pull of non-rotational universe physics from the Harvester Universe. When they first tried taking us to their universe, it was under the pretense of bettering our existence. That might not have been true. Relative to the way they process intelligence, perhaps, but Derringkite did not imagine in his madness how the Harvesters were physically communicating with him. He didn't realize that Von Neumann type probes were leaking information. That's not good news for a universe that had reached the Omega Point. It means the infinite simulation running the eternity of every being's life is going to end. The Harvesters needed a new influx of primary experience. It has been billions of years since they existed as actual physical beings."

JuneMary cocked her head. "You mean the Harvesters are body-snatchers?"

"I wouldn't put it that way," Alex said. "That implies some ill intent on their part, which is really impossible to know."

Just then, Alex felt a wave of vertigo. He grabbed JuneMary's arm to stabilize himself.

"What's wrong?" JuneMary asked.

Alex straightened up. "I just got dizzy for some reason." He held up his hand, looking at his thumb. It was throbbing painfully.

A two-tone chime sounded. The ship reported that an external hatch had been opened.

The screen showed someone in a mobile thruster unit.

"It looks like President Innsbrook has gone out to get George," Odessa said, shooting JuneMary a knowing look.

"Darn right, I unlocked his door," JuneMary said. "You got a problem with that?"

JuneMary must have been as surprised as Alex at her outburst. Not only would she normally never get angry like that, but under the universal empathetic influence of the Harvesters, no one should ever get angry.

Something wasn't right at all.

Alex's thumb really hurt. It felt like it was on fire. A sharp pain shot up his arm so intensely that Alex actually screamed. The unbearable searing pain in his thumb was coming from the Harvester chip.

"Help me!" Alex cried, grasping his right wrist with his left hand as the pain continued to intensify.

As everyone rushed to his side, they could actually see light coming from Alex's thumb. Then there was a sizzling sound and a sickening smell of burning flesh as the Harvester chip burned its way out of Alex's thumb and landed on the floor.

JuneMary held Alex upright as he stumbled in shock.

Odessa and Horace looked at where the small glass chip was superheating the floor, the surrounding area bubbling as it liquefied. In seconds, the chip melted its way through the floor.

An alarm sounded alerting them to a hull breech. The chip had burned its way straight out of the ship.

The *Virgin Mother* automatically applied an emergency epoxy filler to the pinhole created by the chip.

Odessa looked up at Alex and said, "I think you've been had."

Alex stood mute as everyone talked to him at once. None of them made any sense; all he heard was a jumble of words. His ears were ringing, his vision blurry. He lost all sense of time. He barely noticed seeing a screen showing President Innsbrook circling the *Virgin Mother* with George Spell under his arm. It hardly registered that JuneMary was pulling at the still irate Horace Witaker's arm. They left the bridge, presumably to help retrieve Innsbrook.

The feeling of dread, that sharp pain that hits somewhere below the gut like a physical punch and spreads quickly to overtake the mind, was enveloping Alex Detail. But just then, he heard a unique sound, perhaps the only sound in the world he would have paid any attention. Five notes played in a small implant in his ear.

Alex Detail never thought he would hear those notes.

He didn't need any other information. The message was from the Generationists, and it meant that Madeline Spell had retrieved the Toolkit.

So that's why she sent Innsbrook here.

CHAPTER 26

•

EXTINCTION LEVEL EVENT HORIZON

George wished he could talk to the cat. Maybe he could if he stretched some space out between his face unit and the rest of his pressure suit, but it was already getting cold, and George didn't want the cat to be distressed just so he could share the beautiful sight he was watching.

As the event horizon grew ever closer to George, he saw the Alex Detail ship sail really fast toward Saturn. The ship actually snipped a slice right through the planet's ring like the leading edge of a razor through a piece of paper.

He watched the ship ride a q-field wave around the outer edge of the rings. George really wanted the cat to see how the rings rippled and turned into a mobius. The sun glimmered off the frozen crystals of the rings in a spectacular golden spray of light, refracted and polarized by George's face mask.

George was staring at the phenomena when something even stranger occurred. The rings seemed to be in several places at once, creating a curving blur that appeared for a moment as a mobius tunnel through space.

George suddenly felt some sense of his mind clearing, opening. He could sense the people on the ship—what they felt—and he understood why. So, *this* was what had everyone so hypnotized by the Harvesters. He wondered if the cat was feeling any better.

But the sensation faded as quickly as it had come upon him. He was looking at the shrinking event horizon and wondering if that too would stop or continue to expand and consume him.

He watched for a while. The *Virgin Mother* came back into his field of vision, gliding above him as he continued on his trajectory away from the Reaper. George had a sudden urge to yell at someone, to be angry. But he had taught himself to analyze things like that, so he put the emotion aside and thought of possible causes. It occurred to him that whatever influence the Harvesters had on his mind, there was an equal and opposite effect, a price to be paid. Like the people who became addicted to drugs and then stopped taking them. They could get cranky.

They are certainly taking their time coming out to get me, George thought, then told himself not to be cranky. Running a big ship like that took a lot of work. Perhaps they were just busy with the business of keeping everything going.

As George continued on his trajectory, he calculated he would pass the ship completely in a few minutes.

Out of the corner of his eye, George saw a glittering green light floating beneath the hull of the *Virgin Mother*. Curiously, the glittering stopped when he turned his head, then reappeared when he turned his head another way. As he drew closer to the ship, George saw that for some reason the glittering green gem was photosensitive to his left eye.

Reaching out his left hand, George grabbed the glittering gem. It was stuck to some thin strand of glass, which looked like toffee that had melted then hardened again. As he held it in his hand, George received a certain sensation. *Interesting.* This was the Harvester chip Alex Detail had stolen from the body of Peevchi Derringkite, the man George had killed. This was the chip George had taught himself to use by peeking into Alex's mind during the past six months. This was the chip George had almost touched when he shook Alex's hand in the planetarium, releasing the particle—a particle that was supposed to collide with the chip and kill Alex Detail.

So Alex must have done whatever he was trying to do with the Harvesters, George thought. And of course, the Harvesters had tricked him. George could see that the chip had burned its way right out of Alex's thumb and melted right through the ship before being frozen in the near absolute zero of space. The chip wanted to get away from Alex!

Those tricky Harvesters.

George was so fixated on the Harvester chip, he didn't notice the person sailing toward him on a mobile thruster until the person nearly collided with him. But George was traveling so fast, he sailed right by his rescuer.

Then, he noticed a wire across his waist. The wire grew tighter, pulling George around in the same direction as the person in the thruster suit. The cat began to squirm and George soothed it with a gentle brush of his hand. As George felt himself being reeled in like a fish, he could make out the face of the person who had come out to save him.

George waved. Though he knew he couldn't make any sound, he said, "Hi President Innsbrook!"

Just then, a beam of light shot out of the center of the giant mobius, originating from some deep crevasse on Pluto. The light shot straight toward Earth.

President Innsbrook held George with one arm while trying to maneuver toward the ship bay with the other. It wasn't easy to begin with, and George had a feeling that President Innsbrook had never done this before. They bounced off the airlock twice. Each time, they had to make a long circular approach to create an accurate alignment.

Finally, Innsbrook was able to clear the doorway of the ship. They landed with a thud in the lander bay airlock. Innsbrook let go of George and hit the panel to seal the bay. As the door quickly slid shut, George felt a tug on his waist.

Turning around, he saw that Innsbrook had nearly been yanked back out into space by the tangled wire. Now, his hand was pinned to the entrance by a tight knot. And there was a lot of blood gushing onto the floor.

Before George could take off his mask, JuneMary and Horace Witaker were in the airlock, untangling Jonathan Innsbrook's hand from the wire knot. George could see Innsbrook's face beneath his own pressure suit mask, and he seemed to be yelling something at JuneMary. He was trying to use his one free hand to take his mask off when she yanked him up and said, "Good job, Mr. President, getting our boy back, but hold still. Looks like I might have to stitch that hand up myself."

George stared. It looked as if the wire had cut through half of Innsbrook's wrist. In his final attempt to pull off his mask, Innsbrook got a look at his nearly severed hand, and passed out.

JuneMary helped Witaker heave Innsbrook up over his shoulder. They stumbled off in the direction of the Wellness Center, JuneMary yelling over her shoulder, "Go to the bridge and help Alex fix this mess. And there's no need to go off and try killing him. He knows the Harvesters ain't no saviors."

After George removed his pressure suit, he was glad to see the cat was okay, although he could tell it was not happy with him. It looked frightened in this strange ship.

George said, "Cat, I have to go to the bridge." He waited a moment to see if the cat would follow him, but it seemed to be more interested in slinking along the wall and sniffing.

George knew his way to the bridge. He had been there before. It was the place where he had taken over the ship and killed Peevchi Derringkite when the man tried to stop him from sending the Doppler shift instructions that sent the Harvester ring ships to their destruction in the sun.

As George walked down the narrow hallway, he noticed a lot of empty rooms. There weren't many people on this ship. Last time he was here, people had been coming and going from nearly every direction. Now, even the weapons locker stood open and unguarded.

George could hear Captain Odessa's voice yelling something from the bridge as he entered.

Alex leaned against a wall, his head resting on his arm while Odessa kept yelling at him to do something. Alex glanced blankly in the direction of George, then pulled his head away from his arm.

"Were you surprised to see Innsbrook?" Detail asked.

"He got hurt, and they took him to heal him," George answered.

"Lucky for you," Alex said. "I just got a message from the Generationists. Madeline Spell infected him with a virus that can kill us instantly."

"What does that have to do with anything?" Odessa asked. "Why would he come here to kill you? Or you?" she said, looking at George.

Alex shook his head. "She probably told him some bogus story about how the virus would kill *him* if he didn't get to us. He would have checked the virus somehow and found it matched our genes. That would be enough to make him believe her. But the Generationists promised they would tell me, if they could, if Spell ever came for the Toolkit. Not that any of it matters now."

"What is that beam of light?" Odessa asked, pointing to the white beam shooting from the crevasse on Pluto toward the center of the solar system.

"It's an energy exchange," Alex said. "But it's only going to go one way. They lied to me."

Odessa shook her fists at Alex. "See what you get for meddling with things? Now, how do we fix this?"

"We don't," Alex said. "That beam of energy will envelop Earth and reverse the light cones of information storage."

"What the hell does that mean?" Odessa yelled.

Alex stared bleakly at the display. "It means I've killed everyone on Earth."

George didn't think Alex was thinking as clearly as he should, so he offered what he thought might be some helpful advice. "Well, why don't we use that big mobius to turn off the beam and let the singularity I created collapse the hole."

"Don't you think I tried that?" Alex asked. "I sent the instructions. But they sent them back to me, then reversed the instructions so the singularity would stop collapsing. And they took their chip back so I couldn't do that again." Alex looked at his red, swollen thumb.

"Do you mean this chip?" George held out the elongated melted shard in his hand.

Alex nearly jumped at the sight of it. He knelt beside George, peered closely at the chip, then back up at George. "They don't know you have it?" Alex asked incredulously.

George shook his head. "No. I thought I would talk to you before trying to use it."

"But I thought they didn't let you use that anymore?" Odessa asked.

Alex nodded. "They can't stop me from using it, that's why they had to get it away from me, after they sent back the patterns I used to create the mobius."

"So it's useless?" Odessa asked.

George understood why Alex suddenly got more pale than before. He held the chip up for Odessa to see and said, "If he uses it again, sends the message to collapse the mobius, then they have to get a message back to him through the chip, reversing that."

"Simple, then," Odessa said. "Send the message. Then take the chip back out."

Alex shook his head. "It's not just an antenna. It's interconnected with the bearer's whole consciousness. The only way I could collapse the hole permanently is if . . ."

A very sad conclusion Alex has reached, George thought. Captain Odessa didn't seem to understand, so George explained. "If he sends the message again, the Harvesters will just do what they did before, then take the chip back. But if they send the message and there's no consciousness left to process it, they're stuck."

Alex took the chip from George's hand. "I'd have to find a way to have a complete synaptic neural failure."

"Poison? A gun to the head?" Odessa suggested, rather quickly.

"No," Alex said. "That would actually take too long. This kind of failure would have to be . . ." He paused.

George said, "It would have to be the kind you'd get if you were infected with the Toolkit, like if you breathed the same air as President Innsbrook."

JuneMary walked onto the bridge holding an orange cat. "Look what I found."

Horace Witaker came in just behind her. "Innsbrook was cut up pretty bad. We had to knock him out and stick his hand in a therma-heal."

The orange cat leaped out of JuneMary's arms and ran over to George.

Alex stood up. "JuneMary, I'm going to go collapse the mobius, but the beam of light is still going to hit Earth in about sixty minutes. Can you get on the m-com to Kelen and see if she can activate the Venus torsion grid?"

"I think she'll do just about anything I ask her considering you got that nice contract of hers for me," JuneMary said. "I'll just send her a wake-up call with the safety code she gave Innsbrook."

Alex started heading off the bridge. "JuneMary, get on the m-com to Kelen immediately. Captain Odessa, Vice Captain Witaker, get this ship out of here as fast as you can or you're going to end up in a black hole. Under no circumstances is anyone to enter the wellness center until the black hole has completely collapsed."

George had seen movies with scenes like this. Usually, before the hero went off to die there was a big speech and a lot of goodbyes. But here, there was none of that. Everyone instantly got to work on what Alex told them to do.

It wasn't supposed to end that way, so George followed Alex off the bridge.

"George, you don't have to follow me. There's no window into the wellness center, so you won't even be able to have the satisfaction of seeing me die," Alex said as George walked down the corridor after him.

Satisfaction? George would be satisfied that the Harvesters were finally destroyed, but that had nothing to do with watching Alex die. George picked up his pace to walk beside Alex. "I had a cat come with me when I left Venus," George said. "I was glad he was with me—even though I expected to die."

Alex slowed a bit, glancing down at George. "So, you're my pet now?"

Yes, that made sense to George. Pets helped their owners, and George wanted to help Alex destroy the Harvesters. "Yes. And I also have a lot of questions still. I won't ever get a chance to talk to you again if you are dead, right?"

Alex nodded. "Yeah, that's usually how it works."

"So, you still talk to the Generationists?" George asked.

Alex tilted his head. "No. I haven't talked to them in years. But I warned them about safeguards they put in the age regression experiments, and they agreed to let me know if it was ever turned into a weapon."

"But you worked with the Generationists, so why don't you know how to keep the virus from killing you?"

"Of course I know how," Alex said. "I'd have to have been in recent contact with Innsbrook, then I'd need to create a general vaccine, just mix a little of my saliva with some other live cell that can't get the flu, like maybe that cat of yours."

"A hair follicle from the cat could provide a good stem cell," George said. "But I would need to know the specific base pair sequencing and then it would take at least a day before I developed some protection from the virus."

Alex suddenly stopped. "Oh, right," he said. "You need to know how to keep Innsbrook from killing *you*, too." He seemed to think about this for a minute, then said, "It would serve Madeline Spell right to have you show up with Innsbrook after all this is over. Do you remember what you said to me in the car, when I was riding with you back to your house from Spell's office?"

George pulled the entire conversation up in his memory, recalling the part that had to do with Madeline Spell. "I said, 'If my mother ever finds out that your involvement with the Generationists was a ploy to develop and implement the technology she used to create me, she will have us both killed and start from scratch.'"

"It seems you were right," Alex said. "Because that's exactly what she's doing."

George didn't say anything because Alex had taken out his hand window and started tapping at it. He was obviously in a hurry; George kept hearing a small sound that indicated the window was autocorrecting a lot of what he typed.

Alex finished and said, "Here. Once I'm dead, this will send you a message. You'll have access to the Generationist research."

George took Alex's window. Inside was everything George had ever wanted besides fulfilling his urge to destroy the Harvesters. Alex Detail had just handed over the files George had spent his entire sentient lifetime trying to acquire—the files showing all the work Alex did with the Generationists, files that were no longer supposed to exist. The Generationist files would show George Spell how he was made, what he was vulnerable to, and why he wasn't a real person.

"Thank you very much, Alex Detail," George said. "That was really nice of you."

Alex made a sound George supposed was the laughing sound people made when something was really not funny. "It's not nice of me, George. It's actually very vengeful of me. Madeline Spell might be getting off easy, but a message from beyond my grave gives me the last word."

"Are you afraid to die right now?" George asked.

"Well, you know what George, it's not as bad as I always imagined," Alex answered. "I'm really more afraid of killing everyone and being left alive."

They were standing outside the wellness center door now. Alex pulled his admiral's pin off his jacket shoulder and slid its edge across the burned cut on his thumb, reopening the wound. He winced as he used the edge of the pin to scrape off some of the melted glass and pushed the Harvester chip back into his thumb.

This was all happening too fast for George. He hadn't gotten the information he needed. "So, what will happen to you, when you go in there?"

"An airborne virus will immediately enter my system," Alex said through a grimace as he squeezed his cut thumb with his other hand. "It has an RNA interference instruction that will pretty much shut down my brain within seconds. I'll have just enough time to send an image of an inverse mobius. By the time the Harvesters try to reverse the message and melt the chip back out of me, I won't have a mind to run their instructions. The mobius will collapse, the black hole will collapse, and they'll be gone for good."

Alex faced the door. "I think you should stay away from this room and Innsbrook. Go put a breather mask on until you figure out how to create the virus antibodies. Meanwhile, convince your mother to deploy a fleet of ships to deflect the beam of light."

"Can I ask you one last question?" George said. "If you had only part of the Generationist research and created an antibody, would you still die?"

Alex turned to George and answered, "It's not very likely. I mean, you would probably be brain dead pretty quickly. However, there would be a small chance that a generalized vaccine would provide enough protection to allow your brain to be repaired. But I wouldn't try it, and I don't have the time to wait for a partial vaccine to become active in my system."

"No, I guess you don't," George said.

Before Alex turned back toward the door, he said, "Goodbye, George Spell."

George said, "I'm sorry, Alex Detail."

That caused Alex to pause and look over his shoulder before opening the door.

George imagined the last thing Alex Detail saw was George aim a gun at the base of his spine and fire.

When George Spell entered the wellness center, President Innsbrook was lying on a raised cushioned table, a table similar to those they sometimes used when doing tests on George.

President Innsbrook slowly raised his head. "I see you cut yourself too," he said, motioning at the cut in George's thumb.

"Yes, but on purpose, just now, when I stole the Harvester chip from Alex Detail and put it in my thumb," George said.

He walked closer to Innsbrook, stopping by his side. For some reason, Innsbrook was taking unusually deep breaths. "I just thought of an inverse mobius. The Harvesters don't like it. They are sending a message back now."

Innsbrook seemed nervous about what George was saying. He stood up, stumbling over to the door. It was locked and encrypted.

"Why did you lock us in?" Innsbrook asked.

"I have to make sure I die all the way," George said.

Innsbrook squinted his eyes. "Why do you think you are going to die?"

"Did my mother say the virus she gave you would kill you unless you came into contact with me?" George asked.

Suddenly, Innsbrook held his hand up to his mouth, like he was trying to keep his breath in. "Oh, damn," he said. "I'm sorry, George."

President Innsbrook was smart. George didn't think he'd like being tricked by Madeline Spell like that.

"I didn't come here to murder you," Innsbrook said. "I should have realized what Spell was trying to do."

George nodded and took a deep breath. The Harvester instruction was about to come back. He was beginning to feel slightly dizzy.

"You have to make sure I die so I can kill the Harvesters all the way this time," George said. "This is very important bus—"

George abruptly lost the ability to speak, but knew he didn't have to explain to Innsbrook. He had spent enough time with him on the way to Venus to know the president wouldn't question what George was doing.

But as his vision went black and he felt himself stumble, George thought about Zarena, remembering the times she touched him on his head. And he thought about the cat he'd never see again.

George was falling sideways. The Harvester instruction was back, just going through the chip, but his brain was shutting off. His left leg and arm went numb as paralysis overtook him. George crumpled to the floor. The Harvester instruction was trying to keep him alive, but it was no use. The neurons in his brain stopped firing. He was moments from death.

The last thing George felt was President Innsbrook's arms, a warm embrace holding him, gently lowering his body to the floor.

Something scratchy rubbed against Alex's cheek. Opening his eyes a crack, he saw a cat licking his face.

Alex tried standing, but a pulse of pain through his head made him drop back to the floor.

Lying there, paralyzed by the pain shooting from his head down his spine, Alex struggled to reach into a patch on the side of his uniform to remove an emergency multi-strip. He put it under his tongue before the pain made him pass out again.

As the strip dissolved, the pulsing jolts of pain ebbed enough for Alex to crack his eyes open again. The cat was pawing at the door to the wellness center. It looked back at Alex, appearing impatient for him to offer some help opening the door.

Alex pushed himself up. He had to brace himself against the wall while a wave of vertigo passed. Inches from where he was leaning, the door panel indicated it was locked and sealed with an encryption. He could feel the ship vibrating—not a good sign.

Why had George tasered him and locked himself in with Innsbrook? Alex looked down at his thumb. It was bleeding, and he could no longer sense the Harvester chip.

Touching a com button on the wall, Alex called the bridge. "Did the mobius collapse?"

He could hear Odessa barking orders over the com. She either didn't hear him or wasn't bothering to answer.

The cat scratched frantically at the wellness center door.

A wave of realizations tumbled over Alex: he had no way to open the door—and if he did the air would kill him; he didn't have the Harvester chip; it wouldn't matter what he tried to do.

Alex decided to head to the bridge.

The multi-strip had cleared enough of the pain so Alex was able to manage a stumbling walk to the bridge, clinging to the wall the entire way.

The moment JuneMary saw Alex lurch onto the bridge, she grabbed him and propped him against a console corner so he could hold himself up. She hurried back to her station. "Glad to see you made it, but we got ourselves some other mess here."

In the center of the holo, a large dark space surrounded by a spinning gold disk was displayed.

"What is that?" Alex asked.

He watched as Odessa manually typed propulsion instruction into the ship while Witaker and JuneMary entered course corrections for every instruction Odessa input. "*That* is a black hole that does not want to collapse," Odessa answered. "And it's dragging us in."

He did it. George Spell had somehow known how to manipulate the mobius and deploy the right instruction through the Harvester chip before the Generationist virus killed him. Why had he sacrificed himself?

Alex thought of the cat desperately trying to claw its way through the door.

JuneMary pulled a multi-strip from her uniform and pushed it into Alex's mouth. As the second dose cleared more of the pain, enough so Alex could think clearly, JuneMary said, "Boy, those old Harvesters know they're doomed. But they want to take us with them."

The ship was moving at an excruciatingly slow velocity. Huge chunks of space debris and rocks from the asteroid belt hurtled past them and went flying into the black hole.

Horace Witaker pounded his console. "There is a shock wave approaching us, reading .31 C."

Almost one-third the speed of light.

"Twelve seconds to impact," Witaker shouted.

Alex recognized the peculiar shape of the gold ring surrounding the black hole. It was the Klein Bottle shape Rosemary had been carrying—the wormhole construct Alex had calibrated for her; the shape of the singularity the Reaper had created.

Alex stumbled to the main display and input the formula from memory, then said, "Adjust course to this velocity curve."

Odessa glanced at the formula. "What? That takes us right into the damned hole!"

Ignoring Alex's new course, Odessa said, "Uncouple the Simmons regulator!"

That would cause a cascade of massive nuclear explosions behind them. Upon hearing Odessa's order, the ship computer estimated a ninety-four percent structural collapse probability.

Then Alex remembered he still had control of the ship. Before Odessa could see what he was doing, Alex engaged the new course.

The ship stopped vibrating, swung around, and accelerated toward the black hole.

"What!" Odessa cried.

Alex collapsed to the floor.

Odessa was yelling for JuneMary to override Alex's command, but it was too late.

The *Virgin Mother* shot directly toward the singularity, accelerating in the massive gravity hole, and somehow improbably striking the impact wave in a narrow area of curved space that sucked the ship through the shockwave and sent it on a sharp turn as it rode the crest.

Asteroids passed at blurring speeds. The acceleration threw everyone against the floor, pinning them down as the ship was pushed out of the planetary plane of the solar system.

As if seeing its quarry escaping, the golden ring contracted instantly to a bright shining point of light, then grew brighter and brighter as the massive amounts of matter fused in a newly formed star. Alex thought he heard a high-pitched wailing, the sound of some otherworldly life screeching in defiance.

Everything went black.

CHAPTER 27

•

HOW TO SAVE THE WORLD AT THE SPEED OF LIGHT

Someone was shaking Alex.

He didn't want to leave the quiet peaceful place he had reached.

"Wake up!"

Alex opened his eyes to Odessa shaking him like a rag doll. "You have to stay awake," she said. Then, in a very quiet voice, Odessa added, "Thank you."

Alex wanted to tell Odessa he was about to throw up on her. His stomach clenched and he heaved, but there was nothing to spew. The wave of nausea passed.

"The singularity has collapsed," Odessa said. "We are safe. But there is that beam of light headed toward Earth."

There were those who believed one could not escape fate, try as they might. Supposedly, Alex's fate was to cause an extinction level event. He hadn't been able to keep George from killing himself; he hadn't been able to be the one to collapse the singularity; and his desperate drive to resurrect the Harvesters' powers in this universe had given them the ability to drag away the essence of every living being on Earth.

It didn't matter to the Harvesters that their portal to this world had closed. Alex explained the nature of the light beam to Odessa: The Harvester light would hit Earth, annihilate the population by ripping away the collective consciousness, and continue traveling throughout the universe until sometime in the future when the Harvesters once again devised a way to recapture the beam of energy they had unleashed.

"How long until it reaches Earth?" Alex asked.

"Just under fifty minutes," Odessa replied.

Kelen had told Rosemary: *Alex Detail's war with George Spell creates an extinction level event that only Venus can survive.*

"JuneMary," Alex asked. "If we were able to bend the light to hit Venus instead of Earth, do you think you could get Kelen to activate her planet's torsion network?"

JuneMary nodded. "Look, Kelen's as deceptive and conniving as any other Rome, but she's not going to sit by and let everyone on Earth get Harvestered away."

Captain Odessa shook her head. "She may be as altruistic as the next politician, but they like to ponder things over, so I would be prepared to be maximally coercive."

The ship vibrated, then lurched, almost knocking everyone off their feet.

"I have to take the Simmons reactors offline," Witaker said.

"Go to the drive room and perform the calibrations manually," Odessa said. "These new ARRAY ships are so flimsy it's a miracle we haven't disintegrated."

Alex looked at the drive schematics. He didn't see anything to indicate a problem with the Simmons reactors. The drive log showing the ship's errant power surge would indicate pilot error just as much as drive damage.

Alex didn't have time to pursue any suspicions he had of Witaker. Odessa was pointing to the Harvester light-beam analysis in the main display. "This is indeed an unconventional light. Apparently photons from the Harvester universe designed to capture humanity's collective consciousness don't actually travel at the speed of light. It's traveling at .97C and currently at a diameter of six thousand ninety kilometers and growing. By the time it reaches Earth, it will be a full twelve thousand eight hundred kilometers in diameter."

"The diameter of Earth," Alex said. "Just enough to engulf the entire planet."

"And just how do you plan to bend this away from Earth and toward Venus?" Odessa asked.

"It wouldn't be too difficult if we had ships take positions at seventy-five hundred kilometer intervals around a single center ship. Then they could bounce nanocup particle beams at magneto inductive resonances. That would be like making a refracting lens. Venus's sidereal time will be thirty-eight degrees from Earth. The questions is, how do we get Spell to deploy ships and create the lens in less than forty-five minutes?"

JuneMary crossed her arms. "That old girl is suspicious of everything. You tell her there's a big beam of Harvester light coming to the planet and you need her to make this big mirror, she's going check it six ways to Sunday and by then it will be too late."

Odessa nodded. "You're right. We will have to induce her using other methods than the current discernable facts."

"You mean you're going to lie to her?" Alex said.

Odessa smirked. "I believe the term is 'a whopper'."

JuneMary whistled. "Ooh-hoo, this sounds good."

"An emotionally distraught mind is much less prone to act on logic," Odessa said. "This is why I rarely make mistakes." Odessa paced past the buffet of festering food as Horace Witaker returned to the bridge.

Grabbing one end of the tablecloth under the buffet, Odessa pulled the entire mess into a ball, then motioned Witaker to open the waste chute. She heaved the whole thing into space.

"Vice Captain, please open a red-level m-com channel to the speaker. I am about to make sure her mind is at maximum emotional distress," Odessa said. "Now, play your parts well. She sent Innsbrook here to kill you, Alex, and George, so please don't speak, Admiral."

Witaker indicated Spell was on the line. "Speaker, the Pluto satellite as well as the Reaper have been destroyed."

They could hear Spell sigh in relief. "How? We've monitored enormous gravitational disturbances on long-range m-com. What did you do to Saturn's rings?"

"I am unsure about that," Odessa said. "Alex Detail was able to temporarily gain control of the ship. But then a rather unusual incident occurred. President Innsbrook came to the bridge to see if he could talk some sense into Alex, and as soon as Innsbrook was within two feet of Admiral Detail, the admiral collapsed." Odessa paused for dramatic effect. "Alexander Detail is dead."

"What about George?" Spell asked, as if the news of Alex's death was expected. "Were you able to retrieve my son?"

"We were, but he must have been deprived of oxygen for too long. Once he was aboard we immediately brought him to the wellness center. President Innsbrook and JuneMary attended to him themselves. Unfortunately he was just out of his pressure suit when he suffered a massive cerebral failure. I am very sorry, Speaker. There was nothing we could do."

Silence on the other end of the line. Then some muffled, sharp breathing, something like an uncontrolled sob.

"Speaker?" Odessa called.

"Stand by, Captain," came Hiramoto's voice.

Madeline Spell's strained voice came back over the m-com. "Thank you, Captain Odessa, for your commendable service. Please take care to return safely."

Before Spell cut the line, Odessa said, "Speaker, before you recall the fleet used to deploy the anti-proton grid, I wish to coordinate with them to perform the Omaha Salute in memorial of Admiral Detail. Regardless of the circumstances, he died under my command."

The Omaha Salute was ARRAY's equivalent of a twenty-one gun salute. It usually involved a number of ARRAY ships crossing one another's plasma trails then igniting them into a starburst. It had not been performed since the last war with the Harvesters. But it was appropriate of Captain Odessa to make the request.

Spell seemed to take a moment to confer with Hiramoto, then Hiramoto's voice came over the m-com. "Very well, Captain Odessa. Coordinate with Captain Sanchez."

After Odessa dispatched the memorial orders to the six ARRAY ships orbiting Earth, it was JuneMary's turn to get her sister-in-law to activate the network of ancient monuments her family had been collecting on Venus for three generations.

Once JuneMary got through to Kelen Rome June at the Kade institute, it was apparent by Kelen's voice that the Venusians knew something bad was coming their way. "What's wrong?" Kelen asked immediately.

Alex could see by the look on JuneMary's face that she was going to take Captain Odessa's advice to be "*maximally coercive.*" "Kelen, I don't know what in heck the Neverstruck Triangles are, but you better go strike 'em!"

Alex expected to hear an argument from Kelen, some denial, some insistence that JuneMary dream up a plea-bargain. Instead, Kelen said, "I have been informed that a single-point consciousness light wave is headed toward Earth."

JuneMary looked at Alex and Odessa. Alex mouthed silently, "Lonadoon."

Nodding, JuneMary continued, "You've been informed right, Kelen, but the light is being refracted outside Earth's atmosphere and redirected to the only place that can absorb it."

"That's very wise," Kelen said. "But I can't just switch on the torsion grid like a light switch. The Neverstruck Triangles were just installed on their pedestal at the capstone antipode. There is no one there to guide a consciousness wave."

"Well, you have twenty-five minutes to get someone there," JuneMary said.

Captain Odessa sent a series of codes to JuneMary. Nodding, JuneMary forwarded them to Kelen. "We left a very fast flier behind on Venus. Here's how to use it."

Thank God for the slowness of bureaucracies, Alex thought to himself as he watched the countdown clock reach its last ten seconds. Captain Sanchez received Odessa's memorial orders and deployed her fleet, all the time issuing questions to Odessa asking for an explanation of this strange memorial that involved positioning ships at such large distances, creating this odd nanocup particle web. By the time Captain Sanchez had worked up the nerve to go behind Odessa's back to Secretary Hiramoto, there were nine seconds left until the Harvester light wave struck.

"Captain, what are you doing?" Hiramoto asked.

Odessa used her most innocent voice to gain the few seconds they needed. "Why, Secretary Hiramoto, this is for the great Admiral Alexander Detail. Certainly we must honor him with a unique tribute."

"I don't see how this tribute resembles the Omaha Salute," Hiramoto said. "I am ordering the fleet to discontinue."

Just then, at t-minus zero, the nanocup grid lit up in a bright white glow as the Harvester beam passed through it, to be refracted thirty-eight degrees from Earth, directly at Venus. The beam continued through the grid for nearly twenty seconds, then traveled forty light seconds to Venus.

The light appeared to stop at Venus and contract into a narrow beam, shooting in a bright white laser to a point in the planet's southern hemisphere.

"Is that where you saw the platform for the whats-it triangles?" Odessa asked.

"Yes," Alex answered. "That is the antipode of the pyramid capstone, the exact opposite spot on the planet."

"Activate the flier's external cameras," Odessa said. "Shunt the image stream through the m-com channels. Use as many as you need."

The main display showed the image from the surface of Venus. Two stone triangles nearly twenty feet high had been placed upright, leaning in against one another like opposite sides of a pyramid. The triangles were engulfed in a dazzling beam of light pulsing with patterns of geometric figures. They could vaguely make out two figures standing inside the triangles, their arms thrown open toward the sky.

"Can you clean that up and magnify?" Odessa asked. "I want to see who they are."

Witaker worked at his console a moment until two figures filled the bridge center display: their mouths were moving, chanting, as the patterns of light poured over them, tearing at them with luminal wind.

The light grew even brighter, its intensity ravaging the two people, whipping their hair and flapping their clothing. One of the figures stumbled and nearly fell to the ground, but the other pushed forward, never taking its arms from above its head, using its upper body to keep the other from collapsing.

Alex's vision began to fade until he saw nothing but bright white light shooting down at him. He received images in his mind: Above him stood two large triangles. Faintly, through the dazzling pulsing beam, he saw the vague outline of a person standing in front of him—Brother Lonadoon.

Blinking the images away, Alex took over Horace Witaker's console and set the cameras to maximum magnification. Two faces filled the main holo. One was Brother Lonadoon. The other was a woman. Alex could hear the sharp intake of breath from the others on the bridge as they saw the resemblance.

The woman was Alex Detail's mother.

The sudden knowledge that his mother was on Venus, working this whole time with Brother Lonadoon, at the very center of the events he was to ultimately unleash onto humanity, caused Alex to fall to his knees.

It wasn't the Generationists, or some genetic change ordered by Madeline Spell, or even his own self-centeredness that had prevented him from thinking too deeply about his mother for the past twelve years. It was his mother herself who had locked out his mind, shielded herself from Alex while she worked to protect the world from the destructive powers that would one day be released by her son.

"My mother," Alex said to himself as he knelt before the glowing holo display of Brother Lonadoon and Zarena Detail struggling to stay on their feet under the increasing intensity of the blinding beam.

The light grew so bright the main holo was almost impossible to look at. But Alex could not move his eyes even as they burned. Tears ran down his face.

Then it was over. The light was gone.

So were Brother Lonadoon and Zarena Detail.

They found President Jonathan Innsbrook sitting on the floor of the wellness center, cradling the body of George Spell.

Even though Alex was wearing a re-breather mask to protect him from the virus floating in the air, he could detect the faint smell of burned plastic. There was a small charred hole in the floor of the wellness center where the Harvester chip had once again burned its way out of the ship.

Alex immediately wanted to ask Jonathan Innsbrook about his mother, but somehow he knew that Innsbrook would have no knowledge of her. Jonathan had delivered the Neverstruck Triangles and George Spell in exchange for an alliance with the separationist faction of the New African government. Nothing more.

Jonathan had watched the unfolding series of events on a holo in the wellness center as he held the small dead body of George Spell. When Alex walked in with the rest of the crew, Jonathan looked up at him and said, "I know what you are thinking, Admiral, but I'm sorry, I never met her."

Alex nodded. "Of course not."

And the only person who could certainly tell him about his mother had also disappeared.

JuneMary patted Alex on his shoulder, then bent down and scooped up the cat before it could pounce on George's body.

Captain Odessa and Horace Witaker helped Innsbrook stand. They placed George's body on a medical table.

"I watched how much pain they caused him," Innsbrook said, referring to George. "But he stood through the whole thing, never made a sound." Innsbrook looked at Alex. "I know he tried to kill you, and according to Lonadoon if we had left him on Earth the danger would only have continued to worsen, but something happened to him on Venus. He did not want to die, Alex. He knew he was sacrificing his life to save yours."

Alex stood above George Spell's body. The small boy's eyes were closed to slits, the faint green of his irises just visible, brushed by the platinum blond hair plastered across his forehead.

Alex noticed the square outline of a small hand window in the pants pocket of George's pressure suit. When he pulled it out, for a moment Alex thought it was the window he had given George earlier, but then he realized this one was a smaller, simpler device than most.

Alex pressed his finger against the screen. The device recognized him as George Spell and lit up.

The screen was filled with genetic formulas that Alex himself had written over four years ago. "How'd he get this?" Alex said.

"What is it?" Odessa asked as the group gathered around.

"He has a file that. . ." Alex hesitated a moment, then realized there was nothing to hide anymore. "This file is the top decile of my Generationist research."

Alex scrolled to the bottom of the screen where he could see George had done some scratch formulas. There was a gene modeled, not human, with a sketch of different protein structures. *The genetic instruction of an antibody.*

Alex checked what species the gene belonged to.

Feline.

Genius. Alex had never thought that about anyone other than himself.

"JuneMary, let me see that cat," Alex said, taking the cat from her. It licked at Alex's face, around his mask.

He showed the cat George's body. Its tail twitched and its paws reached for George. Alex set the cat down on George's chest, and it immediately began licking George's face, working its way around his cheek, above his lips and to the tip of his nose.

George's body suddenly convulsed. He took in a sharp breath. His eyelids fluttered and he coughed.

Odessa pulled a drawer open. "Get him a hypostick of adrenaline and an oxygen patch."

"Wait," Alex said. "He doesn't need any of that."

George stopped coughing, his eyes opened, and he looked at the cat sitting on top of him. "Hi Cat," he said in a raspy voice.

Alex helped George sit up as the boy caught his breath. "Hi, Alex Detail." He looked around the room and said, "Hi President Innsbrook, Captain

Odessa, Ambassador JuneMary, Vice Captain Witaker. You all look very happy. Does that mean you stopped the Harvester beam?"

"Yes, we did," Alex said. He held up George's window with the Generationist research. "Where did you get this?"

"That?" George said. "When I was on Venus, our mom gave me that."

CHAPTER 28

IN THE INTERESTS OF THE GREATER GOOD

Madeline Spell sat in her office, staring out the window, not seeing a thing.

She knew she was in shock. Hiramoto had insisted she have her doctor stop by, but she couldn't talk to anyone, not even Hiramoto, her closest companion, the man who had helped her rule the world for all these years.

The Harvesters' last remaining threat to the world had been destroyed, but Alex Detail and George Spell were dead.

She tried consoling herself that the loss of two more people in what could have been a global extinction was well within acceptable collateral damage parameters. She reminded herself she could not have taken the risk that the remaining chunk of Pluto not be demolished. Had George failed and died in the process, then Alex Detail would destroy humanity with his continuing Harvester quest. Had both George and Alex survived, then the exacting war between them would have led to the extinction level event Lonadoon had warned her of.

No, Madeline had played the only hand that would assure her that neither the Harvesters, Alex Detail nor George Spell would ever again threaten the world.

But George *had* been successful. The remains of Pluto had been consumed by a black hole. And according to Odessa, Alex was in the middle of some massive experiment with the rings of Saturn when he had been interrupted by President Innsbrook. Had Spell not sent Innsbrook to the ship with the deadly virus, who knows what would have happened?

But there was just no way of getting around it—she had killed Alex Detail and her son.

It's why we made George, Spell kept saying to herself. She'd been trained to be detached, like a farmer who raised animals destined for the slaughterhouse. Hiramoto had successfully not allowed George to imprint on him, but Spell knew she had utterly failed in that regard. Her love for her son had blinded her to the dangers he posed. Her selfish emotions had almost led to the extinction of humanity. She had paid the cost in great pain—the pain of having to sacrifice the life of someone she truly loved for the greater good of the many.

Lonadoon had once counseled her that Alex Detail and George Spell had come into the world as a consequence of the universal mind creating a defense against the Harvesters. To die destroying the Harvesters would simply be the fulfillment of their linear potentiality.

Lost in her thoughts, Spell slowly woke to the fact that her desk had been chiming for a while.

A mission update had just been forwarded to her from Odessa. "Go ahead, Captain," Spell said. "I've received your mission report. Does it explain the light phenomena we just witnessed on Venus?"

"Yes, Speaker, but I was contacting you personally to inform you of a significant occurrence."

"Yes?" Spell asked.

"Alex Detail and George Spell are alive."

The room spun, and Madeline Spell grabbed the edge of her desk. "Thank God! How? You said—"

Odessa cut her off. "Their apparent deaths were the result of having succumbed to a particular virus. However, their bodies were able to create antibodies. They recovered."

Spell couldn't understand. "How were you able to . . ."

"I think it would best if we continued this conversation in person," Odessa said.

So she knew about Innsbrook. "Of course, Captain. Please return safely." Spell scanned through Odessa's report. It detailed the Harvester beam that needed to be bounced off Earth. It commended Spell for her quick decision to deploy the fleet to create a virtual lens. It detailed their observance of the light being absorbed by the two figures in the Neverstruck Triangles. It did not, however, identify them. Spell wondered who these people were and why

Odessa was hiding their identities in this report. Presumably, she'd had a close enough view of them through her access to the flier's cameras to know who they were.

There was a special addendum to Odessa's report. She noted that the Harvester chip had burned its way through the ship and into space. It was impossible to tell if the chip had been sucked back into the Harvester universe through the black hole, or if it remained floating in the solar system. If the latter were the case, and someone were to develop the means to retrieve it, that person could be wielding the most deadly weapon known to man.

Spell forwarded all the information to Hiramoto. He arrived at her office moments later.

"I don't think you should allow them to return," Hiramoto said.

Spell had been expecting that. "George will understand," she said. "He will know what I did was out of necessity to ensure the safety of the world. He has never had any difficulty understanding such things."

"And what of Alex Detail?" Hiramoto asked. "How will he respond to your attempt to kill him?"

"Well, since he had been accusing me of that his entire life, it should be nothing new."

"Madeline, they know you have the Toolkit!" Hiramoto nearly shouted.

"What better way to keep them both under control," Spell said as she stood up from her desk and walked over to the windows. "The Harvesters have been booted out of the universe; Alex and George are alive and no longer at war. I cannot think of a better outcome."

"Really?" Hiramoto asked. "How long do you think you will be able to hold off both Alex and George? They will do whatever they can to get the Toolkit. They will be relentless."

Spell sighed. "I will deal with them." She turned to face Hiramoto and said more confidently, "I have always found a way to deal with them."

"Brother Lonadoon was pretty mad when Mom gave me the Generationist files," George Spell said as he sat in Alex's quarters, petting the cat curled up on his lap. "She touched my hair sometimes. I could tell she was thinking of you when she did that."

"Did she say how long she was there?" Alex asked.

"No, but it seems like she knew Brother Lonadoon forever," George replied.

Alex had never imagined himself sitting in a room with George Spell, talking to him as if they were brothers. But that's what the conversation was like. The *Virgin Mother* was still over a day away from its return to Earth. Meanwhile, George sat petting the cat and told Alex everything about his time on Venus. How Zarena had planned for Alex's birth to thwart the Harvesters, how she had taught him about the ancient torsion networks of Earth and Venus, and how she was very nice and very smart.

"So, do you have any idea what happened to them?" Alex asked.

George shook his head. "I don't understand everything about how the whole torsion network thing works. The power is created by certain monuments and shapes. Pyramids are especially important. Mom didn't tell me enough to be able to know what she and Brother Lonadoon did with the light that hit the Neverstruck Triangles. But they're both really smart and powerful magicians. I think they are okay. I hope so anyway, because I'd really like to see them again."

Yeah, me too. Staring out the window, Alex could just see the faint blue speck that was Earth. "How do you feel about Madeline Spell now?"

George shrugged. "I told you she would kill us both one day. She did what she had to do." George stopped petting the cat and stared blankly for a moment. "But that wasn't very nice of her."

"Usually when a person does something that's not very nice it's because they think it's very necessary," Alex replied, his gaze drifting to the floor.

"Does that mean you're not mad at Rosemary for fooling you?"

Hearing Rosemary's name startled Alex. Was he mad at Rosemary for betraying him? For spending time with his very own mother and plotting against him, all the while playing the part of innocent hostess? He wasn't sure. He was more concerned with what Rosemary thought of him. Alex had consoled her in the Radius Arboretum, only to use that intimate moment to steal Kelen's communications code. She must think he was even more manipulative and selfish than he was portrayed in the worst rumors about him.

"We both did what we thought was very necessary," Alex finally answered. They sat quietly for some time until Alex began to feel a chilling dark sensation. "Can you sense the Harvester chip out there?" Alex asked. "I can, almost like it's still close by. It didn't get caught in the singularity."

George nodded. "It's going to find someone else one of these days. But it will never come back to either of us."

Alex sighed. "I've had just about enough of the Harvesters."

"They're mad at us," George said. "Both of us. I ruined their link to this universe and you tried to trick them."

"Whoever that chip finds, the first thing that person is going to do is try to kill both of us," Alex said.

"Yup," George replied. "And that's why I have to go back and be mom's son like everything is normal. And you have to take over ARRAY. Because if they make another war, it's going to be really bad."

Alex wondered if he'd ever get to live his life without the threat of a war looming over him all the time. "Maybe the chip will never find a person. Maybe there won't be another war."

"Maybe," George said. "But if there is, you and I both have to be alive to fight it together."

CHAPTER 29

UNTIL NEXT TIME

Madeline Spell had offered to hold Alex's promotion ceremony at Carnegie Hall, the place where the young Alex Detail had first addressed a crowd of adoring fans.

But Alex knew if he was going to be a successful chief admiral, he was going to have to start by projecting a more responsible image. He chose the general assembly chamber of the old United Nations building.

Alex had already been summoned to this building earlier in the day to answer questions from the House Judiciary committee regarding the auto-record shut-off he authorized during Madeline Spell's meeting before sending them off to rescue George.

He expected it to be an all-day affair, but Chairman Schleiff simply read an account of the meeting from Madeline Spell: "I, the Speaker of the House of Nations, do attest that for interplanetary security reasons, we authorized discontinuation of the house auto-record to confirm that the accident in the planetarium was not an act of terrorism. Having done so, under an abundance of caution, we provided Ambassador JuneMary with transportation back to New Africa aboard the ARRAY warship the *Virgin Mother*. Subsequent events are now a matter of public record."

Chief Justice Schleiff peered down at Alex, and asked him one question. "Admiral Detail, to the best of your knowledge and recollection of events, do you agree that Speaker Madeline Spell provided an accurate accounting of the meeting, has not redacted any critical information, and has acted in the best interests of the House of Nations?"

There were no questions about Harvester chips, clones, or the disappearance of the rings of Saturn. Madeline Spell had packed the courts with loyalists: the only people subject to this question would be Secretary Hiramoto and Alex.

Alex looked up at the Chief Justice and answered, "I agree."

The justices then congratulated him on his upcoming promotion, saying they very much looked forward to attending later.

Alex was scheduled to meet with Madeline Spell an hour before the ceremony, but decided to drop by her office early. She was in the middle of a holo-conf when she saw him standing in her doorway. Cordial as always, she excused herself and ended the meeting.

Alex took a seat across from her desk. Spell normally would have gotten up and sat with him on a chair across from the sofa. He didn't think he'd ever sat across from Spell at her desk, like a subordinate reporting to a boss.

"The admiralty is impressed with your planned reorganization," Spell said. "And I must admit I am surprised and pleased by your initiative."

Of course she was surprised. Alex knew what Spell thought of his abilities as the next Fleet Admiral—nothing more than a boy playing at being Chief Executive. But she had better be pleased, and ARRAY had to start doing things a whole new way. The Harvesters had seen how they fought the last war. It was time to throw away all the old game plans and start from scratch.

The ARRAY reorganization plans that so impressed Spell and the admiralty were nothing more than a ruse to blind them to Alex's true intent. While ARRAY would soon be busy strengthening a military system that had been largely ineffective against the Harvesters, Alex would be tapping into a greater power. The only true defense against the Harvesters was the force harnessed by the torsion network, mysteriously linked by thousands of ancient monuments now spread across the planets. As with any power, it had been subverted by its very protectors, those who would use it to their own ends: Lonadoon, the Romes, the Junes, Zarena, and untold others. Soon, Alex would be undertaking a covert reunion of the protectors of the torsion forces into a new ARRAY defense system.

Paramount to Alex Detail's Reunification was keeping it hidden from the likes of Madeline Spell.

"I didn't come here to talk about ARRAY," Alex said. "I came to ask you about my mother."

Spell leaned forward against her desk, hands crossed. She shook her head. "We have no way to determine what happened to her and Brother Lonadoon. JuneMary herself confirms the files from New Africa are accurate. If they were killed in the light beam, then it left absolutely no trace of them on the Neverstruck Triangles."

Alex wasn't concerned with the fate of Brother Lonadoon. From what George had told him, Lonadoon had been around for a long time. Alex had a feeling he was still somewhere, or someplace. But what about Zarena? What was his mother's true nature?

George had not revealed much to Spell's people in his several debriefings other than a kid's excitement at his fun trip to Venus with all the nice people. Alex was careful not to let Madeline in on anything he and George had agreed to keep secret.

"I was just wondering," Alex said, "How long were you in contact with my mother after I came to ARRAY?"

Spell sat back, rubbing her hands. "We were friendly, as much as possible, at first. I agreed to keep in regular contact with her regarding your progress at ARRAY. She was very assertive with her suggestions on how to best utilize your abilities. For a time we were actually very close. But then, we began to differ on . . . matters."

"I don't remember any of this," Alex said.

"Nor will you ever," Spell said. "Zarena thought you were too attached to material things. She suggested radical methods of expanding your abstract thought abilities. Trances, inducements, interruptions in your memory storage coding. We grew concerned and began limiting her contact with you until we finally had to have her barred from communicating with us or you. But by then, I suppose, she had accomplished whatever it was she was after—because that was when she began the charade of sending me the imploring letters to visit with you. I was always struck by the sudden change in her personality. She was very good. I never had any idea until now."

"It's not like you to underestimate someone. She even succeeded in reprogramming George where you failed," Alex said with a smirk.

Spell frowned at that. It was an obvious attempt to goad her, and she wasn't going to bite. "If anything has *reprogrammed* George, it's the fact that the Harvesters are gone once and for all." She added for good measure, "Lucky for you."

"Lucky?" Alex said, pretending to hold back anger. It was important to his plan to keep Spell under the impression he could still be petty and petulant. "Lucky that the assassination attempts have stopped? I'd say *you* are the lucky one. I'm sure George is just fine with the fact that mommy tried to kill him. It's a Spell family trait."

"What I did to George, and you, was no different from what Zarena did putting George on that Reaper, or what she did handing you over to ARRAY." There was a hint of anger in Spell's voice, but she took a moment and calmed herself, then continued in her usual patronizing tone. "Your selfishness is still your greatest weakness. Both your mother and I had to put our personal feelings aside and serve the greater good, as did George. George stopped you from walking into the wellness center, saved you from being killed by President Innsbrook's virus because he wanted to make sure the job got done right, even if it meant sacrificing his life, just as he risked his life when Zarena gave him the Reaper."

Alex crossed his arms. He might actually buy her argument if he hadn't heard her rationalize away each and every one of her immoral actions in the name of the greater good.

"Why do you suppose Lonadoon never mentioned her?" Alex asked.

Spell shrugged. "He would say that if I had listened to him, heeded his warnings, it never would have mattered."

Alex nodded. "Do you still have the letters she wrote?"

"Probably not," Spell said. "I began deleting them after a while. I can have someone see if they can recover some and forward them to you. If you really want them."

Huh. Spell seemed to like the idea of him seeing his mother as someone perhaps as manipulative and utilitarian as herself. "Yes," Alex said. "Whatever you can find, it's something."

Something to keep you occupied, looking in the other direction, dealing with the sentimentality of a son for his mother while I carry out my true work.

There was none of the pomp of the coronation-like ceremony that had previously been planned at the New York Planetarium. When Alex entered the general assembly chamber in the old United Nations building, the members of the House of Nations were present and seated, and so were the Speaker's cabinet, justices and the ARRAY Admiralty.

Alex walked through the grand entrance, feeling tall in his dark blue ARRAY admiral's dress uniform, five stars on each shoulder epaulet, shiny metallic blue rank insignia on each arm, dark metal buttons running the length of the double-breasted jacket that reached mid-thigh.

Behind him marched the ritual two-person procession of hand-picked ARRAY officers. Captain Odessa, stubbornly wearing her old-style orange Captain's dress uniform. It was the one concession Alex had allowed her, to make up for the fact that she would have to suffer this event stoically, as no food would be served. Odessa had not been so insulted since Kelen June served them a meal of celery. JuneMary walked beside Odessa, wearing her old Commander's uniform from the days of her service under Captain Odessa aboard the *Cronus*. Alex had asked Horace Witaker to accompany Odessa, but Witaker had politely refused, as Alex imagined he would. Alex didn't think Horace would welcome the image of him accompanying his commander and former love interest. Relieved that he wouldn't have that sad-sack Horace walking behind him, Alex was happy to be able to ask JuneMary to do the honors.

As Alex walked the center isle toward the dais, the crowd began to applaud. Alex didn't look at them, or wave, or get carried away with any of that other self-indulgent nonsense he might have done before. He kept walking straight to the dais, took his spot in front of the flat podium, and saluted Madeline Spell. She returned the salute and said, "Admiral Detail, please place your right hand on the great seal of the House of Nations and repeat after me."

Alex placed his hand on the flat panel, on top of the great seal, a circular map of the inner solar system, inscribed in a wreath of crossed conventionalized olive tree branches. Madeline Spell issued the oath, and Alex repeated it.

"I, Alexander Detail, do solemnly affirm that I will, as Chief Executive of ARRAY, support and defend the Articles of the House of Nations against all enemies, foreign and domestic; that I will bear true faith and allegiance to the same; and that I will obey the orders of the Speaker of the House of Nations and dutifully command the officers of ARRAY, according to regulations of the Uniform Code of Military Justice."

Madeline Spell placed her hand next to his on the great seal, and the House computer officially registered Alex Detail's biometric signature under the office of Chief Executive of ARRAY.

"Congratulations, Admiral," Spell said and shook his hand.

As the assembly applauded, Alex thought he caught a glimpse of an orange cat peering out at them from behind the floor-to-ceiling curtains. He looked again, but there was nothing there.

After the ceremony, Captain Odessa stopped Alex as he was walking to his new office. She didn't shake his hand or offer congratulations, though she did offer him a bit of the protein roll she was eating, then led him to her office and shut the door.

"I have something to show you," Odessa said, activating a display on her desk. "I was in the process of sending a deca-pulse wave to deactivate the other spydrop that I somehow lost on Venus, the one that mysteriously ended up in Kelen's conference room. Well, I was reviewing the recording from the time we left Venus, you understand, looking for clues as to who placed it there."

Alex rolled his eyes. He wanted to tell Odessa to get to it, but he let her continue her verbal charade.

"Well, apparently they have a need to waste perfectly good space on New Africa, because Kelen never once stepped into her conference room, but the spydrop did pick up some audio from her office. I thought there was one bit you might be interested in."

Odessa tapped her desk; the audio played. It was Kelen's voice saying, "Rosemary, would you please ask Zarena if she has a moment for me to say goodbye before she leaves?"

Alex looked up at Odessa. "When?"

"Twelve hours ago," Odessa said.

"So my mother survived? Have any ships left Venus in the past twelve hours?" Alex asked.

Odessa shook her head. "None that we know of."

Alex stared at the desk for a minute, as if he might hear his mother talk to him. He looked up at Odessa. "Thank you, Odessa."

"You're welcome, Admiral. Oh, and be sure to pass the information along to George as well."

Alex would tell George and only George. Their mother was alive. It was all they needed to know. There was no need to go look for her. When the time came, Zarena Detail would find them.

EPILOGUE

Horace Witaker sat in his sparsely appointed ARRAY quarters, holding the charred Harvester chip in his palm. Even separated from his nerves by the thick skin of his hand, he could feel the connection with something greater than any force that existed in this universe. He could understand how possessing the chip had consumed Alex Detail and driven him to open the portal to the Harvester universe.

Horace might be the only person who could understand, having experienced the unity of consciousness, the brief understanding of immortality he'd gained from examining the memories of his death aboard the *Cronus*—the death that happened and did not happen. And, of course, Alex had been tricked by the Harvesters. Alex's materialistic drive to power would put him at odds with the Harvesters no matter how clever he thought himself.

When Witaker saw how the chip burned its way out of Alex's thumb and through the ship's hull, he felt an overwhelming sense of hopelessness. How could Alex be so stupid? How could they ever hope to relive the super-consciousness the Harvesters had offered them?

It was nothing less than a miracle that George showed up at the ship with the chip. Horace knew it was a sign. The chip had returned. He wasn't going to let it get away.

Horace was able to duck out for a moment and grab a bolt of carbide used for emergency hull repairs. The material had one of the highest melting points of any compound. He spread the material like a tarp in the storage space beneath the wellness center.

Later, after the singularity had collapsed and they were in the midst of stopping the Harvester beam, Witaker caused anomalous drive readings to give himself cover, and slipped away from the bridge. He found the chip, which had recently burned its way out of George Spell's thumb and through the floor of the wellness center.

The chip was still hot but no longer burning with whatever fuel the Harvesters used to summon it. Witaker wrapped it in the carbide tarp. He applied a drop of corrosive to the floor and extended a light-knife in a narrow beam through the six inches of material between the floor and the hull. It was a simple matter to allow the ship to fix itself with the same emergency epoxy. Later, when Alex and the others checked below the wellness center, they found the same type of hole the chip had burned through the floor of the bridge.

After they had returned to Earth, the *Virgin Mother* had been put in a space dock for repairs. Alex Detail himself had led the inspection of the ship, looking for any signs of the Harvester chip. There were none. The hole beneath the wellness center was identical to the one on the bridge.

Now, the Harvester chip is mine.

Horace held the chip and imagined it shining bright, burning away the shadows, including the biggest shadow of all.

Exhausted from the last several days, Horace lay on his bed, the Harvester chip gripped tightly in his hand. He fell into a deep sleep and dreamed of the great shadow that encircled life, the eternal darkness to which all life in this universe must ultimately return.

Horace drifted in his dream, and began falling further and further away from the light as the dark void drew him closer. He kicked, reaching for something to hold onto, but the darkness was overtaking him, enveloping Horace as his body began to shiver in the painfully cold depths. Horace could no longer see or feel. He fought to stay conscious in his dream, but knew he was dying. He had been here before, when he had died aboard the *Cronus*. The darkness knew he had escaped, and it hunted him, always on the verge of his vision, always on the horizon of his thoughts. Now, the darkness had come to reclaim him.

No!

Horace would never go back there.

His hand tingled. He began to feel warmth spread up his arm, returning life to his body. He held up his hand. The Harvester chip glowed bright, and the darkness withdrew.

As the power of the Harvester chip filled Horace's body, it created a powerful aura of light around him. He boldly stepped toward the darkness, and it parted, powerless to stop him. Horace fearlessly walked deeper and deeper into the void, bringing the light with him as the cold black haze screamed for his warm flesh.

Horace was floating above the image of himself in his dream, watching himself part the black sea, knowing he was dreaming.

But he let himself keep dreaming.

He knew that when he woke up and returned to the real world, he was finally going to step out of the shadow of Alex Detail.

www.ingramcontent.com/pod-product-compliance
Lightning Source LLC
Chambersburg PA
CBHW020610310726
48979CB00008B/1421/J

* 9 7 8 0 9 8 1 9 3 1 1 5 9 *